DATE DUE			

my worst date

my worst date

david leddick

st. martin's press
new york

Book design by Scott Levine

Library of Congress Cataloging-in-Publication Data

Leddick, David.
My worst date / by David Leddick. — 1st ed.
p. cm.
ISBN 0-312-14689-2
1. Gay youth—-Florida—Miami Beach—Fiction.   2. South Beach (Miami Beach, Fla.)—Fiction.   3. Mothers and sons—Florida— Miami Beach—Fiction.   I. Title
PS3562.E28444M9   1996
813'.54—dc20   9623004
                                                              CIP

First Edition: November 1996

10   9   8   7   6   5   4   3   2   1

For Adam Budzius

I would like to thank:

Steven Pressfield, author and very good and longtime friend, who was the first to read "My Worst Date" and assured me that it was really a novel.

Jennifer Rockford, my agent's assistant, who was second to read this book and whose enthusiasm convinced him that this was indeed a novel.

Paul Gottlieb, the nicest neighbor anyone could have and President of Abrams Books, who sent me on my way to see other publishers with my infant novel.

Michael Denneny of Crown Publishers, who was warm and friendly and made a bridge for this book to St. Martin's Press.

Darren Scala, who typed the manuscript so beautifully when I couldn't face it anymore.

Keith Kahla, my editor at St. Martin's Press, who truly edits and has impressed me, which is not easy to do.

my worst date

glenn elliott paul

Here's what I think of first. He was dark. Not too tall. With his clothes off he had beautiful definition in his upper body and his stomach was very flat.

He came across the yard, not using the sidewalk, to my mother's real estate office. She was out, showing Art Deco houses to some New York people who wanted to move to Miami Beach because they'd read it was chic in *Time* magazine. Estella, my mother's secretary, said she was out but would be back soon. I crossed the room in a kind of businesslike way and stepped through the door, picking up some papers from a desk as I passed by. To make us look like a real office with things going on. Having nowhere to carry them to, I went into the storeroom, where we kept the typing paper and the toilet paper, and realized I'd just have to stay there for a while.

"Maybe that young man could show me something," he said. "I'm just looking for a small house or a nice apartment to rent." "That's Mrs. Carey's son," Estelle said. "He's just filling in today. He's still in high school. Well, maybe. Why don't you fill in this card and we'll see how soon Mrs. Carey comes back."

While I stood in the storeroom he filled out his card. I looked at it later. Name: Glenn Elliott Paul. Address: Waldorf Towers, Ocean Drive. That was it.

I came out of the storeroom. Estella said, "Find out what you wanted?" The bitch. She knew exactly what I was doing. She's the smartest one in the office, and the best-looking, too. Fortunately, non-Hispanic men were of no interest to her.

"Oh, here's Mrs. Carey," she said. Mother cut across the lawn, too. She was looking pretty good today. My mother had once been a famous model from Italy. With bangs and long straight hair and those dark blue eyes Italians sometimes have. Not blue at all like English people or Scandinavians. But that blue I call "contact lens blue." Unreal looking.

I was born when she was living with someone important in South America. I don't know who he was. I'm not sure that he was my father. *That's* taboo. But she left him, took me, and came back to the United States to model some more.

Now we live in Miami Beach and her hair has those awkward kind of blond streaks they put in dark hair down here. So you're sort of blondish but not in any way that fools anyone. That's the Hispanic mentality. "Of course I wouldn't want you to think that I was pretending to be really blond."

She came in the office and the man said, "Mrs. Carey, I'm Glenn Elliott Paul.

"You seem to have a lot of first names," Mother said.

"Everyone says that," he answered.

Mother suggested several small houses she had for rent. The apartments would have to wait until tomorrow as she had to call the superintendents and set up appointments.

"Why don't you come with us?" he said to me.

"He has better things to do," Mother said.

"Like what?" I asked.

"Like your homework for one thing. And aren't you supposed to be learning that monologue for your entrance exam to Talent High?" Talent High is where I want to go next year, over in Miami. It's a school for the artistic. Not the autistic.

"You want to be an actor?" he said, looking at me directly for the first time.

"I'm thinking about it," I said.

"You could be a model first," he told me.

"No I couldn't," I answered. "I'm too short."

"You'll grow," he said.

"Six inches?" I asked.

"Well, that would be a start," he answered. Mother was looking at us both, jangling her car keys.

"I don't want him to be a model," she said. "I was a model. It stinks. He can try to be an actor if he wants to, but a model, no. Let's go, Mr. Paul."

They left and I got my bicycle. I tooled over to Ocean Drive and rode slowly along to see what was good.

It was October. My worst month. Everything happens to me in October.

There were a couple of really great-looking guys on roller blades. One had cut-off bib overalls with nothing on underneath. You know that look? The pecs under the bib top and the side buttons undone so you can see the white places on the hips that a bathing suit covers. Very humpy. He gave me that "I'm not gay, just good-looking" look models do. I thought, If you're not gay why aren't you wearing any underpants? Those guys.

The girls are much better. They just pull their hair back, put on a T-shirt and jeans, and go. Only the ones who aren't going to make it run around with their tits hanging out and wiggle when they walk.

Ocean Drive has changed a lot. When I was fourteen there was nothing here but old folks stumbling around in the sun and drugged-out Cuban hoods stumbling after them. The beach was always great, of course, but nobody was on it.

Except for that weird guy with the black glove, running every day. Nice body, but that glove. I think his hand is missing, and he's got a plastic hand in there. And then he wears those black shorts and old-fashioned basketball shoes. It's a little spooky, though you do have to kind of wonder what it would be like with a guy with a beautiful body and a plastic hand. I just gave myself shivers.

As I turned the corner on Thirteenth Street to go home, there was Mr. Paul at the light in an old Volkswagen convertible. Very cool.

He called out, "Where do you go to the beach?" I stopped beside his car and put my legs down. I'm not that short.

"Here," I said. "At Eleventh Street. That's the place to go."

"Are you going tomorrow?" he asked.

"Yes." I decided.

"What time?"

"Right after lunch. So I have some chance of getting cramps."

He smiled like he didn't understand me. "Okay. Maybe I'll see you there."

"Fine," I said.

The light changed and he zipped off up Collins. I went over to Drexel and on home. Up Royal Palm. Mother was already home when I got there. She was sitting on the couch with her jacket off and her shoes kicked aside. She looked cute. She didn't ask me where I'd been.

She said, "He took the first one."

I said, "Who he?"

"Mr. Paul. That man at the office this afternoon. The first apartment I showed him, that one at Twenty-first and Michigan, he liked. He hardly looked around. He just said his furniture would fit fine and it would be fine and wrote me a check."

"And," she added, "I'm going out to dinner with him tonight."

I did a long Bette Davis–style take. I walked across the room and looked out the window. That's where the camera would be in one of those scenes so you can see my face in close-up and my mother behind me on the couch. Then I said, *Are* you?"

Mom had the Miriam Hopkins role. "Yes. I'm even kind of

excited. He's good-looking, don't you think? And nice. Polite. Do you think I'm older than he is?"

"Mom darling," I said, "you aren't older than anyone."

I went to the kitchen where the cats were screaming to be fed. Three girls and two boys, all brats. Mostly black and white. Phyllis, Fern and Alice. Ned and Ted. We're quite a family here on Royal Palm.

I heated up some frozen shrimp cannoli while she was getting dressed. I was eating it and studying my speech from *East of Eden* for my Talent High audition when he showed up to get Mother. You know, that one James Dean does with Julie Harris that makes everyone cry. I couldn't get a copy of the script so I got the movie on cassette and copied it down. Everybody else does dip-shit stuff from *Bye Bye Birdie*.

Mr. Paul was wearing a blue blazer and looked very smart. His hair was slicked down and he was wearing a tie. I wondered what he'd wear at the beach tomorrow. A seersucker suit maybe. He smiled and said hello to me. I smiled back as though very absorbed in my script.

They left. Mom looked really great in her white suit. Her best one. And her hair pulled up on one side. Nothing gets past me.

"Good night, darling," she called out. At least she didn't come over and kiss me. That would really have been overdoing it.

"Good night, Mom," I said. "Have a great time."

"Will you be all right?"

"Yeah, I'm going over to the Club Deuce later."

"You're *not*. I mean it."

"Just kidding. I don't have fake ID," I said. "I'll talk to Macha and go to bed. I'm fine." They left.

Macha is my best friend. She's very cool and so are her parents. They have a place over on North Bay Road but they are excellent.

I called Macha and asked her if she wanted to go to the beach the next day. They have a pool and she never goes to the beach. She doesn't want her skin to age. I said, "I'll buy the sun block." She must have figured I had my reasons and agreed to go. I didn't tell her about Glenn Elliott Paul. I figured, what if he doesn't show up? Plus, this is beginning to get complicated.

The next morning Mom said Mr. Paul had taken her to dinner at Tiberio's up in Bal Harbor and that he was a perfect gentleman. She thought he wasn't new to Miami because the staff at Tiberio's seemed to know him. And then they'd gone down to Ocean Drive for a drink at the jazz club in the basement at the Waldorf Towers. He obviously hadn't tried to get her to go up to his room at the Waldorf Towers. The bed probably wasn't made. And he didn't want her to see the KY on the night table.

on the beach

This is how it happened when we met at the beach. Somehow something less than I thought would happen and somehow something more.

Macha came with me. I wanted her to see him and I also wanted to make sure it didn't get too heavy right from the start.

We went to the beach right off Eleventh Street. That's the cool part. I thought about what kind of suit to wear. I decided on short boxers. Not too brief, but brief enough. The models are all wearing long boxers. Like they're not at the gym three hours every day. No, short boxers were right. You can see I've got a nice body but I'm not showing it off.

Macha wore a big T-shirt and shorts. She was staying out of the topless competition all the girl models are staging down there. Who could compete with all that plastic?

We threw our stuff over three of those kind of beach couches and paid for them so there'd be no arguing later. And got them at the end of the row. With the last one empty for him. Get that, *Him!* He shall remain nameless. Until I introduce him to Macha. I told her someone might show up.

I went in the water. I love Miami Beach. The water was Jade Green. The sky was Baby Blue. The sand was Dusky Lavender. Every color a designer shade. Beyond the palm trees the Art Deco hotels in all their jagged shapes and pastel bands, zigzags, squares, circles. Like one of those cut-out walls in a nightclub with the lights coming up behind them.

Overhead 1930s and '40s airplanes are coming and going, hauling drugs in and out of Opa-Locka Airport. At the end of the beach the cruise ships parade out, one after another. High in the water with all those thousands of socially ill-adapted aboard. Heading for the ports of the Caribbean where the shopping is so fantastic. Or maybe just to go out and ramble around in the Atlantic for a few days, trying not to catch on fire.

As I bobbed up and down, far out I could see something brilliantly yellow. Coming toward me. I kept my eyes on it and wave after wave it got larger and larger. And yellower and yellower. It would pop up into view as the waves lifted it . . . yellow . . . and then sink from sight.

After much bobbing up and down on both our parts the yellow thing became a rowboat. With a small dark man rowing. He rowed and rowed and rowed, up and down, up and down. It was pretty rough to be out in a rowboat in the Atlantic, but he managed well.

Reaching me, and I was beyond the other swimmers, he rowed past me, without a glance, straight for shore. I followed him. Rowed right up through the final breakers, leaped out, and pulling the boat up, turned it over, put it over his head and shoulders like a yellow turtle shell, and marched off across the beach. Steadily and sturdily even if he had rowed in from nowhere. Out fishing? I didn't see any fish. In from Cuba? The beach in Miami Beach was certainly a great place to land. No one was going to stop him. Wherever he was going, he knew where it was.

Close to shore I could see Macha on her beach lounge. Around her was a selection of male beauty. A row behind her was Mr. Bodybuilder That Was. Still good body but bulky. Dark glasses. Several impressed male cronies. Looked like a drawing for Flash Gordon. The cronies were of the Eve Arden school. You know them. Thin, never good-looking. The wise-cracking girlfriend role is for them. If Eve Arden had never made movies to be seen on *The Late Show* or *Our Miss Brooks,* what would they have done?

In the sand nearby was a younger, Latin-type bodybuilder. All greased up. With his girlfriend. He wasn't too built up. But short. Would definitely get fat later. But certainly very okay. Those were the best selections of the day.

Other than Mr. Paul, who was standing at the back of the beach bunks looking about. White shirt, navy blue shorts, no shoes, big white towel. So far, so good. What you wear and take to the beach says everything, doesn't it?

I came out of the water and lifted one arm toward him. I slicked my hair back with both hands. It's a nice gesture and makes your body look good as you're approaching someone.

We met at the benches and I introduced Macha.

"Macha, this is Mr. Paul. He's a client of my mother's."

He said, "I'm glad to meet you. Actually an ex-client of your mother's, Hugo. I took the house. Signed for it this morning. And I think I'm young enough that you can call me Glenn." He sat down. I sat down between Macha and Mr. Glenn Elliott Paul.

He said he thought the water looked good. I told him it was. He said he thought he'd go in. And asked if we'd join him. I said I had just come out. Macha demurred. We were supposed to think it was her period, I suppose, so she wouldn't have to run the perfection gamut.

Glenn Elliott stood up and pulled off his shirt and his shorts. He was wearing a snake-green bikini. On the edge but on him definitely all right. He had some body.

One of those natural hard bodies that just come that way. Lean. Pecs, but not the saggy kind, biceps but the long inter-woven muscles, not grapefruit. Plus a very nice ass with a faint white line across the back where his bikini wasn't up quite high enough. Nice thighs. And it all went with his thirtyish Paul Newman face. He walked down and dove in and swam strongly straight out to sea.

"Can I handle this?" I asked Macha.

"Very major league," she said. "I'd certainly take my time."

And then we just lay back and took the sun until he came back in.

"Wake up," he said. And flicked water on us. Just like another high school kid.

He stretched out on his bench on his towel and propped his head up on one hand. "Well, what do you think?" he asked. He wasn't asking Macha. Just me.

"What do I think about what?" I said.

"Oh, you know. Life. Everything," he said back.

"I don't know. Everything is pretty good right now. I'm doing okay at school. Mom is doing okay at work. I've got my friends. We're having a good time. I guess at sixteen that's about as much as you can ask. Don't you?"

Then he said, "And what's next?"

Sex. I thought. "You mean, what's after high school?" I said.

"Yeah, that'll do," he said. "What's the plan?"

"Well, let's see. Macha and I have been talking about the both of us going to Barnard. Where her mother went. It used to be only girls . . . women . . . but now they have men. It sounds cool," I said. I thought I sounded really silly. Just like a sixteen-year-old. An extremely cool guy in floppy yellow shorts came over and lay down in the sand where we could see all his muscles clearly. Yellow seems to be the color of the day.

Macha sat up and said, "Barnard sounds like fun. They kind of let you figure out your own curriculum and you can study what you want."

"Which is?" he asked in a kind of inquiring voice. Definitely not sucking up.

"I think I'd like to be an actress," Macha said.

"She's really good." I told him. "She's in all our plays at school. She did Tennessee Williams, *This Property for Sale,* for Talent Night. All the parents got very shook up."

"Well, there's certainly a very great demand for actresses these days," he said. There is maybe really something to this guy. Then he looked at me with those kind of light blue husky dog Paul Newman eyes and said, "And you? Do you want to be an actor?"

"I'm thinking about it, but actually, I think I either want to be a reporter or go into the diplomatic corps. Or be a high school teacher. Nothing too great. Just something that I think would be interesting to do."

"Come on," he said. "Come in the water with me again. I've got to get going." He leaped up and jumped right over Mr. Cool in the yellow shorts and dove in. I got up and followed him.

He bobbed up out of the water behind me and put his hands on my shoulders. I heard him say, "I just want to know, do you go out with guys?"

I said, "I don't know if I go out with guys, but I sleep with guys."

"That's all I wanted to know," he said, letting go of my shoulders and sinking under the wave that came cresting over his head. Coming up he said, "I'd offer you a ride home, but obviously your pal has a car."

"Yeah," I said. He sounded a little jealous. He didn't like Macha, that much was clear.

"You coming in?" he asked. And I nodded that I was and we walked out of the water. I wondered how we looked together. Did people think he was my father? I'm sure they thought I was his tootsie. And that he could do better. With them. Ha!

He just pulled on his shirt, leaving it open, and said goodbye, his towel and his shorts in his hand. "It was nice meeting you," he told Macha. "It was nice meeting *you,*" she answered.

Quite civilly, for her. Although I'm sure he wondered what that meant. I did. And he walked away on those great legs. With that great ass. Not at all gay. Just a god, that's all.

"Where will all this end?" I asked Macha.

She said, "I wish I were a guy. A gay guy. All the really humpy, fabulous guys are gay. It's not fair. That guy—Glenn—is great. If my father looked like that I'd consider sleeping with him. Fortunately for him, he doesn't." I said nothing.

Mr. Yellow Shorts interrupted us. "Could you tell me the time?" he asked. We both looked at his waterproof watch. "It stopped," he lied.

"I think it's about four o'clock," Macha said. I dug around in my bag and found my watch.

"Four-ten," I told him.

"Thanks," he said. "By the way, my name is Ken."

Ken was all right so I said, "My name is Hugo. And this is Macha. We're both pleased to meet you."

Ken said, "Are you from around here? You don't seem to be models."

"Is that a compliment?" said Macha. "Or not?"

"No, no, no," our Ken said. "Well, it's not really a compliment but it's not an insult either. You just both seemed so nice and relaxed and having a good time with your dad or whoever he was." So, I wasn't a teenage hooker on the beach. Anyway.

We found out that Ken was from Chicago. He was trying to be a model. He was with Models One. He was staying at the Breakwater. And he was going out to dinner with Macha.

He had made his choice between us, and it was only fair. Macha needed a love interest. I'm sure Ken had no idea she was only sixteen. And besides, I had Glenn—my Mr. Paul—to mull over. Actually, I think Ken picked up on that. He may be from Chicago but you don't model for more than twenty-four hours and not learn something.

the bomber club

I needed money. For a lot of things. The real estate business was dead in Miami Beach so Mom was just squeaking by. I suppose I'll go to college when I finish high school in two years so I ought to be getting ready. I'm not really into clothes, but even so, the Reeboks, the Gap T-shirts, the leather jackets aren't free.

I knew if I just took care of things Mom wouldn't notice, and I could always say I worked down at the Perfect Pizza with Macha.

Macha has a thing about asking her parents for money. She does real well on tips. One of the old men there the other night said, "What's a shiksa like you doing working in a place like this?" She said, "Oh, come on. Wake up and smell the cappuccino. I'm not a shiksa." He said, "You're not, with that cute little nose?" And he tapped her on the nose and left her a big tip. It's the long blond hair that does it. But as Macha says, "In this day and age, if you don't have it, you get it."

It was really Macha's idea that I work at the Bomber Club, the male strip disco down on Washington. She goes down there all the time even though she's only sixteen. She was going there when she was fifteen. Her best girl pal graduates this year and has her own car so with the car and fake ID they both hang out all over town. They tell Macha's parents she's staying overnight with Elouise, and she does, eventually. Macha's parents have a lot of mileage, you'd think they would have figured that one out, but evidently after forty the "figuring it out" switch goes off. Even Mom's is pretty closed down.

I said, "But you have to be eighteen to go into the Bomber Club." And Macha said, "You may have to be eighteen to go into it but I don't know that you have to be any age to work there. Look, you dance like gangbusters. You have a very nice body and you could make it even nicer if you went to my gym once in a while. You're blond. You're no movie star but you're young. Let's go to Fred Faricanelli, who owns the place." It seems she knows Fred well. Chats him up at the bar all the time, even though she never drinks anything but Evian. Macha could chat up the Pope and make him think maybe it would be nice to be Jewish.

So I practice a little at home. I think House sucks myself, but if that's what they're going to play, I'll make my moves to it. And I look in the mirror. I'm no Marky Mark, but he isn't blond, either.

And we see Fred Faricanelli. Macha called him up and we drop down after school. "Is he eighteen?" Fred says. It's a little like I'm invisible. Or more like I'm the product. Macha is the saleswoman. She says, "Would I bring him in if he wasn't?" She's so smart.

"So," says Fred, "let's see what you can do."

"Should I take my clothes off?" I ask. Fred just looks at me like I'm speaking Swahili.

"You've got your jams and T-shirt on. Just take it from there," Macha suggests. So I get up on their little stage, Fred turns on the music, and I pretend I'm at home in front of the mirror. I hear Macha yell over the music, "How long is each number?" Fred holds up one hand with all five fingers up. "That's long," she shouts back. Fred tucks his thumb in. I take off my T-shirt and pull my jams down so you can see the top of my skivvies. I thought I'd wear boxers and under them

14

Calvin Kleins. So I show Fred this move I thought up where I move on one foot kind of like the twist while I pull my shorts off one foot and then shift to the other to get them off all the way. I do my boxers the same way. This is the longest five minutes of my life. I pull my Calvin Kleins down a little and the music ends.

Fred says, "Will you go all the way?"

"I'd rather not," I said.

"Yeah, none of the guys want to," he says. "Gives ya more longevity in the club. You can show them something later if they get tired of you."

Macha says, "You're going to use him?" I can hear a little hint of excitement in her voice. Fred probably can't. But she's *so* cool, a little bit of uncoolness shows.

"You his agent or something?" Fred asks. "How much do you take off the top?"

"How much is on the bottom?" Macha asks. For sixteen this woman is incredible.

"Okay. He only works Friday and Saturday nights. I don't need him during the week. He does three shows a night. I can give him a hundred dollars for the two nights."

"What do the other boys get?"

"They get more because they're professionals. And they do other stuff."

Macha says, "Well, that's their business. And please, professional. You forget I hang out here a lot. Hugo dances better than most of them do."

Fred says, "He's a little stiff."

Sacha says, "Don't you wish." (Where does she get this dialogue!) "I think he should get a hundred fifty. And two hundred in six weeks if people like him. After all, he's a nice boy from a nice home who's doing this to earn money for college. He's not some twit off the boat from Cuba."

"Okay, have him here Friday at ten o'clock. We'll see how it goes." And Fred bids us adieu. When we walked out the sun seemed twice as bright as usual. Really bright. I squinted. And now I had to keep my nerve up. Mom was no problem, I'm always out on the weekends and she's asleep when I come in.

Friday night I go in a little early. Macha and Elouise go with me, to wait and take me home afterward. I could walk, actually, but it will be late and I'll be excited.

We go in the back door and Fred's cousin Walter is there. "This the new kid?" he asked. I nodded. "You girls can't hang out back here. No women in the dressing room."

"You probably let men in," Macha said.

"Give me a break, Macha," Walter said.

So the girls left and I went into the dressing room. Go-go boys don't wear makeup but they sure look at themselves a lot in the mirror anyway. There was a long counter, a big mirror over it, and a row of chairs, each one occupied. I held out my hand to introduce myself down the line. "Hi," I said. "I'm Hugo." "Oh, what a great name," said the short dark boy with an extremely beautiful body in the first chair. "We'll call you Huge. Are you?" I let that one pass. "I'm Coco Rico. That's what I work under anyway." And there was Maximum Shell. Very big. Very blond. A Dolph Lundgren lookalike. Very beautiful. And three others. Only one was swishy. He worked under the name Myrtle Beach and did a kind of drag strip, I guess. But he had a great body. They all did. I closed the door, bang, on any cubbyholes called Romance. This place was the Gaza Strip of sex if I ever saw it. With land mines under every step.

I didn't feel so nervous. I already had on what I was going to wear. And I was doing what Macha does. When I asked her how she could be so swift when she was talking to Fred, who is after all a grown-up, if a kind of unimpressed one, she said, "I just pretend I'm my mother. You know what she's like." So I pretended I was someone like Matthew Broderick playing the part of a teenager going to work in a disco strip club.

Walter came and said, "You're on, Coco." I went out and

watched a little bit from the wings, but that made me nervous. "Just go out and hit it," I thought. "Don't think about it." Though I could hear a lot of yelling going on over the music. Some of the other guys worked. They all did pretty much the same thing.

I heard Walter's voice over the mike saying, "An' now somebody new, just in town from San Francisco. Hugo. Some people call him Huge." He must have heard Coco in the dressing room.

So the music started. Not "Blue Hotel," which I'd requested, but a really bad cover of "Besame Mucho" by the Red Hot Chili Peppers. I walked out. It was surprising. The club was full of guys but I could hardly see them, the lights were so bright on stage. I just kind of pulled my clothes off as though I was just undressing. I mean, I didn't even know what they might like so I couldn't very well be suggestive. I was down to my Calvin Kleins when I could see well enough to see Macha and Elouise at the bar. They were looking enthusiastic. Next to Macha, who was turning to him from time to time to talk, was Glenn Elliott Paul. Mr. Paul. He didn't look anything at all. Very deadpan. And I split, leaving Walter to figure out what to do with the rest of the music.

iris's soliloquy

Let us say, what I can tell you? Probably first, my name isn't really Iris. It's Irene. I've always thought it was rather a stupid name. Like a nurse. Nurses can be named Irene. There's something clean about it. I heard a song once years ago, "Good Night Irene." I used to sing it. "Good Night Irene, I hope you're clean." Horrible name.

I was born in Trieste. My other name is really Mayer. At least my father's name was Mayer. But I was always known as Caratelli. Irene Caratelli. My mother's maiden name. We used it after my father went back to Germany. I shortened it to Carey when I modeled.

Caratelli was my mother's name and I never asked her if it was *her* mother's maiden name. Not to say that my mother wasn't married to my father. She was. But he was German. You can see I have blue eyes. Gentian, someone once told me. Did you ever see a gentian? I never have. One of those flowers that grows in the Alps, very likely, that no one has ever seen. Dark blue, in any case. At least they're not cornflower. Ever see a cornflower? Me either. Light blue, I suppose.

In any case. I was born in Trieste. I vaguely remember my father. I was four I think when he returned to Germany. They had met after the war, of course. Does this sound like a terrible motion picture? It always has to me—in a really rather ordinary way. He had something to do with shipping things out of Trieste. He was a good bit older than my mother I think. Mother was his secretary. She was pretty. The war hadn't been over very long. Everyone was poor. I suppose it was a romance of a kind.

I think the concentration camps broke up their marriage. Of course, the Italians shipped some Jews out, but not many. And they certainly weren't very cooperative. I think when my mother thought about it more and more, she developed a real horror of my father. She used to bring it up from time to time. Yes, I think that's true. I think she just couldn't get into bed with him anymore. Haven't you ever felt that way about someone? Suddenly you just can't bear to have them touch you. Sometimes I think that includes everybody. It probably depends upon how many people have touched you.

So we lived together in Trieste, my mother and I. I went to school. She worked as a secretary. She called herself Caratelli and so did I. I suppose my father must have continued to send money, as we lived fairly well. I mean, I never didn't have plenty to eat and nice enough clothes. I wore school uniforms until I was almost eighteen. Thank God I look good in navy blue.

Of course I didn't have any boyfriends. Italian girls never do. But I knew something about the outside world because my mother loved Capri and in the 1950s we used to go there on our vacation in August. Perhaps my parents went there on their honeymoon or something. I still like to go there and did when Hugo was little. Now I don't want to take him because he's a nice-looking teenage boy and you know what Capri is.

My mother was funny. She was very correct but she always rather liked that Capri atmosphere. She explained to me when I must have been about ten that there were men who preferred the company of other men. Which made sense to me, because the few boys I did know in Trieste always wanted to hang around with other boys their age and play marbles or make airplanes or something.

We used to see all the movie stars and famous people from all over the world wandering around in those little streets. And that's how I started modeling—Roberto Capucci saw me in Capri with my mother. I guess I sort of looked like Audrey Hepburn. I had short hair at the time. And I was small for a model. I preceded the bigger ones like Tilly Tiziani and Mirella Freni. And Isa Stoppi. She was the greatest. I think she had Tunisian or Moroccan blood. She had a very tawny skin but was blond with pale blue eyes. Yes, she was remarkable. Probably still is. Tilly's dead but the others are still storming around somewhere.

At any rate. Roberto asked my mother to bring me to the atelier. My mother was very reluctant because to her modeling was just one step up from prostitution. She wasn't wrong, of course. But she did it. Vanity, you know, is a very strong motivation. Her little duckling was beautiful enough to model. Roberto was sort of the Italian Dior at the time. Very young, very talented, very structured clothes. It was like climbing into the Tower of Pisa to wear one of his dresses. And of course I could model them well because I had *no* body. To wear couture you have to have no body at all. The duchess of Windsor, Gloria Guinness. Strange to think of those great femme fatales who married such famous names and great wealth. Men certainly didn't get all excited lying down on top of *them*. I suppose they did things in bed that the nice girls those men knew or were married to before hadn't even heard of. Funny how women don't think of doing that stuff until men instruct them. Men, the great experimenters.

So Mother said yes, and I lived with some very nice people who were friends of our family and went every day to the atelier. Except for my little hat and gloves I still wore navy blue and might very well have still been with the nuns. There was certainly no one at the atelier to try to seduce me.

But then we did the shows, and the American magazine editors were there and there was a big fuss about me that season and I came to New York to do pictures for *Vogue.* Honestly, I wasn't much. A little girl with brown bangs. But they had just been through those really big glamour girls like Suzy Parker and her sister Dorian Leigh. And Sunny Harnett. Ever heard of Sunny Harnett? *The* blonde of blondes. And Dovima, but honestly Dovima was always something of a joke. I was a change of pace, I guess. But nobody asked me out. Eileen Ford had me live with her. None of the photographers were interested, and I was sent back to Rome to Roberto still a virgin. It pleased me that I could assure my mother that this was the case and not be lying. And then I met Baby Baroncelli.

I wonder where Baby Baroncelli is now? I was crazy about him. I think it was my pictures in *Vogue* that captured his interest. Not me. Because when I came back, Italian *Vogue* used me, and French *Vogue.* Even English *Vogue* a bit, although they were really into their English thing then. I was a hot ticket there briefly.

At a dinner party I met him. I think he wangled an invitation because he was not usually running around in those kinds of circles. The friends I was staying with were a count and a countess, so when I went out with them we did see some nice people. And you know Rome. If you don't have a title you might as well kill yourself. But Baby tracked me down and started taking me to lunch from the atelier and I thought he was just wonderful. Which he was.

He didn't work. He didn't have to. He was the heir to the Baroncelli fortune in Brazil. Yes, he was Brazilian really. I don't know how long the Baroncellis had been out there, but they made millions abusing the natives in one way or another. Baby was tall, he was handsome, he drove a wonderful convertible, he always had a tan, and he was great fun. I don't know about intelligence. He was intelligent enough to know how to live life in a really great way and make things seem exciting and won-

21

derful to everyone who was with him. And he was married.

I know this. He had a very publicized marriage to one of those South American girls whose father had made zillions in tin. And they were both Catholic. And I don't think either of them were particularly eager to be unmarried. They no longer lived together and they hadn't had any children so it was just a handy excuse to not marry whomever they were seeing at the present time. Like me.

So of course I ran off to Brazil with him. He really loved me at the time I think. And I was still a virgin until I left for Brazil. Really.

We had a huge penthouse on top of a building right on Copacabana Beach, which was really quite nice at the time. Rio was a city where you could venture forth carrying a purse and wearing jewelry in those days. And I had Hugo and we had a kind of dream life. Baby was always with us. We went to polo matches. We went up the coast to his beach house. We went nightclubbing. He had wonderful friends. The women were always beautifully dressed and had fabulous jewels. The men were witty and fun. It *was* a kind of dream. Imagine me from Trieste just a year before. I wasn't twenty yet. It was so different from what I know as real life it *felt* dreamlike. And I had no background. All those people around me, they were having a very different experience. They saw the surface and knew beneath it who was sleeping with whom, who really didn't have any money, who hated their wife or husband. I knew nothing. I learned Portuguese so I could speak to the maid and that was about all I learned in Rio. It's funny, you know how everyone is wearing aquamarines these days? Showing off their new aquamarine necklace? When I lived in Rio the maid wore aquamarines.

And then Baby fell in love with another man. When I look back it was in the cards that he fall in love with someone. We'd been together two years. Hugo was something over a year old. I was a sap. What did I know about hanging on to a man? What

22

do I know now? I'm Italian. Once you have a baby all you think about is him.

I was good company. And not stupid. I was well read for a girl my age. I could keep up in conversations. I don't think I bored him particularly. It was just that he was a millionaire who was used to getting what he wanted, when he wanted it, and two years of me was about what he wanted. I figured this out when I came back from the beach early and found him having fun naked on the white couch in the living room with some guy named Larry, a young American, who had turned up in Rio a few months before.

You know how you are at that age. I wasn't just stunned or furious or shocked. I was crazy. When you are really rejected in such a thunderclap way, you just have to run out of there. And I ran. The next morning Hugo and I were on our way to New York. I didn't even stay in the apartment. I ran out and downstairs to my friend Sybil's. She was English and knew how to handle these things. She went upstairs. Saw Baby, picked up a suitcase, took our passports, and we were gone.

I couldn't go back to my mother, obviously. So I went back to Eileen Ford. She always told me I could make a lot of money in New York anytime I wanted to, so that's where I went. I just arrived in a taxi in front of her apartment building with Hugo under my arm, and I have to say she was great. Also she knew I was going to work. I was only twenty-one. I still looked good. I was young. She helped me get a little apartment, and a little baby-sitter, and gave me a little money to get started. And I was off.

I don't think the people who worked with me at that time had any idea I had a baby and no husband at home. Women didn't do that then. Or very rarely. Eileen passed me off as an Italian divorcée, which is really a joke when you think of it. There have been about four of them in Italy.

I did very well. *Vogue* grabbed me up, and then I became the Lady Lillian brassiere girl. You remember that campaign.

"Imagine me at the Waldorf with Lady Lillian." That was me. My little Hugo and I had some money. We had a better apartment. He went to a nice school. I was always home in the evening. Models didn't travel constantly in those days. Most of our work was in studios in the city. And then we'd do catalog. Day in and day out for mucho dinero.

How did I get to Miami Beach? I met a man. Don't all my stories start that way? He had the idea of starting a real estate business here with my money. And now he's gone, but I've still got the business. And although it's been rotten since just after we got here five years ago, with this new Art Deco revival things are looking much better. My English is very good? It should be. I've never lived in Europe again. My mother and I are reconciled and she's been here twice, but Hugo doesn't speak Italian, so their relationship is limited. Well, that's the story.

hugo nails glenn elliot

He was waiting for me when I came out of the club. It wasn't so late, we'd just done our third show. It was Saturday night, my second night, three shows a night. I came out the front door, we don't really have a back door, and was planning to ride my bike home. It was locked up to a tree down the block. The club hadn't closed yet but we'd done our last show. Myrtle Beach (his real name is Fred Gooley, which probably started his whole fantasy) came out with me. The other guys were hanging around in the club, trying to get lucky I suppose. Myrtle was really cool. He saw Glenn Elliott over by his car across the street and just walked away and left me, didn't offer me a ride, nothing. He got the picture in a flash and wasn't going to embarrass me or anything.

I said, "What about my bike?" He said, "We could just put it in the backseat." It was one of those Miami Beach nights. It's so stupid. I've seen millions of them. That navy blue sky. That dumb moon. The little flickering colored lights on the jets overhead. Where could they be going so late at night? Leaving for Europe I suppose. I wished I was on one. Instead of sitting here in this convertible beside this very handsome guy who looks like a movie star going where? To do what? I was really nervous.

He got the picture. "I just thought I'd wait and take you home, Hugo." "Thanks," I said again. "You're a good dancer, Hugo," he said. "Thanks," I said again. I really felt stupid. Well, what *were* we supposed to talk about? "Your mother would probably call the cops if she knew you were doing this." "I know, I know," I told him. "But you know, I think I'm going to earn a lot more money doing this than bagging groceries at Woolley's supermarket. It's for college," I added.

"Is it really?" he said, and looked at me out of the side of his eyes. "I thought it was just because you couldn't get dates and didn't want to stay home on the weekends." Then he laughed and laughed and pounded the steering wheel. "You are quite a sketch, Hugo," he said. "Quite a sketch. Thank God, you're a good dancer or I'd run you right home by the back of your neck and tell your mother on you. Fortunately, you move that beautiful little body of yours around pretty well so I don't have to be embarrassed for you. Just promise me one thing, will you?"

Here it comes, I thought. Just don't go all the way, etc.

"Just don't get a tattoo," he said. "They're fine on Henry Rollins but you're not the type." This guy has something, I thought.

"I was thinking of just a little one," I told him. "Oh really?" he says. "Yes, I'm undecided between a nice, plain 'Mother' in a heart or 'Death Before Dishonor.' "

"Where were you planning to have this tattoo? Exactly?" he said with another one of those looks of his. We were driving beside the golf course, which stretched off under the moonlight like some kind of magical country. A couple in a convertible like ours had just pulled off ahead of us and were getting out of their car with a big dog of some kind. The man had short hair. The women had shortish hair that was blowing around her head and her skirt was blowing in the trade winds around her legs. The dog went romping off across the course and you could hear them laugh together as they strolled off after it. That is what it should be like, I thought. That is what love should be like, strolling across a golf course at midnight in the moonlight.

"Would you like to stop and take a walk?" he said, noticing that I was watching them.

"No," I said. "Not tonight. But some night I would. Very, very much." I can get the skirt but where am I going to get the dog?

We drove slowly up Royal Palm. "Where were you planning to put that tattoo?" Glenn asked me again.

"I was thinking on my behind. But everybody does that. Or maybe on my ankle. But Stephanie Seymour has already done that. So I'm kind of stuck. Under my navel? Under my hair?"

"Some model in Paris has already done that." How would he know that? Does he read *Vogue*? Mr. Paul was certainly a lot different that the fathers I knew, like Macha's dad, who is *quite* cool but doesn't read *Vogue*—that I know.

"The best thing to do is to put it on somebody else. Like me," he said, pulling up in front of the house.

"Then, wherever it was I could see it easily," I said, getting out of the car and lifting my bike out of the backseat.

"Whenever you wanted to, whenever you wanted to," he said, his voice getting lower than it usually was.

"I'll see you again, Hugo," he said, looking up at me standing beside the car with my bicycle.

"Will you?" I said. "This is kind of strange." I could see through the screen door where my mother was lying on the couch reading under the lamplight. "This is kind of strange," I repeated.

"Strange is best," he said, and pulled away. Where was he going, I wondered? I didn't know if he'd moved into the house Mom had found him yet or not.

I fastened my bike to a pillar on the front porch.

"Hi," said Mom. "Shouldn't you bring that inside?"

"Yeah, maybe you're right," I said, unlocking it again and

wheeling it into the living room. Mom was lying on the wicker sofa reading a sizable book.

"What are you reading?" I asked her.

"*The Romanoffs,*" she said. "A very wild family. But not boring."

"Didn't they just identify the bones of the last czar and his family?"

"That's what the paper claims," she said, sitting up. "I thought you'd be home before this."

"I had to stay and help with the glasses," I told her.

When you lie, you must lie with conviction. The slightest hesitation and they're onto you. Mom told me once, "Don't ever underestimate how intelligent other people are, even if they seem stupid." And I don't, I don't. "I thought I heard a car?"

"One of the guys gave me a lift home in his convertible. I put my bike in the backseat," I told her.

"A nice guy?"

"A very nice guy." Telling some of the truth.

"Earn any tips?"

"Not bad, not bad at all." Which was also true. I hate lying to my mom and maybe I won't do this very long. Maybe I can figure out some other way to make some money. I really hate not being up front with her. But she also told me, "Don't lie and pretend you're not guilty of something if you are. If you're guilty, you're guilty. You'll never be not guilty, no matter how much you pretend. Just hoist that guilt on your back and keep trucking. Not being guilty isn't important. It's realizing that we all become guilty as we proceed through life. Just tuck it away and keep going." At the time I wondered what she was guilty of that she had tucked away. Now I was beginning to get the picture. I didn't like it but it wasn't going to hurt my love for her.

The next day, Sunday, I called Macha and asked her if she wanted to go to the beach. "It's raining," she pointed out.

"You're right," I said, "but we could put on our raincoats and walk on the boardwalk."

"Right," she said and came over and picked me up in her car. Macha just learned to drive this year and her parents got her a Miata, which her father really considers *his* car, but she zips around in it all the time. They're happy if she's just on Miami Beach going to school and driving her friends to the beach, instead of raging down to Key West in the dead of night.

I like the sun, but I think I love the rain. Walking on the boardwalk in the rain is a Miami Beach most people don't know. No one is on the beach. The lifeguards are huddled up in their little pavilions on stilts. And real Miami Beach people come out to see the gray waves, the birds scudding low over the water, the line of freighters offshore, waiting their turn to come into dock.

You never think about the people on the boats when it's sunny, but in the rain you can imagine all those little Chinese cooks sitting about tossing the *I Ching* or playing mah-jongg or smoking opium. Killing time until the sun comes out and it's our usual old Miami Beach again.

"Now here's the story," I told Macha. "This is like very big-time action I've got myself involved in and I'm not sure I've got the nerve to go through with it. Plus [don't you just hate people who say 'plus' ?] I have to think about my mother, too. This guy, Glenn Elliott, is way, way out of my league but fabulous. He is also going out with my mother, which I think is great. He picked me up after work last night and I'd say from what happened, and nothing happened, that something could easily happen. Know what I mean?

"I don't like deceiving my mother even about working down at the Bomber Club, but what if she's falling in love with Glenn Elliott herself? What kind of person is that, who takes his mother's boyfriend away from her?"

Macha had the hood of her yellow slicker up and she looked real cute. Rain was running down her face and making her eyelashes stick together and she was licking the raindrops off her lips.

"Go for it," she said. "Go for it, Hugo. This isn't like you just want to get laid. You won't say it but I can tell you're really interested in this guy. And you know, Hugo, it doesn't really matter who he is. Most likely he's some Miami Beach phantom and we're probably going to find out he sells drugs or he does drugs or he's in the Mafia or something. They usually are. But if you run away from this just because it's too much for you to handle, that's bad for you. We're just here for the experiences, you know. When we lay down to die, it's what happened to us that we're going to remember, not whether we're famous or rich. Look at all the people we see all the time at my parents' parties. They're rich. Lots of them are famous, at least around Miami Beach, and they look terrible. Nobody really loved them, they never really loved anybody."

Where does she get this stuff, my Macha. She says the things I vaguely think about but can't get off my lips.

"You're grown-up enough for this, Hugo. What if you never saw another guy in your whole life you could really be crazy about? Unlikely, but it could happen. And then all your life you'd be wondering about Glenn Elliott Paul and what happened to him and where he was and even if you found him he'd be old. You've got plenty of time, Hugo. He doesn't. How old do you think he is? Thirty-five, -six, -seven?"

"My Mom is thirty-seven," I said. I felt like seven myself, personally.

Macha was on a roll. "And for your mom, Hugo, you've got to think of yourself. If you cool it with this Paul guy, that doesn't mean he's going to fall in love with your mom. And your mom is another person as well as being your mom. She's got to take her chances, like anyone else."

"But Macha," I said, "she doesn't have as much time as I do. And she's a woman. And he's a man. And I'm a boy."

"Pshht!" Macha was expressing disgust. That's her noise

she makes that's somewhere between "shit" and spitting and throwing up. "You act like you can control other people. You can't. He's who he is. She's who she is. You're who you are. You just have to step aside and let the good times roll. I'm soaking wet. Let's go to my house and watch some television."

When I left Macha's it was dark. I'd asked Mom that morning where Glenn's apartment was exactly and she told me it was a little Spanish type in yellow in the middle of the block, west side, on Michigan between 21st and 22nd.

So, romantic fool that I am, I decided to walk down past there and see if I could catch a glimpse of him. Sort of *Camille* style or something. It was still raining slightly but I'd dried out and figured I'd walk past, hang a glimpse, and go home and study history for tomorrow.

Michigan is a good hike, but not too far, and I knew the building. More like a beaten-up Italian villa. I walked down the opposite side of the street and all the lights were on in all of the rooms. I stood under a palm tree in the shadows and looked. Upstairs the blinds were open and the overhead lights were all on. He came to a window and looked out. He was wearing a T-shirt and blue jeans. He looked right across the street and right at me. He couldn't possibly have seen me. I was really in the dark. But he just stood there and stared at me and stared and stared. I came out of the shadows and walked across the street until I was standing right in the light from his windows. He continued staring down at me. Then he said, "Hugo?" I didn't say anything. I couldn't. He said, "Don't go away. Stay right there. I'm coming down." He came out the side door and came toward me very slowly. When he was almost up to me I started crying. I just couldn't help it. He put his arms around me and held me very tightly and said, "Don't, Hugo. Don't." But I couldn't stop. I was all wet outside and all wet inside.

He walked me up the stairs and continued to hold me. He didn't really have any furniture. Just a TV and I could see a mattress on the floor in the next room, unmade, with some sheets and a blanket messed up on it. "It's all right, my baby. My little Hugo. It's all right. You're all wet. And you're cold. I think you should take a hot shower." He turned off the lights except for the bathroom and slowly took my clothes off. I just held my arms up and let him strip off my T-shirt. He was very gentle and loving as he unbuttoned my jeans and pulled them off after kneeling down and untying my sneakers and pulling them off one at a time. I balanced myself by putting my hands on his shoulders. I was like a zombie, I couldn't do anything but stand there and snivel and shake. I was a mess.

"Come on," he said. "You'll feel better when you get warmed up." He turned on the water. "Here, get in." He looked at me all forlorn and ashamed under the shower and said, "Hold still. I'll get in myself." And that was how it really began.

In about an hour, when we got up, there were clothes all over that apartment. I felt wonderful.

I pulled on my wet jeans and he gave me one of his T-shirts. I put my undershorts and my socks in my raincoat pocket and he took me home. Mom was in her room so I was able to scoot upstairs without her seeing how wet I was.

bomber club 2

Backstage we got pretty bored between shows. Just sitting around that dinky dressing room with our feet up on the edge of the dressing table.

One really slow night Coco suggested that we play "My Worst Date." Everyone said they had really never had a bad date, or not really bad. And Maximum Shell told that stupid joke about "What's the definition of a really terrible blow job? . . . Fabulous."

Coco Rico said, "Everybody always says they never had a bad date but then they start to remember. I'll go first."

And he tells us about the guy he hung around with in high school in Ohio who always wanted to fuck him, but Coco never wanted to do that. But he was very much in love with this person, who was a forward on the basketball team and was dating a cheerleader as well as seeing Coco. And finally in the heat of the backseat of a car or somewhere like that Coco gave in and took it up the bum.

"It hurt," he said. "And more than that, in a few days I knew something wasn't right. You know. I said, this couldn't be come still coming out after all this time. So I had to go to the doctor. But I wasn't so dumb. I went to a doctor in another town about twenty miles away and pretended I was visiting there. Turns out

33

I've got the clap. Nice, huh? My virgin butt and the man of my life gives me the clap.

"But. Really stupid me, I give the doctor my real name and address. I could have lied so easily. But no, I give him the real scoop. And whaddya know? In that county all the doctors exchange lists of their patients with venereal diseases. That's right. And my dad's best friend is our family doctor in this little burg I come from. They went to high school together. So, you guessed it. He tells my dad. My dad goes through the roof. Mostly because it makes him look bad, obviously. I refuse to tell where I got it. I'm not going to blow the whistle on Rufus. And voilà! You find me here, stripping in this sleazy hole in Miami Beach. Not directly, of course. But I had to get out of that town."

"What about Rufus, what happened to him?" I wanted to know.

"Last I heard he married that cheerleader. I hope he got rid of the clap before he did." And Coco laughed like crazy, pounding on the dressing table.

"Yeah, that was my worst date. So far," he said.

Then one of the dancers, named Calvin, chimed in. He's known as Calvin Fine at the club. A great set of pecs. Dark hair. Blue eyes. You get the picture. You could kill yourself.

"I was working in Chicago at Marshall Field's. A salesman. And there was a company we were always ordering things from on the West Coast and I used to speak frequently with this girl there. Sally. Very flirtatious and cute sounding. And she kept saying things like, 'I hear you're very cute. Why don't you come out here? It would really be worth your while.' I was pretty AC/DC at that time and even though I was living with another guy I thought, why not?

"So I called a guy I had spoken with at that company and I said, 'What's the story with this Sally? She must be a real dog going on like she does with some guy she's never seen.' And the guy says, no, she is really cute. An Oriental chick, very nice body, definitely worth checking out. So we're talking on Thursday and she says if I came out we could go to Palm Springs and spend the weekend together and then she says, 'Maybe you're not man enough for this,' and that does it. So I tell her I'll be there the next evening. I book a flight. And you know, I have zero money. And I tell my lover that I have to go to California for the store over the weekend. Which he definitely finds a little curious. And off I go."

"I get to the airport, LAX, and pick up my bag and nobody. I think this is a complete farce. A hoax. All these people at the supplier's are probably laughing their heads off at this jerk who flew all the way across the country because some woman dared him to. And then I see this Oriental woman coming towards me, and she is ugly. Very ugly and not young. She walks right toward me and I'm thinking, Oh, no, I'm going to tell her I'm not Calvin. Definitely not. And she walks right past me. It's not her. I'm about to call after her, 'Sally?' And then I think, wait a minute, are you crazy or something?

"And then, when I had just about given up, through the glass doors comes this great-looking chick. And it's her!"

Some of the guys were beginning to look up at the ceiling at this point. All this kind of gung-ho heterosexuality wasn't going down so well. But I was interested. And Max was kind of into it, too. I think Calvin and he are the switch-hitters in this crowd.

"So," Calvin goes on, "she has her car. A convertible. And we're on our way to Palm Springs and I've never been to California before and I'm thinking this is definitely hot. So hot that by the time we get to Palm Springs we don't wait to look around. We pull into the first motel. Grab a bite and we are in our room. And I kind of roll over and grab her.

"And get this. She pulls away and says, 'What are you doing? I just came here to be friends.' Friends? Friends! I couldn't believe it. I was shaking. I couldn't even stay in the same bed. I jump up, I'm getting dressed and screaming at her. How she's fucking lucky she didn't get raped. And she's saying over and over, 'But I just want to be friends.' This is a nut case, right?

"So I get out of there. Go to the motel office and spend every cent I've got to take a taxi back to LAX and take the red-eye back to Chicago. Leaving that cunt to cuddle up to her pillow in Palm Springs. Of course when I get home I tell my lover that I just had to rush back I missed him so much. And believe you me, he got his about five minutes after I walked in the door."

"I don't get it, Cal," Myrtle Beach said. "There's got to be more to this story than that. Maybe she didn't like you when she saw you?" Calvin gave him a look like *he* was the crazy one. "Obviously, that's hard to imagine," Myrtle said.

"No," Calvin said. "She had done that lots of times, evidently. I talked to the guy at her company and told him what had happened and he asked around and found out she had even got some English guy to fly from London to see her. And pulled the same thing."

"Maybe she was dying to get raped," Max said.

"Well, it wasn't going to be me," Calvin told him. "Imagine some guy pulling this routine. He'd have walked out of that motel with one very sore asshole."

Then Max told us about the guy who picked him up when he was still living in Westchester County, north of New York City. "There was this man who hung around the bar we used to go to. Very good-looking. Sort of like Alan Ladd." Everybody looked blank. "Tom Cruise?" Their eyes lit up. "One of my friends took him home with him one night and he told me later, this man immediately wanted to know, 'Do you have any toys?' and my friend said, 'Do I look so young I still play with toys?' and the Alan Ladd type says, 'No, I mean sex toys.' My friend realizes this gent is trouble and so he tells him, no, he doesn't have any sex toys. And the guy asks him, 'Well then, do you have a hammer?' He gets rid of him. But I'm intrigued. These crazy types interest me."

"You could get into big trouble, Max," Myrtle said in the kind of voice that suggested he might have been there.

"I always take my own car," Max said. "So I can always leave. And I'm big."

"There's always drugs," Myrtle answered.

"Well, yeah, you do have to avoid anything in a bottle you haven't seen opened," Max answered.

"Even then," Myrt responded.

"Okay, so I was probably crazy myself, but a couple of nights later he comes into the bar and comes on to me.

"I remember it was Memorial Day the next day. You know, the day when all the soldiers died."

I looked around to see if anyone else found this description of Memorial Day surprising. Nobody did.

"And I think, I want to see what this guy is into." Max is beginning to reveal some interesting aspects to his character at this point. I would never have thought this big blond lug would be this bizarre. Lesson number five thousand and forty-two in life, I suppose.

"I tell him I'm taking my car, too, and I'll follow him. And I do, right into the fanciest part of Bedford Hills."

"He was really weird. He walks into this big, lavish house and says, 'Let's get comfortable' and takes off all of his clothes. And he's not bad. He asks me if I'd like a drink and I take a beer. He pees in the sink. He's really drunk. And he wants to show me something down by the pool. It's dark down there but he's mumbling about some bricks he's put down and he wants me to see. I'm ready for anything. He's got a flashlight and he's kind of shining it around and I back into something sharp. I look, and it's deer antlers! Yeah, deer antlers. I say, 'What's that?' and he shines the light over my way. He's got a dead deer in a wheelbarrow, right beside the pool. 'Where'd you get that?' I say and he says, 'Road kill.' He didn't kill it I guess but found it along the road and brought it home. 'For what?' I ask him and he looks at me and says, 'Oh, you know.'

"Okay, is this a bad date or what? So we go back to the house and go up to his bedroom and he says, 'Time for the toys,' and opens the closet door and pulls out this collection of dildos and fist fuckers. You wouldn't believe it. So I got him talking about himself. He had a wife and kids. And had just gotten out of jail. Maybe that's where he got into all this dildo stuff. His wife had left him and was divorcing him. He had this crazy laugh. Every once in a while he'd interrupt himself and laugh like this, 'Ha, ha, ha, ha.' Hard, you know, like it hurt. Sort of like the Joker in *Batman*."

I said, "Max, weren't you scared? This guy was really dangerous." Max said, "Nah. Not really. You know, I had control over the situation. I knew he was kind of showing off for me. And I get a kick out of controlling things. You know, going out just as far on the edge as you can go. It was like that.

"I asked this guy, 'Don't you ever discuss any of this stuff with your kids, your going to jail and so on?' He gave me a look like *I* was the one that was crazy. And I split. But that was definitely the craziest date I ever had."

We had to go on in a few minutes, but Myrtle was dying to get his worst date out of his system. "It wasn't so terrible. Not really. But it just struck me as kind of a disaster all the way around. This guy is on my case, when I was working down at that place where we used to paste frocks on Godey Lady prints. You know, those awful pictures of women's dresses back in the nineteenth century. Like a shadow box with lace and stuff pasted on the picture. Anyway, there is this guy there who is real nice and he really likes me so I think, Well, come on, you're not exactly the White Virgin, give the guy a break. He comes home with me.

Myrtle Beach went on. "We're in bed and I say, 'What's wrong, honey? Can't you get it up?' And he says, 'It is up.' Wild, no? I can't help myself, I have to sit up in bed and laugh. I'm laughing and laughing and laughing. Not trying to be rude, you know, but it really struck me funny. So he gets up and goes home."

Coco said, "That doesn't sound like *your* worst date. It sounds like his."

"Yeah," Myrtle said, "I heard later he killed himself." That electrified everyone. They really sat up and took notice. Myrtle looked around and hurried to reassure them, "Later. Much later. It wasn't on account of me. I heard he was looking all over the world for his identical twin and couldn't find him." "He had a twin?" Coco asked. "No, but he thought if he could find someone exactly like himself he could be happy with him. But he could never find him."

"That figures," said Coco. "You don't like yourself but you think you could be happy with someone just like yourself. People." And started putting more body makeup over his bathing suit lines.

Our new dancer, Mickey Mick, had been sitting over in the corner through all this. I thought he probably was like me, our worst date was still coming up. Mickey's probably about a year older than I am. Dark. Cute. He's going to be cuter in a couple of years. From Connecticut, I think.

Suddenly he pipes up, "Maybe you wouldn't even call this a date. I don't know. It sure was the worst. When I was a sophomore in high school, about three years ago, I was very hot for this guy named Gary. He used to come around and we'd watch television down in the rec room. Well, you know, one thing led to another. I'm laying on top of Gary. This part is funny. And he says, 'What do we do?' And I said, 'Just improvise.'

"Anyway, Gary is sprawled across the couch with his pants down, I'm sucking his cock, and my brother walks in. My older brother. And he gets pissed off. Gary leaves. I realize I am in deep shit.

"So when my father comes home, my brother tells him. And he goes ballistic. He drags me into the bathroom yelling his head off about he isn't going to have some little queer in the

39

family, you know, all that stuff. And then he says, 'You want to suck something, suck this.' and he pulls out his cock. And get this. It's already hard.

"So I was crying and begging him not to make me do it, but he grabbed me and pushed my head down. And I could hear my mom outside pounding on the door screaming at him to come out and the other kids crying. It was heavy.

"So I did it. He didn't come. He let me go. And I went upstairs and put some clothes into a shopping bag and here I am."

Max said, "God, that's disgusting."

Myrtle Beach, who is really the toughest of the whole bunch, said, "I would have bit the bastard's wiener right off. What a piece of shit. Sorry, I know that's your dad. But that's a dad for you."

Then he turned to me and said, "What about you, Hugo? Haven't you had a terrible date or two? Are you too young? Or are you just not talking?"

Walter saved my bacon when he stuck his head in the door and yelled, "What gives with you guys? I've been yelling for you for ten minutes! Get the hell out there. Outta nowhere there's a mob out there." And we all pulled up our jockstraps and went out, me thinking about my dates and knowing when the worst one showed up, it was going to be a honey.

sex with glenn-iris

My experience isn't so great that I can compare him to a great many other men. But he certainly is different from the other men I've slept with. My first husband—well, not really husband but I always thought of him that way—Baby, was pretty much the standard Latin lover. Oh, got the job done and off. He liked it when I had an orgasm but he wasn't concentrating on that. And he wasn't so high on fooling around. I never minded oral stuff, I've always rather liked the penis. It's such a surprising kind of phenomenon. I mean, imagine if a man's ear or his little finger or some other appendage suddenly blew up five or six times its size just when you touched it. God certainly had some unusual ideas about propagation. It could just as easily have taken place in our armpits. Imagine, two penises, two vaginas, and you have to get them together at the same time. A broad-shouldered man and a narrow-shouldered woman would be in a lot of trouble.

Anyway, back to Baby. He definitely was not keen on reciprocating oral activities. I wonder how it worked with his boyfriend? He was so macho I'm sure he had to do his on-again, off-again routine even if the holes differ. Some English Lady somebody said in a court trial about someone's perversion, "Well, we all have orifices." And we do, we do.

Glenn's force field seems to be my pleasure. He's not so much into climbing aboard and getting on with it, and he's not really kinky. What he likes best is to use his tongue to get me to orgasm. And if more than once, even better. Personally I'd like to have a little more physical contact with that gorgeous body of his than just his tongue. But I was brought up to give a man his pleasure. And if his pleasure is my pleasure, I shouldn't really complain.

I've tried doing the same thing for him at the same time and we did it successfully once, but I don't think he liked it so much. Me either, frankly. That lady who wrote "Latins are lousy lovers," what's her name? Helen Lawrenson, wrote that she didn't like to do "soixante-neuf" because it was like patting your stomach while you made a circle over your head. You could do it, but she never knew quite where to concentrate. And I got the impression that what he really didn't like about it was he couldn't *see* me. He's very visual.

Glenn is uninhibited. He's out of his clothes in a flash. I certainly get the impression that he's been in and out of his clothes in a flash many times in many places.

He does not want to talk about other women he's known. He never said if he has been married or not. I don't really know where he's from except that I do know that he came from California or Miami. I don't know where he gets his money. Drugs? Well, anyway, we were talking about sex.

He has this very beautiful body which I think he thinks of as a sort of gift he has to offer other people. He's very quick to pick up on what you like to do and will humor you to an extent. He'll *do* it, but it doesn't become part of the repertoire without your asking.

He's a good kisser, which is very high up on my list. He has a very beautiful mouth. Classic. I think you can tell everything by people's mouths. Men learn to fake it with their eyes, but when you look at their mouths, it's all there. Those narrow lips that will give nothing and were never born to kiss are for staying away from. I even know one guy whose lips sort of went inside. When I knew him in his twenties he had a beautiful, curvy mouth and kissed very well. But I saw him recently and, though he's still handsome, there's just this little steel-trap line where those lips used to be. His ego devoured his lips. It was just me-me and my-my until all that taking and no giving just pulled those little lips right into his mouth.

Glenn's mouth isn't like that at all. And he's old enough that if he was a nongiver, it would begin to show.

Also, watching someone walk away from the rear tells you a great deal. So many men look forceful when they walk toward you. But when they walk away they walk like very large babies. That kind of toddler walk. It looks cowboy macho coming on, but you see you have another big child to handle when they walk away. So I say, let's keep them walking away. Glenn looks like a man when he walks away. I love to see him walk away from me with his clothes off. That white butt, the rest of his body nicely tan.

Certainly he's interested in sex and I don't have to talk him into it. In fact, I think I could say he's very interested in sex. And gets more interested the more you let him have his way. I've been experimenting with him a little bit, and he can really stay down there a long time if he thinks there's a chance I'll have another orgasm. And I frequently have a number of them now that I'm kind of getting into what he wants from me.

But the lights are always on and his eyes are always open.

He has a very nice cock, too. Circumcised. Rather heavily. Dark skin, and lighter where the circumcision is. Large head that kind of takes on a bell shape when he's really excited. I think he really likes me to masturbate him after he's seen me have a number of orgasms. He told me that one of the mistakes people make is in thinking they should both have an orgasm at the same time. For myself, I like to go all to pieces in the arms of someone who is going all to pieces at the same time.

This occurs to me, and I don't let what occurs to me take the

43

form of gospel truth in my head, but it occurs to me that when Glenn is watching me have an orgasm it's as though he's imagining what it's like. And that *he* is *me* having the orgasm, having sex with himself. As though I'm some very exotic form of masturbation. I think he'd love to have sex with himself. But being a gentleman, and kind, and realizing it's impossible, he's found a solution to loving himself better than anyone else. And probably loves me for doing it for him. I have a pretty nice body, my breasts are still up there. There was never very much to collapse in the first place. I think that's how he loves someone.

What do I really like? I'd like to be a large, fleshy, pale blond woman. And I'd like to make love to a small, very handsome man. Who would aggress my body like the Wehrmacht losing its way on the Russian steppes.

sex with glenn hugo

I don't know that I'm in the mood for all of this. You may find out more than you want to know. First of all, let me say right here that any sex with Glenn is good sex as far as I'm concerned. I am absolutely nuts about him and it's about all I can do to keep him from figuring that completely out, although I think he's pretty well guessed.

When we first started making love he was very romantic and we did it boy-girl style. He was the boy, obviously, which I don't mind. He's very careful, uses condoms, knows what he's doing, and plenty of foreplay. I don't know if I could say he loves "me" but he certainly loves my physical being. He likes to lie next to me and run his hands over my body and talk about how beautiful I am. Honestly, I'm not *that* beautiful because I've seen beauty and lots of it in this town. But I'm nice and I'm not a dork and I'm not a slag, so that adds up to something.

If I have to be terribly honest, it's not the fact that he's in me that's so terribly thrilling, but it's the fact that the man I love is making love to me and enjoying it that makes it gratifying. The most exciting part is when he has his orgasm.

I think I must be basically very feminine because it's seeing him and knowing we're going to make love that gets me all worked up. The minute we are behind closed doors I want to get out of my clothes and get at it. He's the one that makes it into more of a ritual.

Lately it's turning out that he really enjoys my masturbating him, which I like to do. And he has revealed a taste for porno flicks on his VCR. What he likes best are those threesome jobs but he only likes the boy-girl sections, not the boy-boy stuff. He told me that he likes the homoerotic stuff better than the heterosexual videos because the men are better looking. It's so complicated, isn't it? I don't really get off on porno videos so much myself. A: I like the fact that someone wants to put the blocks to me. With video there is no victory. They don't even know you're there. B: I don't like to make love with videos playing because it demoralizes me that I'm not hot enough to be exciting all by myself. C: I'm not into threesomes, foursomes, you name it. I like romance. And with a video there is definitely a third party in the room. And D: it's quite obvious that you can really get into video and sex magazines and that stuff, and that's just like a drug scene. You start a little and sooner or later it's the only thing that turns you on. And you get real weird. With black leather stuff hidden in the closet and straps and strangling and all that stuff. If it doesn't feel good I don't really dig it. Of course, I'm just a kid but I don't think things are going to sort themselves out in that direction for me.

In fact I wasn't so keen on it the other night with Glenn. He puts on a video, throws a sheet over the couch, and we strip and plunk ourselves down. He pulls out the grease and says, "No condoms tonight. Just wanking." He really got into that video and he didn't want me to do the hand work. He wanted to do it himself, and he really kind of forgot I was there. He had his other hand on my winkie, but he was really enjoying himself and when he came he shot halfway across the room. I sort of felt I was like one of those inflatable dolls.

I tell you what. He certainly has a big crush on his own dick. It's a good one, but I can tell he really enjoys looking at his own body and his winkie in action. I suppose that's good from an

46

ego standpoint. Maybe someday when his own hot looks skid a little he'll change. Who knows? All I know is that things change all the time and obviously we're never going to get married and have kids. (He's too old for me, ha, ha, ha!) My job is just to stick with him and really try to love him. Although I don't know exactly how that is going to shape up in the future. I mean, I am planning to go to college and I certainly don't plan to be a kept boy.

at the gym

"You must come with me to the gym," Macha said.

"Why? Doesn't my body look good enough now you've seen Glenn?" I asked. We were on our way down the hall from our economics class. We were in the second half of our course and I'm still not clear as to what it's about. Although I'm getting good grades in it. It's kept interesting because Mr. Burley, our teacher, is having a nervous breakdown or something. A very extended nervous breakdown. It's been going on since last fall. Today he almost lost it. He suddenly got all red and burst into a sweat and just stared into the back of the room and held tight onto his desk. LaVerne Engels was reading something and she at least had the wits to keep right on reading after she got to the end of the paragraph. She must have read about three pages when he finally snapped out of it. It wasn't all that terrible. We've all seen our friends get into a drug snit or two, if we haven't ourselves.

Actually there isn't a lot to Mr. Burley, but I think we all like him better because of his nervous breakdown. We'd probably hate him if he wasn't falling apart right in front of our eyes. Anyway, he kind of snapped out of it and said, "That will do, La-Verne," and gave us our assignment for next time. None of us discussed it because we don't want the principal to know.

"Burley almost didn't make it today," I added. Macha ignored this. "It's not your body. Your body is fine. Come on, you're on the swimming team. I want to see somebody there and I want him to think it's just by chance. That we go there all the time."

"I don't even have a membership. You go to the Fountainbleu Spa, don't you?"

"I'll take you on mine. I can have six visitors a year and nobody's come with me yet," she said.

"Who is this we're going to track down?" I wanted to know.

"You'll see. And you owe me this. I sat through that ordeal with you on the beach."

"Ordeal?"

"Wasn't it an ordeal for you? Or was it just a breeze? A whiz? You get in bed with men in their thirties all the time, right? You don't even know if he's married. There could be a Mrs. Glenn. And lots of little Glenns. He could have syphilis. He could have AIDS!" This she screamed so loud that about twenty people going into French class ahead of us turned. "What are you looking at?" Macha demanded. She can get very belligerent so there was no big reaction. Some girl said, "Oh, be cool, Macha, for God's sake."

"Are you coming?" she added in a slightly lower tone. I said, "Yes."

"Are you going to take this French class?" I asked her. "Or what?" She said, "Yes."

The terrible thing about the gym, and this goes for *any* gym I've been in, is that the guys are all so terribly self-conscious and there's this kind of cruisy atmosphere, which if you're not cruising makes you so nervous you have trouble getting the key into your locker. I've never been to an all-girls' gym, but it would be kind of a relief.

The Fountainbleu isn't bad. I've been to the gym on Lincoln Road Mall once and it was unnerving. When I was there this great big humongous guy put down these weights and said, "I've got to get out of here. Bill will kill me if I don't have dinner on the table by the time he gets home from work." But the Fountainbleu has more of a New Yorky atmosphere. People who go there seem to be in more of a hurry to get in and get out. And there were definitely some unattractive guys in the aerobics class who were there to come on to girls. Maybe I'm the one who sees everybody being cruisy.

Macha came in from the women's dressing room. She was wearing sweatpants and a T-shirt. Plain. She was just letting you see she has a nice bosom. Actually she has a great body and nice legs. Nice proportions. Normal like. But she keeps it pretty well covered up, which I think is great. I wore sweat pants, too, because I have nice legs and like Macha, want to err on the side of not flaunting things. I sound just like my mother when I say something like that. "Err," you know, not "error." She heard someone say "To error is human" once and sat them down to explain that it was "err." So much for educating the masses.

But I wore a tank top. Swimming has given me nice shoulders and I'm not going to keep *everything* from human view. Our teacher wore short shorts and one of those tank tops that hangs open so you can see the nipples on their pecs. Nice. Not. He had dark, curly receding hair and one of those tight, little nervous faces with little dark eyes that flick all around the room all the time to see if there is anyone who doesn't think he's sexy and beautiful. I'll bet there's some guy at home that he gives a real hard time to most of the time. Did I say that his tank top was peach?

He gave all the standard aerobics stuff. To his credit he did it. I hate those teachers who start off the exercise and then walk around as though they're checking the class out to make sure they're doing it right. You could be upside-down with your toe in your mouth and they wouldn't notice.

After class Macha said, "So. Let's go do some weights."

"He wasn't here, right?" I asked her.

"Don't get smart. You could use some weights. Your body is your living, you know." And she snickered loudly and pinched my ass.

As we walked into the weight room I got the picture. There was Ken, the guy from the beach. Still wearing yellow. That must be his color. He must have told Macha he goes to the Spa and despite her being cool, Ken must be on her agenda.

Instead of going over to Ken, Macha went over to one of the instructors and asked him to show her what weights he thought she should use on the bench. The instructor weighed about four hundred pounds without any fat. I could kind of get into body building if you could keep your neck. I don't fancy having one of those necks that's the same width as my head. And then having a crew cut on top of it. It's like your head *is* your neck. And maybe you should have an even larger head on top of it. So I went over to Ken. I will repay my debt, I thought. "Hi," I said. "Remember us? From the beach?" He was doing those weights on pulleys on each side, for strengthening your armpits, I guess, and staring into the mirror at his normal-size but perfect body. I have to admit it. There was nothing wrong there. "Hi. Uff," he grunted. "How are you? Uff," grunting again.

"We're fine. See you later," I said, and wandered off to one of those sit-down jobs where you force some enormous weight up with both legs and hope your kneecaps don't pop off in your face.

I really looked meager compared to the other guys there. They all had these big leather belts and upper arms like my waist. Most of them aren't too tall, although some of them were. There's a lot of that Boys' Town camaraderie, with slapping on the back and diet exchanges about powder drinks.

I think they get started thinking they'll be more attractive to women, and then it dawns on them that actually they've made themselves more attractive to men. They stare into the mirror so much that finally the only thing that can satisfy their love would be a body just like their own. Going to bed with one of them would be like climbing in with a couch. And two of them together? Two couches making bamboola. Kind of beyond human. Also, here's my sex thought for the day. The bigger you get the smaller your penis looks. It's true. You see these little wiry guys in the showers at gym class at school and they always look like they've got quite a bit of equipment there. And the big thugs always seem to not have enough. And probably side by side they're the same size. One of the magazines had this picture of Arnold Schwarzenegger nude and you think, "A great big guy like that ought to have a great big kazooka." And then everybody's talking about compensation. They're building their bodies because they don't think their winkie is big enough. I don't think that's true. They're all probably about in the same ballpark, with some exceptions. And there's that Jeff Stryker out in Hollywood who does the porno films, who's so famous for his dong. But he's tiny. He's a real small guy. Whatever he's got would look big on him. That's my theory. If you're into size, go after the small guys. The optical illusion will please you.

And what do you know? I see that Yellow Ken is over talking to Macha. He's showing her how to use the armpit strengthener. And she is being very sassy, of course.

And so we leave with Ken. After running the gauntlet of the showers and the dressing room. I make a point of not checking out his equipment just so I don't have to have an opinion for Macha later. He checks mine, I notice. "Got time to have a cup of coffee with us?" I suggest as I'm pulling on my boxer shorts.

"Macha already suggested that. Yeah, that sounds great. Except I don't drink coffee."

"Well, you could have a diet cola." He made a face. "Evian?"

He said, "Something like that."

We walk out, leaving behind all the hulks, studiously observing the interiors of their lockers while they pull on their bikini underpants. Don't let anyone ever say that they made themselves available at the gym.

We went in Macha's car down to Arthur Godfrey, to the Purple Banana health food place. Is that name for real?

A friend of ours from school is our waitress. Minelle Fury. Macha says, "Minelle, what gives with the name of this place? The Purple Banana. Have you ever seen a purple banana? Wait a minute. I didn't say that."

Minelle was wearing her hair pulled up on her head like one of those Betty Grable movies. You know. The bangs come from all the way back on your neck. I think she styles her waitressing on Betty Grable. She holds her little order pad up and says, "Relax, Macha. It's been the Purple Banana since Arthur Godfrey was around to order our whole wheat blinis. Hi, I'm Minelle," she adds and reaches across the table to shake Ken's hand.

"This is Ken," Macha says.

"And I'm Hugo, Minelle," I tell her.

"Oh, really, Hugo. Who could miss you?" Minelle tells me. We sit near each other in Speech. We did an improv for them one day where it started out that Minelle was the mother and I was her delinquent son and then halfway through we switched roles. When I said, "And now they tell me you've got a tattoo. Where, Freddie? Where?" and Minelle said, "Right on my dick," it was hot. Even Miss Munro, who is not uncool, laughed and said, "We are definitely starting on radio announcing tomorrow. So I won't have to hear anything that can't go on the air."

So we ordered our wok-fried green beans and Fourteen Fruits milkshakes (what did I tell you about the name of this place?) and got to know Ken. Did Ken get to know us? Wait and see. Wait and see.

Ken is from Memphis originally. He graduated from UCLA with a degree in hotel management. He has been in Miami

Beach about six months. He works the night desk right at the moment over on the mainland at the Coconut Grove Tropics, the big glamorous hotel over there. But lives in Miami Beach. He's subletting a little apartment just up the block from the Fountainbleu, which is why he was walking when we picked him up at the gym.

It didn't seem to bother Ken that we are high school students. Of course, we are high school students with a difference. There's probably not a person in our school who wouldn't say that. Ken didn't ask us what classes we were taking or what our teachers were like and the usual stuff. He sort of dealt with us as though we were out working somewhere on the night shift ourselves. Which in my case wasn't so far from the truth. Tomorrow was Friday and I was back at the Bomber Club.

We dropped Ken off in front of his building and he said, "Maybe the three of us could do something together this weekend. Go to a movie or something like that?" Macha scribbled her number on a piece of paper from a notebook. Ken handed her a card from the hotel. We said probably Sunday. No need explaining the Bomber Club to a nice guy like Ken. But then, everyone seems nice when you first meet them in Miami Beach.

"What did you think?" Macha asked me. "Is he being sort of fatherly or uncley? We *are* still in high school."

"I don't know," I said. "Maybe he doesn't know many people."

"The way he looks it shouldn't be hard," she said.

"Maybe he's entranced with your exotic teenage allure," I suggested.

"Or yours," she said.

"Please. I've got my hands full. And I didn't get that message, did you?" I asked her.

"I didn't get any message," she said.

54

hugo's sexual history

Are you sure you want to hear about my sexual history? I thought everybody's was sort of like mine, but when I start to talk to people I realize it isn't. Macha, for instance, doesn't even have a sexual history. Which in all honesty is sort of nice, but I wouldn't like it. You miss a lot. To put it mildly.

People are always talking about their virginity, and when they had it. Or lost it. Or whatever. I don't even remember being a virgin. Well, hardly. When I was in kindergarten I already had a boyfriend. It was really cute, everyone thought. He always said that when he grew up he was going to marry me. I remember thinking there was nothing wrong with this, but I wasn't sure when the time came that he would be my choice.

What our teacher, Miss Vanderstealth, didn't realize was that we were actually getting it on. Randy was precocious, no doubt about it. They sure gave that kid the right name.

His father had a small but choice collection of pornography that he kept in the night table. Both Randy's parents worked and he was left with a Colombian maid a lot so he explored the house. I think he probably learned to read looking at those magazines. Randy's folks lived in the same building we did. And they were always eager that Randy and I spend a lot of time together. And after I discovered what Randy was up to, I was always willing to go over and play.

I mean, this wasn't anything decadent. It was just sort of one step from playing doctor. But we would get undressed and Randy would climb on top of me and punka-punka. What could happen? We would look at the magazines and make punka-punka and we thought it was fun. It *was* fun. I guess we just thought we were doing what his parents did in their spare time.

Anyway. I never felt guilty about it. It was just how things were.

And do I still see him? Socially. Sexually? Not really. He's one year ahead of me in high school here. He graduates this year.

I don't know. Maybe it's something about me. But when you get to be that age—eleven or twelve—where you start staying overnight with your pals, all my pals seemed to be interested in sex. Maybe it's the tropics. That's how you learn to masturbate. Flog the dog. Pull your pudding. Wank. But the first time I had an orgasm it was having sex—with a friend of mine named Phil. Of course I jumped up and said, "Wait a minute. I've got to pee." Of course nothing happened. And I began to get the idea. It's fun, you know. Here you've got this thing that belongs to you and you can have fun with it, all by yourself. I don't blame women for having penis envy. It's something to envy, it really is. Just from a toy standpoint.

My worst sexual experience. It didn't warp me, but I don't know why. It was with Phil's father. I sometimes think Phil and he set it up. We were at Phil's. We sort of knew his father was in the house. I was lying under Phil, while he flailed around on top of me. We must have been about ten. The door was open a crack and I looked into that black slit and thought, someone could be watching. And a moment later Phil's dad walked in. He didn't seem upset. He came over and looked at my cock while we were leaping around getting dressed. Then he said,

"I want to show you something," and sat down on the other side of the bed and pulled open his pants. I remember he took a neatly folded white handkerchief out of his pocket and opened it so he could wank on into it. He started and then insisted Phil take a hand at it. I stood at the end of the bed gripping the footboard, frozen. It wasn't so disgusting. It was just simply beyond anything I had ever experienced. Then he asked me to come over. I said, "No, thank you." Well brought up, right? Then he said that if I didn't want him to tell my mother I would have to. So I came over and relieved Phil of his duty. Pulling on that rubbery old World War II cock was no pleasure, let me tell you. It just wasn't sexual. I can remember thinking that this was something children shouldn't be doing. It never occurred to me to run out or wonder *what* he'd tell my mother exactly without incriminating himself. Finally he took over and brought himself off into his handkerchief and then neatly zipped up his pants and walked out. He was wearing jockey shorts, which has kind of left me outside the Calvin Klein jockey shorts sex-symbol explosion. Phil's father was sort of devilish-looking, evil. I went home and sat in a chair and looked out the window and felt sort of upset to my stomach. But you know how kids are, they forget or it all becomes part of the drill.

Another time I was at Phil's in his room. We had been reading and Phil had to go on an errand. While I was lying there the old man came in and sat behind me on the bed where I was lying on my side reading. He touched my butt with his hand and said, "Is that where Phil does things to you?" This time I had the presence of mind to just get up and go home.

And it's only recently I've been wondering if Phil and he kind of set these situations up. And if I wasn't the only one. I mean, if the old fart wanted to score with kids, that was one sure way not to make it, right? The will to fail. You see it all the time.

That was the worst. The best so far was George, the guy on the football team I was in love with last year. We never slept together, but we really have had a kind of love affair. I was in high school assembly and I saw him with another guy from the team walking across the stage setting up some equipment or something. And I was just struck with this feeling. You know, that electric charge. Maybe I just needed to have some electric fascination for someone and George came along at the right moment. But anyway, there it was.

I know some of the guys that ran around in his crowd so I started hanging out more with them, and then George would be around when we went to the movies. And we'd talk, and eventually George and I would be going to the movies by ourselves. Oh, I can be crafty when I want to be.

What's he like? He's sort of innocent, sure. At least for me. He has this kind of pale, muscular body without much hair. I think his family is Polish or Czechoslovakian or something. And this roundish face with roundish blue eyes. I sound like I'm describing a doll, don't I?

We go down to the beach at night and talk a lot, and we hold hands and sometimes he puts his arms around me and I lean back against him. He sort of likes to do light necking with me, but I get the idea that he doesn't really register what he's doing. And I think he double-dates with some of his other pals and goes and nails girls who are really available. But I don't think he connects the two things. Weird, huh?

Well, anyhow, that was my big romance till Mr. Paul hove into view. So you see I don't really have a lot of experience, but I think I have a knack for love. I mean, it's really important to me. More important than having the lead in the class play or being big on the sports team. Or even making money. I really want to be in love and I think I could really be in love with Mr. Paul. Where could it go? Who knows? Not far. But far enough for me to find out what it feels like to have a real love affair. Of course, I imagine that he's going to want to stay with me forever and we're going to go away to a desert island or something and be happy forever. Right? I can dream, can't I? I'm not really that crazy, really. But when you're in love you kind of live in two levels. Your imaginary one, and on track two you sort of keep going along in the world of reality.

iris mulls it over

Miami Beach is very treacherous. You step out the front door in the evening. The clouds rise up black against the sky, pink from the light from Miami across the bay. The trade winds clack the palm leaves against each other and flow over your skin, which feels warm and glows from a late-afternoon swim. The moon hangs up there in a sky that is navy blue to the east. You're all in white. Convertibles are moving slowly down the street in what is forever a summer night. Why wouldn't you fall in love with whoever pulls up in front of your house in their convertible? It's almost an obligation. Like a Fitzgerald novel you're never going to get out of. And they all end so badly. But you're sure yours won't.

Until Hugo was six, romance didn't really matter. I had my hands full changing diapers, finding nursemaids, paying the rent, modeling. But since we've come down here and I'm working in real estate, I've thought of a father for him and a hubby for me. Obviously, no one has turned up. Part of it has to have been my fault. I don't think I was really in the market. Or else I'm just stuck in some kind of teenage romantic mode so no one is really good-looking enough or interesting enough or nice enough.

Everything is like a speeded-up movie in Miami Beach. Or

an LP playing at 78. What takes months or years to happen in the temperate zone just zips by here. Restaurants open. They're popular. They're gone. People meet, fall in love, get married, fall out of love, get divorced, and it's only eighteen months later. Maybe it's because we're always under this tropical moon. All we've got is the rainy season to tell us another year has actually gone by. Otherwise, it's always the same time.

So Hugo has never really had a father and it doesn't seem to bother him. He just came out of the womb sensible. Even as a little boy you could explain to Hugo why he couldn't have something or why he had to wait and he'd sober right up. He always wanted to be neat, hang things up, put things away. I never really needed a man around to keep him in line. He was always ready to help me with the dishes and do the laundry. And now our Mr. Paul shows up and I'm right back where I was before I even had Hugo. Very attracted to a guy I know nothing about. Another good-looking man in a town full of good-looking men with no real story. Where do they come from? What have they been doing before they came to Miami? You know they have to be con artists of one kind or another and you're just standing around, shifting from one foot to the other, waiting to be conned.

iris and glenn dine out

I really wanted to talk to Glenn Elliott. There were some things I wanted to sort out. Like his money. Where did it come from and what was he doing with it? So often with men you assume they know what they're doing because they act like they know what they're doing. And then suddenly you realize they don't have it together at all. And things fall apart. Things fall apart mostly just after I've met them. Scenario. I meet handsome, intelligent guy with money. We kind of reach an understanding. Then it turns out he owes money. Lots of money. Then it turns out that he is prone to depression. Lots of depression. Plenty able to handle all this until he meets me. Then once on the solid ground of my life, kaflooey, his life falls apart. With Glenn, I'd sort of like to get a little hint of this in advance if I can.

So Wednesday night I asked him to go to the Mulberry Street Café with me. Hugo was going to the roller hockey game with Macha and his new friend Fred so I didn't have to get dinner. I like the Mulberry Street, the tables are far enough apart that you can talk. And the ceilings are high. I hate New York restaurants because the ceilings are low, the noise level is unbearable, and you're always jammed in cheek by jowl with someone named Dana who is telling her best girlfriend about her abortion, ignoring the fact that her elbows are touching strangers on either side.

Glenn Elliott was looking cute. He is such a cute guy with his little short haircut and his navy blue blazer. One of those guys who know absolutely nothing about fashion but always knows what looks good on them and how to maximize their cuteness. It's kind of a European thing. Nothing effeminate about it but well put together. And good shoes. Always good shoes.

After we ordered Glenn said, "Well what is it we *must* talk about?" "Did I say we *must* talk about something?" I said.

"Iris, let's face facts. We've been seeing each other for a few months. We like each other. We've had some fairly dramatic sexual episodes. And you haven't made any moves to advance our relationship, or drop it. You've been very cool. So obviously the time has come to discuss what's going on."

"You're a real gentleman, Glenn," I told him. "But actually I wanted to talk about money." He had a slightly apprehensive look since he'd picked me up but now he laughed and took off his jacket and hung it over the back of his chair. "Okay, let's talk about money then. Yours? Mine? Where to get it?"

"Yours, really. I don't want to know how much you have or how little. But as a real estate person, I'm rather interested in what you're doing and whether I think you're doing the right thing. There are so many barely legal people around Miami Beach I don't want you falling into the wrong hands. Or maybe you're one of the barely legal people."

Glenn said, "I'm definitely one of the barely legal people, but not when it comes to money. I have a certain amount I've pulled together and that you don't really need to know about. It wasn't from robbing banks. I like it here, I think I want to stay here, so I'm investing, or investigating really, to see if I can't make some more money here."

I asked him how and he told me he'd been talking to Larry

Rodriguez, a recent arrival in town who supposedly had been involved in some big deal property developments up north. What developments he'd been involved in seemed to change a lot depending on whom you were talking to. What made me uneasy about Rodriguez was that he was very present at social events around Miami Beach. Too present. He was trying to establish credibility, I thought. Those too-nice gabardine suits, that too-good car, a Jaguar. Slightly bulging eyes behind his glasses. No real woman in his life, but probably not gay. When there's nothing really to check out, no clues, that's one of the biggest clues of all.

I said, "What are you thinking of doing with Larry Rodriguez? Go in on one of those big Ocean Drive hotels? Like the Amsterdam?"

"No, Gianni Versace's buying that. He's very interested in the Tides. Larry is," Glenn said. The lobster had come and it was good. Except a single order is enough for a family of four. I put a napkin into the front of my dress. White linen with dark green piping. It's one of my best looks but somehow I always wear it when there's a lot of tomato sauce plopping about. I decided to keep my feeling about Larry Rodriguez to myself. Men always think intuition is worth nothing in the marketplace. If the guy's got a big car and a vague prestigious reputation, that's quite enough. My theory is that the big problem with guys like Larry Rodriguez who are out to take people to the cleaners is that they always get taken to the cleaners themselves. Their big blind spot is that they are never suspicious of people who are exactly like themselves. You'd think they'd twig onto a charlatan in moments, being one themselves, but they never do. So. I really don't like the idea of Glenn Elliott being involved with this guy. If he really does have some money.

I ask, "How about a similar building all on your own?"

"Do you know of one?" Glenn looks at me instead of his lobster.

"Glenn, I'm a real estate lady. I know of many."

"Any you like?" He's back to his lobster.

"Here's my concept, Glenn. People are buying the big hotels on Ocean Drive with the idea that they'll renovate superficially and turn around and sell for a big profit. Leaving the hotels to be really renovated by the next owner. That is definitely for somebody who wants to come in, make money, and leave. From what I understand that isn't your plan. Plus, who knows how fast this boom will move along? If you're stuck with the hotel and no immediate buyer you have to run a hotel. And that's complicated. Maybe too complicated and you have to sell at no profit. Or maybe a loss. Or maybe no sale, just sitting there paying the mortgage payments with no income from the hotel. I'm not crazy about this plan for anyone who isn't already in the hotel business and can survive. It's actually the next buyer, who really wants a hotel, who's going to make the money. But a small apartment house, who couldn't run it? Renovations, you can do them one apartment at a time if you don't want to spend the money. You'll always have some income, because these apartments are always rentable at some price. And if Miami becomes the New York of the next century, your property is going to increase in value enormously."

"You've got this figured out, haven't you? Why don't you do this?" Glenn asked me.

"Because I don't have any money. But I'm trying. I'm saving my money as best I can. You've seen my car. And when I can I'll make my move and Hugo and I will move into it and fix it up as we can," I said.

"Hugo and you can invest in it together," Glenn said.

"Whatever money Hugo has he's keeping for his college," I told him. "I want him to go to a very good school. He wants to be a writer. He's got his head on straight, Hugo has. He knows his life is more important than his money."

"Thanks to you."

"Maybe yes, maybe no."

"Oh, I think definitely yes, Iris. Definitely yes."

"So that's my plan."

"Do you have any buildings in mind for me, Ms. Real Estate Lady?"

"There's one I love, not far from the police station on Drexel. Four stories, I think about fourteen or fifteen apartments. A very nice-looking building. Balconies. Asking about three-twenty-five. They'll take less."

"And how much work has to go into it?"

"Cash, you mean?"

"No. How much renovation."

I told him what I knew, roof seemed good, it was fully occupied. About eight grand a month in rents. We agreed to go over there and take a look the next morning. I don't know if I was steering him away from Larry Rodriguez, but at least I was beginning to have some idea of what kind of money he had and how smart he was about using it. I'm not planning on marrying this guy but on the other hand I'm not planning on supporting him either.

macha and ken

The trouble with life is that nothing ever really happens. Which
leaves it sort of up to you to make things happen. Like falling
in love. You fall in love and then something is supposed to happen. Right? Except nothing much does. You're in love and then
what? At least with two guys. With a guy and a girl, woman,
whatever, I think that's why there's the whole ritual of getting
engaged, getting married, getting babies, getting bored. At
least something happens. You know what the next steps are.

This is what our conversation covered when I had lunch with
Macha. We passed in the hall at school and she said, "I want
to have lunch with you."

"Lunch?" I shouted at her down the hall. She turned around
and came back.

"I have some serious things to discuss with you and my
mother always has lunch to talk things out so I think we have
to have lunch."

"That serious, huh?" I said.

"Oh, definitely that serious," she said and disappeared toward the science labs.

So Saturday we had lunch. At the Blue Star down at the
Raleigh. Very Esther Williams, the Blue Star, with that pool and
all. The big deal seems to be that Macha has fallen in love with

Ken, the guy we met at the beach. The guy we saw at the gym. Mr. Yellow Shorts. She's been keeping things from me and I had no idea that things were so advanced.

I said, "Okay. So if you're in love with him definitely you're sleeping with him. Am I right?"

"Almost."

"Macha, that makes my blood run cold to hear that someone is almost sleeping with someone else. What does that suggest to me? That you both take off all your clothes and run around the room. That you get in a backseat and dry-hump. You know how I hate the idea of dry-humping. Or you take off all your clothes and he doesn't. And he fondles you. Or he takes off all his clothes and you fondle him. Read hand job. Really, Macha, what's going on here? I want to know."

"Well," she said, in that long-drawn-out way that makes me want to kill her, "I have seen him with all his clothes off. And he has seen me with my clothes off."

"At the same time?" I wanted to know.

"No," she said, with a kind of admiring look that meant, "You *do* ask the right questions, don't you?"

"You don't have to give me the details," I said. "So, what's the problem?"

"I just kind of consider you the expert. You're having this all-out affair. You're very much in love. I assume Glenn Elliott is very much in love with you. And I'm not sure of what I'm doing or what's going to happen next." What a laugh. As if I had any idea about what was going to happen next in my life.

"I'd say I'm becoming more of sex expert than a love expert," I told her. "But shoot. Spill the beans and we'll see what we can piece together here."

"Okay. You remember we met Ken on the beach. And I happened to see him going into the Fountainbleu health club one afternoon, so I figured hanging around there I'd probably see him. And see if he got interested. I think it was just because I was jealous of you. You had this very handsome guy on your case and I wasn't seeing as much of you. So what was I supposed to do? Find someone similar. And Ken dropped into view. You've got to admit Ken is handsome. And has a great body. And the usual drill. We went out for coffee after gym. We went to the movies. Obviously I can't go out with someone from school. They're like kindergartners. And Ken is twenty-two. That's only five years older than me."

"And then. And then?"

"Well, it's really strange. You know I'm not a virgin. Even if I am almost. I went to bed with Freddy Fischer a couple of times to see what all the hue and cry is about. It was definitely not about Freddy Fischer. But I think a lot of it has to do with how interested you are in the person. Ken is really weird underneath that kind of nice guy-jock look of his. For instance, he doesn't want to sleep with me. Holds me on his lap. I can move, but not much. He doesn't want to kiss because he says it would get him too excited."

"This guy must be from California."

"Chicago. They must be similar."

"They're so self-centered. They don't want anything to happen to them. Even have emotions. Don't you think he's afraid of getting AIDS? Even from a high school virgin?"

"Almost a virgin," Macha said.

"As good as a virgin," I told her.

"Maybe that's it. But lately I told him I was tired of being the only sex object in this arrangement and he had to let me do the same things with him. And so now I do. I undress him and play with him."

"Literally?"

"Oh, yes. It gets quite big and hard."

"You know about masturbation, I suppose," I asked her. She gave me quite a look.

"Please. Could anybody get past the sixth grade in Miami Beach and not know it all?" she asked. "That doesn't seem to be it. He sort of wants to hover around the threshold of getting really excited. But that's it. And now I don't know if I've just gone so far I want to really get into it. Or if I am really in love. I think I'm in love. I'm not the slightest bit interested in anyone else. I can't imagine going out with anyone else. I feel like we're sort of a twosome. He's quite intelligent. Reads a lot."

"Do you think he's gay?"

"I think he knows the score. I definitely get the impression that he's no amateur sexually. I'm the amateur sexually and I know all this stuff isn't brand new to him."

"Where is all this stuff taking place, if I may ask?"

"He has a little flat in Coconut Grove now. He left the beach." Macha always refers to apartments as "flats" since she made that trip to England two years ago. "And a couple of times he's been over to the house when my folks were away on trips."

"What do they think of him?" I asked.

"My mother thinks he's gorgeous. She would. And he reads *The New Yorker* and they talk about whether the new one is as good as the old one. She thinks he's fine. And my father doesn't like him as he has never liked any guy I've hung out with and never will. So what's new?"

"And what's his plan, Macha?"

"This is weird, too. He wants to be an actor, but he doesn't want to model because he thinks that no one would take a male model seriously as an actor." "He's right."

"Have you told him you're in love with him?" I asked her.

"Oh, Hugo. People don't do that," she said.

"Yeah, they do, Macha. The next time you see Ken I think you have to tell him you love him. You've gone far enough with this fooling around stuff. And it's not good for him, either. He's going to get all that semen backed up and get an infection."

Macha said, "You're kidding."

"No, honestly, Macha. I don't know very much but I know that things have to move forward or they go off the track and strange things happen. Or they stop. Or you have to stop them. You're not really suffering from all this, are you?"

"Not emotionally," she said. "But I will if this goes much further like this. And I don't want to suffer. I wasn't brought up to suffer."

"Oh, that I'm sure of. That I'm sure of."

As I rode my bike home I thought that this was relatively heavy stuff for us to be talking about. But then, maybe the kind of things you see on the old television shows about teenagers, maybe that is relatively light stuff. I mean, *Romeo and Juliet* and all that. Maybe we should be into heavy stuff early on. I mean, if we're old enough to think about it we must be old enough to do it.

The very next day Ken called me. There was a message on our machine when I got home from school that Ken, Ken Weitz, had called. Wanted to speak to me. At Macha's suggestion. Macha is my very good friend too. And I do want her to have a full and happy life, true. But the picture I got on Ken after our lunch is that this is a guy who doesn't know his own mind, to say the least. I could just imagine that Macha had told him that she was in love with him. He had told her she wasn't. And she probably had told him that I told her to declare her love. I thought I'd better speak to her first, because Ken was obviously calling me to tell me to mind my own business. But Macha wasn't at home. And I can't resist calling Ken to see where destiny was taking us. It's so rare when anybody wants you to do anything.

Ken was at home. He doesn't report in at A Fish Called Whatever until 7:00 or so. Ken wanted to meet and talk with me. Macha had said that I was an excellent person to talk to about, exploring new directions (Really!). And he wanted to talk about becoming an actor. He was actually rather charming. He said, "Macha told me that you give very good advice."

Flattering, no? So I agreed to go over to his "flat" after school the next day. He was going to pick me up and run me over to his place so I could see his videocassette.

You know how I'm always grousing that nothing really happens in life. It's only what you make happen. That's not entirely true.

But when things do happen, they come so completely out of left field. You're never really prepared for them. It's like you see this person approaching; you may not know them very well, but you think you've got the picture on them. They have a little tray and they say they're bringing you a tomato surprise so you just assume that's the tomato surprise on the tray, and when they put it in front of your wondering eyes, the surprise is that it isn't a tomato at all, it's a time bomb. And before you can decide what you're going to do with it, it goes off.

Thus, Mr. Tomato Surprise Ken. My theory was that he was hustling Macha in order to make contacts. Worst possible scenario, he was going to try hustling me for the same. Like who do I know? Even though sexual intercourse is no substitute for a formal introduction, it's worth a try. So, I'm braced. Mr. Ken looks very cute. He's wearing white shorts. Short shorts. A white sweater. Very tan. And his legs are his feature. He's very pleasant. He has a kind of empty apartment but nicely done. The guy has some taste. This isn't a flophouse. He gets me a Coke. Do you get the picture on this fellow? A younger Robert Redford type, who gives the impression he might like to fuck. Which Redford certainly doesn't.

He said he had a video he wanted to show me to get my opinion.

He puts a cassette into his machine and I immediately see that this is no actor's showreel. There's a kind of dumb title, *Sailor, You Suck,* or something like that, and I see three sailors coming down a street and going into what looks like a fifteenth-rate hotel.

I'm cool. "This doesn't look like your showreel, Ken." One

of the sailors was Glenn Elliott. This film isn't new. It looks like sometime in the seventies, I'd say, and Glenn Elliott looks really young. But it's definitely him.

"No, but I thought you ought to see it," says Mr. Ken. I look at him. He looks at me, face empty. Very cool. I am very cool. Even cuu-uul. "Gee," I said, "are you trying to turn me on or something?" By this time the sailors were down to their underpants and they weren't navy underpants. Sailors don't wear jockeys. That much I know.

"No, I just thought you ought to see what kind of guy your mother and you are hanging out with." Now on the film they're opening beers and there is a close-up of a bottle going into a guy's mouth. I wonder if Madonna has seen this film. There's a lot of clinking of bottles on glasses and some roughhouse so all three of them fall on the bed. Striped bedspread. This is all sort of pre–Bruce Weber but of that ilk. Terrible lighting.

"I don't get it, Ken," I told him. "Why would you care? And where did you get this movie? They don't have stuff this old in the stores." I didn't ask him to turn it off, you'll notice. Now the sailors were tussling, pulling each other's briefs off. Glenn was a lot better looking than the other two.

"Well, I care about Macha and you're such a good friend. I don't like you running with a porn star," Ken said.

"Has she seen this stuff?" I asked him.

"I don't want her to see this kind of film. She's too nice," he said.

"I'm not, I suppose?" He is absolutely right, of course. I'm not, but how does he know that? And then, bingo. I got it. You know how sometimes the story is right there and you don't even have to figure it out. It's there.

"Glenn's an old lover of yours, isn't he, Ken?" Sometimes I surprise myself. I *am* only sixteen. And I wouldn't say I was this calm, but I wasn't running out the door screaming, either. But this had to be it. Straight guys don't wear those kinds of shorts. Ken didn't look quite so cool but he was holding it together.

"What if he is, that doesn't change anything, does it?" he said.

"Well, it could mean you're trying to scare me away from him. You've got to have figured out that he and I are sleeping together." I was on a roll and lights were going on all over the place. "And that's probably why you were on the beach that day. Checking us out. And tracking Macha down at the gym. Am I on the right track or what? What's the story here, Ken?"

By this time one sailor was sitting backward on another sailor's cock and sucking Glenn Elliott, who was standing on the bed in front of him. There were some close-ups. It was definitely Glenn Elliott.

He looked at me in a kind of admiring way. "You're a smart kid, aren't you, Hugo? Very smart. You got this all figured just like that. One, two, three." He wasn't being sarcastic. "Yeah, we were together in Philadelphia. Before he came down here."

cold christmas

While I was pondering Ken's porn video, Mom was planning to go to Key West for Christmas. "Let's invite Glenn to go with us," she said.

Not, not, not.

Fortunately she was too late. Everything was already booked. I don't know why anyone would want to go to Key West anyway. Unless you drank so much you wanted to go somewhere that people drank even more than you did. Beaches? Zero. Architecture? Two on a one-to-ten if you like dinky little frame cottages. People? Please. There is no beauty in Key West. Only torn off jeans shorts. I think Mom thinks it's more relaxed. I'll give her that. If a coma is your idea of relaxation.

I was very happy to stay in Miami Beach. And besides, what would the sleeping accomodations be in Key West? A motel room with two double beds? A cottage with two bedrooms? There could be no good solution.

And then it turned cold. I kind of love it when we have a kind of winter here for a few days. Everyone gets hysterical that they have to wear a cardigan sweater. They run around saying things like "It's 65 degrees!"

This Christmas will be a special time because of the chill. There's a cold wind blowing in the night, right through the cracks of the louvred windows. Glenn has been staying with us every night so he went out and got a big roll of plastic and stretched it over the screens in the bedrooms to cut out the wind. The bedrooms are all on the back in the direction of the beach, so they were getting the most wind. Mom dug out blankets from the cedar-lined closet, so we can all huddle under our heaps of wool at night.

In the morning the sidewalks have a kind of glaze from the fog having frozen in the night, and the air is silvery. No clouds, just this silvery air going up and up and up.

Actually, I hate Christmas. All these Moms and Dads trying to fake feelings they don't really have for each other, and probably hardly have for their children. And certainly don't have for their own parents, the old doddering farts. It's all that sort of "Let's Pretend" kind of stuff that people run out at Thanksgiving and the Fourth of July carried to the maximum. And the children are all excited about the things they're going to get for nothing. Stuff, stuff, stuff. And it's all for free, free, free. Do I go too far?

Mom and I always try to make it as real as possible. Since we're in the tropics we don't have a Christmas tree but try to do something festive in a Christmassy way. Last year we bought a lot of red lights and wound the entire trunk of the royal palm tree in our front yard with them. So the trunk was this glittering kind of pillar rising as high as the house. I had to climb the ladder and do the top part. Mom held it at the bottom. It was fun.

This year we're going to make miniature palm trees of the pillars on the front porch and use the red lights to wind around the pillars. I cut fake palm leaves out of green cardboard and taped them around the top of the pillars. There are only four of them and not so terribly high. Tomorrow I'll start winding the lights. We'll probably have to buy some more.

It's all right that it's cold. Let's just hope it doesn't rain. And melt my cardboard palm leaves. And electrocute us all when we put on the lights.

We'll have Christmas dinner at The Strand. Neither Mom or I like the kind of food people eat at Christmas. Turkey really isn't very tasty. And all those mashed potatoes and yams and things. I do like stuffing, but it seems kind of silly to eat something just to get at what's inside. And then there are those broccoli sprouts. Where did anyone get the idea that they were food?

We'll have a nice supper at home on Christmas Eve and then we'll exchange our presents. I've been shilly-shallying around trying to decide what to get Mom and decided I'd get her an old silver Hermes bracelet I saw in one of the Deco antique stores. It's made like miniature horse bits I guess, but each link is a different design. It's cool, with a very secure kind of little clasp so it can't fall off. I want to get her something that won't wear out, like a cashmere sweater. And I'm certainly not going to get her something practical like a new ironing board. She needs one but she can get that for herself. I want her to have something that she can look at years from now and remember how I was, how we were, what our lives were like way back then, that Christmas long ago when I gave her a silver bracelet.

I don't know what to get Glenn. Maybe a cashmere sweater. I can afford it. Navy blue. That will eventually wear out.

Yesterday we went for a walk down on the beach. The three of us. The seas are very high. Pale green and silvery, piling in and crashing high. Glenn went in but I was afraid to. Mom and I stood and hugged each other while he tore in and dove over a wave and then gestured to us to come in. We just huddled and shook our heads. I had this feeling that the sea was like my life. I wasn't sure but what it was too strong for me. That it might just sweep me away. I've never been in such stormy, strong seas, and maybe right now isn't the time to try it out. I wondered what would happen to us, Mom and me, if Glenn was swept away and we never saw him again. It's too much of a chance, tearing lives apart just by jumping in the ocean.

When he came running out, water running down his body, his hair slicked down over his eyes, that beautiful body rushing towards us, shivering, reaching for the towel with its arms outstretched, it was sort of like Jesus running towards us. Our savior. Is there a crucifixion waiting down the line? For which one of us I wonder?

hugo models

And then I grew. It was really strange. Suddenly I was getting taller. My legs were getting longer. I felt like Alice in Wonderland in that part when she's eating bits from the mushroom. The boys at the Bomber Club noticed it right away. "Hugo is finally growing up," Coco Rico said one night when we were standing beside each other in front of the mirrors, adjusting our jockstraps. "You used to be just a little taller than I am. But look, I'm only up to your ear. Where will this all end? Our baby is growing up and is going to leave home."

Maximum Shell came over and stood beside me. It was true. Really big. I wasn't as big as he was but I was getting there. And my chest and shoulders were filling out, too. I felt like an impostor. It was still me inside.

I decided to work up a new act. All the guys were doing it. The manager encouraged us to develop different stuff to hang on to our regulars. I got the idea to do a bicycle messenger thing. We don't have messengers in Miami Beach but I've seen lots of pictures of them and they're a big fashion item. Getting out of those Lycra shorts was kind of a problem, but I rode in on my bike, which made a big hit. And there's lots of gear to take off, what with the helmet and the goggles and the gloves and the sneakers. I went down to a bikini but I kept my socks on. That little creative touch. Then put all my clothes in the bike basket and rode off. It was a pretty good act if I do say so.

Maximum was doing his swimming bit then. He didn't really strip but came on soaking wet with one of those rubber caps and goggles and a big towel and worked with the towel. He was good, Maximum. For a big guy, he could really move.

Coco Rico was doing his number on skates. Tricky. Roller blades. He wore all that real outsize stuff so he could get it off over the skates. He went down to one of those Brazilian butt-barers and kept his cap on. He was always a big favorite since he has such a good time doing his act. He loves the attention.

Myrtle Beach was in trouble with his Top Model number because Linda Evangelista and Christy Turlington and that bunch were going out of style and all those little waifs were coming in. So he threw the whole thing over and did a Carmen Miranda bit. He made all his own costumes and he got a look going that was excellent. Myrtle is a biggish guy and when he put on those wedgies he was *big*. The MC introduced him as the Towering Inferno. It was true. With that turban with all the fruit on it he could hardly get onstage. He put a real banana in the headdress, which he took out and ate during the act. Kind of obvious but the crowd loved it. He told me he got the inspiration seeing an Andy Warhol retrospective over at the Alliance on Lincoln Road. They had a short with a drag queen called Mario Montez on a couch, eating a banana. It was called "Normal Love." Great, right?

I kind of thought my little bicycle act got lost in the shuffle with all the other acts, but one night there was this guy waiting backstage who wanted to talk to me. He said, "Hi, I'm Mike Merkin. I'd like to talk to you." Yes, Merkin was the name. Can you imagine being called Merkin? Wouldn't you change it to anything? Even Jerkin? Anyway. He said he represented Sophie-Louise Models in Miami Beach. I'd heard of them. He had been a model himself I was sure. He still had kind of ruined good looks. Soft and crumbling. You *know* he had to be just like his looks. His face wouldn't look that way if he wasn't soft and crumbling himself. "I want you to come see me," he said. "You shouldn't be here. You're wasting your time. These other guys have nothing going for them."

"I'm just doing it for the money," I told him.

"Everybody's just doing it for the money. Even the ones who are giving sailors blowjobs for fifty cents. What kind of money is the question. At least if you were modeling you could tell your mother."

How much does this guy know about me, I wondered. "Why do you say that about my mother?" I asked him. He looked at me. How old was Mr. Merkin? Thirty-five, forty?

"Does she know?" he asked.

"No," I said.

"No one who works in a place like this tells their mother. What are you going to tell her? That you take your clothes off in front of a bunch of gay guys? This is not show business, Hugo, my dear. This is not show business." He added, "Come over to Sophie-Louise sometime this week and we'll talk. You're the right size to fit clothes. You've got a good look. You're blond, which isn't that common. And you've got a nice body but you're not too muscly. I think Gianni Versace would like you. And we're doing a lot of stuff with him right now. Where are you in school?" This guy knows something. How does he know I'm in school?

"I've got one more year to go, after this one," I told him.

"You might have to quit school." He saw my face. "No? Well, we can always work something out. There are those classes you do at home."

"I'm planning to go to college," I told him.

"Jodie Foster did it so I guess you could. But she was already a big star. Let's not worry about things like that yet. Can I give you a lift home?"

Everybody had cleared out by now and we were all alone backstage. I could hear all the noise out front. Coco must have just gotten there. "You don't have to mingle, do you?" Mr. Merkin said.

"No," I said. "Nobody has to. The rest of the guys like to. But I'm too young."

"How old *are* you, Hugo?" Mr. Merkin asked.

"Sixteen, I'll be seventeen in June," I told him. "I guess if you're big enough, you're old enough," he said. "That's from a Judy Holliday movie," he added.

"Yeah," I said. *"It Should Happen to You."* He nodded his head at me.

"Very good, Hugo. Very good."

"Thank you, Mr. Merkin," I said. I shook his hand. "I have my bike so I don't need a lift. And I *will* come see you this week."

"I'm there all day," he said. "You know where it is probably. We have our own building." I knew exactly where it was.

"I'll come down. I'd be glad to," I said, and Mr. Merkin left. Not back into the bar but out the door.

I rode my bike downtown and saw Mike Merkin the next afternoon. They had a big office upstairs over a café on Ocean Drive, the walls covered with pictures of models. Many of them, most of them, I came to find out, were not in Miami Beach and rarely came there. But it looked great. Lots of the faces you saw in the magazines everywhere were there on the walls.

Mike Merkin showed me the portfolios and the composites of some male models who were actually in Miami Beach working. Not to be vain, but I thought I looked as good as most of them. He gave me a list of photographers to call. "You have to have pictures done. We have to put a portfolio together for you. I want you to call these people and see if they'll do tests with you. Most of them are going to if you tell them I asked you to call. Some of them are straight, and the ones who aren't are going to come on to you, obviously. What you do about that is up to you. But you don't have to put out. Anybody that has to put out isn't going to make it as a model. Do you think Cindy Crawford put out to get started? Give me a break. If you've got it, you've got it. Putting out can get you into a couple of magazines, but it isn't going to make a career. Hollywood? That's a different story. I'm talking modeling. Nobody puts out for Bruce Weber, believe me. A, he wouldn't have it. B, it's not on the schedule. All he's interested in is the look. So get out there, and let's see how you do. I've got a cattle call for Versace Friday. He wants a whole bunch of guys and you don't need a portfolio. Can you be here about three?" I thought I'd have to skip phys. ed. but what the hell. That wouldn't affect any grades. So I said I'd be there.

And that started the whole rigmarole. Versace took me for one of his ads. You can just see my pectorals in the back in the yellow shirt. Macha was thrilled. For being so anti-modeling, she certainly got off on her best friend being a model. Mom wasn't so sure it was such a good idea. Of course she had been a model and knew what the story was with most male models. "If it's only to make money to go to college it's okay, Hugo," she said. "But I don't want you to think about it seriously. You're too smart for it. You've been brought up in a nice home. It's not as though it's a big step up from feeding chickens in Oklahoma. But if you miss out on your education, you'll miss out on spending the rest of your life with people who are smart enough so you won't be bored with them. It's not being rich, it's the boredom of spending your time with stupid people that's the big trap of not being educated." My good mom. Excellent woman.

And Glenn Elliott, about whom nothing should surprise me by now, turns out to know some major photographer and said he'd call them and see about setting up tests. How major? Like Richard Avedon, although he *did* say, "I'm sure I could never get a test for you with him, but he does do some of the Versace ads so it probably wouldn't hurt to talk to him about you. Let's wait until you've got some pictures from somebody else and see what he thinks. I know Richard Noble out on the coast, Frank Scavullo, and Harry Monteverde." I knew Harry Monteverde because he had just done this big section in "Details" on Jean-Claude Van Damme. Very cool. So he called Monteverde, who said he was coming down to Miami to do a shooting in a couple of weeks and would definitely do some pictures of me. How did Glenn Elliott know Monteverde? Best not to ask. But he told me. "We were in the Marines together. Kind of crude. But a very okay guy. Very talented. Started out doing photographs on reconnaissance flights. You'll see. Funny, too." What was happening here? Suddenly lots of things were happening that I couldn't tell whether I should be excited about or not. I went upstairs to study chemistry.

I did a couple of those Versace ads and even did a PR thing where they photographed Mr. Versace surrounded by his boys. It was interesting being with some of the famous male models they brought in for the occasion. Most of us were local Miami guys, or at least the models that have located here. But they did bring in some names, like Dack Cardozo and Billy DeWere and Gunther. Very interesting how careful everybody is to not be too sexy. Not at all like the boys at the Bomber Club. They handle their bodies as though there is a camera somewhere all the time. Always making good poses. And talk about very masculine things like baseball or television. Though they do talk about clothes a bit. Because they've worn all the famous designers' things. And they talk about their girlfriends a lot. What it is, I think they're all in training to become movie stars. They're living their pasts right now. So later nobody can talk about them, like they do about James Dean and Rock Hudson. Of course, when it comes to sleeping with somebody in order to get a part in a movie, that's another story altogether.

It's really weird. They've seen people like Kim Basinger and Sharon Stone make it big from modeling to movies, now with the Baldwin brothers it looks like men can do the same thing, so they're being careful right from the start. So strange. Nobody gets to know who they really are or what they're really like. It's not even of any interest. They're just busy making themselves into a product that the movie business will be interested in. I can't really be like that. Of course, I can flex my pecs when the camera starts clicking, but this business of being careful, careful, careful all the time. No way.

deceit in the bathroom

As Glenn came down the hall I reached out and pulled him into the powder room.

We were very face-to-face in the tiny room. I undid Glenn's belt, unzipped his fly, and pushed his trousers down as well as his jockey shorts. He had a look of resignation on his face although he was already very erect.

I reached behind myself and turned on a tap. With my wet hand I took the Roger et Gallet soap and slimed Glenn up.

"Let me get out of these shorts," I said, dropping them and stepping out of them. I wasn't wearing underpants.

Sitting on the edge of the sink I braced a sneakered foot on either side of Glenn against the wall, framing a Redouté rose print.

"Okay, get at it, big boy," I said.

Glenn came and groaned loudly. My mother, coming down the hall, rapped on the door and said, "Darling, are you all right?"

In a very normal tone of voice, Glenn said, "Yes. I just realized I forgot to pay the light bill."

He pulled up his jockey shorts and his pants and left the powder room buckling his belt. I heard him say to my mother, "Come on, let's see what you have in the kitchen that will make me forget I won't have any lights when I get home."

iris at the gym

Here I am on this damn rowing machine. Fifteen minutes and have to keep the rate under 4,000, whatever the hell that means. However, my legs look good. Just tan enough. Funny how these Reeboks and sweat socks make thinnish legs look good. Who would ever think something like gym shoes would be a fashion enhancement? Hugo sort of has my legs.

I wonder if anyone has ever written anything for one of the fashion magazines about the gym slut phenomenon? That poor creature over there on the bicycle machine, all flowing locks, blusher, and slipping and sliding torn sweater. I'm sure her mental picture of herself is that she is driving all these husky weight lifters mad with passion. Dream on, sister. She's not so young anymore and there's something about those leg warmers that makes me think she's a dancer . . . was a dancer . . . has had dance training. What do they call those in Hollywood? MAW's. Model/Actress/Whatever. A poor-grade one that must read too much *Cosmopolitan.* You wouldn't have to be around gyms very long to know that most of these guys aren't interested in anyone with a bosom. At least that kind of bosom. How could a woman like that have a relationship with anyone anyhow? She's so stuck in those Cosmo Girl fantasies she'd just be acting out the fantasies of wonderful her. Now she's talking to a friend but with her face turned toward the room so we can all see her adorable expressions of surprise, horror, laughter. Poor thing, I'm being awfully hard on her. Who knows? She might in fact be a wonderful person. Unlikely when you know so little about how to apply blusher correctly. I wouldn't be so bad-tempered if I didn't hate this damn machine so much.

And that kid next to her doesn't know she's alive. Not a bad-looking boy. Not as handsome as my little Hugo, but he's got something. Nice skull. Nice profile. So young he's probably dreaming about being a model and hoping someone will see him here. And then what awaits him. To be one of that second-rate gang that hangs around Versace. For someone who's able to afford anybody he wants, he doesn't seem to have great taste. So different from when I was modeling. I suppose there must have been teenage boys who did catalog or something, but who ever saw them? Male models then were guys who looked great in evening clothes, smoking. I suppose somebody's idea of what a successful New York businessman looked like. Slender, good hair, chiseled features. You really worked with them rarely. They did menswear. We did womenswear and never the twain did meet. Sometimes in a television commercial. They held you in their arms, laughing at the end. Three-second scene. Bill Loock is the only one I really remember. Still very handsome.

When I look around this room there are probably half a dozen guys here I could have an affair with. How many really? Maybe many more in fact who are available and if I went after them could land them. But how to know? Maybe I should stand up and in a loud voice say, "Will all the straight guys who might want to have an affair with a still attractive older woman please line up against the far wall?" Then I could go take names and addresses and take it from there.

Maybe that's how God or Destiny or whatever protects us from ourselves. Think of the long and exhausting process of finding out each one of these guys is not bright, not faithful, hung up about making bamboola with the lights on . . . When you think what goes into a relationship of any depth even for a few years it's overwhelming. Fortunately they come, pass by, not sure what they're looking for or why they're working to stay attractive, and go their way. Otherwise we'd be up to our necks in starting affairs, in the throes of affairs, getting over affairs. Five more minutes to go.

There's the Handsomest Man in the World. I always count it a good day when he shows up here. I think he's French, even if he does look like Guy Madison with dark hair. He's got his look down cold. Very tan. Always wears green and turquoise. Turquoise eyes. I wish I could see him better but I'd have to be close and he never does the rowing machines and I'm not going to wear my glasses at the gym.

Big muscles. Large thighs. Not too tall, and not really all that great proportions. But he definitely has allure. A star waiting. He's the sort of guy you can fall head over heels in love with, knowing nothing about them and not having to know anything. It's just "come over here and let me slot you right into my fantasies." His skin looks like it would be very smooth. He doesn't seem to have any body hair. Probably a male stripper. Can a male stripper make it to Hollywood? I'm sure some have. Probably poorly equipped. Probably stupid. Isn't that what they always say about beautiful women? At least beautiful women can get those tits right up front so there's no question about equipment. And now with the implants nobody needs to run around being sneered at anymore. Men are lucky. They just tuck it away in their little jockey shorts and it all has to be left to the imagination. When you get these gigantic hulks lumbering around here, no matter what they've got it would look ridiculous. Someone should tell them that. Finally. Zero Zero. Now for the inner thigh machine. Thirty times. In four sequences.

Should I feel guilty finding these kids attractive who are only a little older than Hugo? I think there's some kind of taboo thing that kicks in so you don't find your own kid sexy. Well, I guess not for everybody. But Larry at the office was saying that when he was married, before he finally clambered out of the closet, he was glad he only had daughters, because it would have been terrible to have feelings for a son. I told him heterosexuals have exactly the same setup. In all honesty, I can see how cute Hugo is but I truly don't feel anything as I might for an equally cute kid who was no relation. Like that guy the Handsomest Man in the World is talking to right now. The Second Handsomest Man in the World. Short legs and not a perfect profile, but he's definitely got something. Funny how shortish men have that "cock of the walk" strut when they walk. Tall men in this country often have that slightly bowlegged walk like their feet hurt a little. Anyway, I think when you've seen someone as a tiny baby and at every stage of their body changing and coming into being grown up it's pretty hard to see them as some kind of studly sex object. In fact, I can't help but think that all these guys were little twerps having to have their diapers changed and being a pain in the ass about eating their cereal. Kind of makes all the stardust disappear.

hugo's pilot

Mike Merkin calls me. I can tell he's really excited. He has a casting for me for a TV pilot. Somebody's planning a teen show, like the Beverly Hills one, set in Miami Beach. And they're casting. He has some scripts. I have to come over right away and start rehearsing.

Mike likes me and I kind of like him. Under those falling-apart Ray Milland looks there's somebody who's really not all that ambitious. I think his looks kind of dragged him into this and he's smart enough to have learned the ropes, but he knows that even if you make it big in Hollywood you still might not have a life. There's something kind of fatherly about him, unlikely as it may seem. And ever since *Miami Vice* bit the dust around here, everybody's been kind of waiting for something major league to happen. *Miami Teenage Vice* may be on its way.

I rehearse my part in an episode of *South Beach*. Macha rehearses with me, and of course, she's ten times better than I would ever dream of being. She's the hot one, not me. I don't know why everybody else doesn't see it. We even improve on the dialogue. I know they hate that, but I figure, I don't really like this a whole lot better than working at the Bomber Club,

I have no plans for going to Hollywood, and Macha and I are having a lot of fun with this thing.

And that's sort of how I got a role in the pilot for *South Beach*. I play Hugo. The writers liked my name so they called my character by my name. What's great is that I got a letter of rejection from Talent High School the same day I got the part on the show. I can put that in my memoirs.

I read those stories in *Details* or *Interview* about how somebody graduates from high school and waits tables for a few months and then goes for a reading and voilà! They're a big star. Sleeping with somebody isn't really the story, but look. Christian Slater's mother was a casting director. You don't miss many auditions that way. And Julia Roberts's brother was already a star and her parents were actors and her fiancé (the one she didn't marry) was the son of a BIG star. Entrenched is the word, I think. Sleeping with somebody is just a start. Marrying someone is more like it. So I was lucky. I didn't marry the casting director. I think they liked the fact that I looked like exactly what they were looking for. Tan, blond, not too tall, full of fun. I mean, I wasn't exactly playing Macbeth when I took that audition.

But they didn't take Macha. They were interested, but she doesn't look enough like a starlet for them.

Macha pulled herself together right away as soon as it became clear she wasn't going to make it. I think the fact she is so involved with Mr. Ken Yellow Trunks helped. I think she is letting herself play the role of pretty high school girl who's got a boyfriend. She's never done it before. She was always too major league for the guys in our school so she'd never really had a full-time boyfriend before. Her folks are not keen on it. Particularly her mother.

She's really seen it all, Matilda, and I think she got the picture right away that Macha is kind of on automatic pilot and her heart isn't in it. And where is there to go with it, really? She obviously isn't going to marry this guy, who is working as a waiter. I think Macha has been kind of jealous of me and Glenn Elliott. The fact that I was so blown away by him. I don't know. I can't be sure of that.

So here I am, working my ass off on *South Beach*. First, most of the other teenagers on the show are in their twenties. Ferdinand Bach, who plays the main lead, is twenty-six. And he can act. When Ferdy and I have a scene together, I really want to throw up. Every take he does something a little different. He knows where the camera is. He knows which side he wants to be on. He's like Pavlov's dog. The minute he hears "Action" it is a different Ferdy Bach at work. He actually doesn't even look like a teenager until he hears those bells. Imagine me. I couldn't really be anyone else than myself. I feel really dumb.

But they are all really nice to me. Missy Maloney, who is my girlfriend on the show, is extremely swell. She is only a year older than me but has been making TV commercials and stuff like that since she was four. But she has taught me a lot, always rehearses with me, and even coached me for my scenes with other people.

And of course I'm seeing a lot of Glenn, too. I started putting it to him from the front and he is digging it. I dig it myself. Don't you wonder what the positions we take when we're having sex have to do with the relationship we have with each other?

I mean, he liked me to kneel so he can see me while I was working him over and he pulled himself off at the same time. We've got very good at it so we're coming together all the time. I fall on him. He kisses me very passionately and gratefully. It's great. But we never stay overnight together. Sometimes I'll stop by on my bicycle on my way to rehearsal and he's still in bed. Or sometimes he picks me up after shooting and we get it on before he comes home with me for dinner. Sleeping with your mother's boyfriend has its points, not many people get suspicious.

94

I think Alan Axthelm, who is also on the show, gets the picture. He's gay and doesn't make any bones about it, even though he plays a football hunk. I saw him sizing up Glenn Elliott when he came around to pick me up one day. And you know how it is with gay guys. Once you sleep with other guys you sort of spot the ones who are capable of it. And I don't mean the screamers. There's nothing in the gesture or look or anything, it's just there. Like some kind of radio signal. The only kind of clue sometimes is that they act a little more butch than is absolutely necessary. You know, that kind of rolling footballer walk. Not even footballers walk *that* way.

The next day Alan said, "That was a great-looking guy that picked you up last night."

"Yeah," I said, "my mother's boyfriend."

"Lucky mother," he said. "She's got you and she's got him."

"Not exactly in the same way," I told him.

"I should hope not," he said. And snorted and walked away laughing and shaking his head back and forth. Alan is an all right guy and I think being involved in a little sophisticated repartee tickled him and made him feel better about playing the football dolt. Actually, Macha would get along great with him. Too bad he's gay. Oh. How many times those words must have been spoken in this world.

Despite our fooling-around conversation I think Alan has figured out something *could* be going on. But what interests me more is what is going on when Glenn Elliott wants me to be the "plugger" instead of the "pluggee." Maybe he wants me to be more masculine and doesn't want me to get used to being the "girl." Or maybe he's always liked being the under partner. Maybe he gets tired of having to hand it out in a masculine way all the time and occasionally likes to relax and have it handed to him. I'll never know. It's the kind of thing even if you discussed it, he wouldn't want to talk about it. Or couldn't talk about it. Or it would ruin everything.

It probably had nothing to do with it, but Glenn Elliott was all of a sudden doing great in Miami Beach. I don't know where the money came from but he bought a small hotel on Drexel and redid it for models. Then the agency Les Girls came in from Paris to open an office and he rented them space on the mezzanine of the hotel. The hotel is called the Lurline. I thought it had probably been named for somebody's mother but it turns out it was a ship that used to run between San Francisco and Hawaii. Then he rented space on the ground floor to some people who opened the Faune there, very trendy with furniture designed by Philippe Starck. Glenn Elliott has a very good sense about things as far as decoration and style goes. How he learned that in the Marines I don't know but he had Barbara Hulanicki design the paint job for the Lurline and for once it doesn't look like an explosion in a confetti factory. It really looks good. Turquoise, white, and navy blue. Nautical. But nice. And the combination of the club and the model agency keep the place filled up with models all the time. The Faune isn't a disco so if you stayed in the hotel you could get some sleep at night. And Glenn Elliott had the windows double glazed and added central air-conditioning so the models could sleep. No matter how thick or how crazy they may be, there's one thing all models are very strict about. Sleep. Sleep. Sleep.

So Glenn is hitting it. Big time. All those little papers like *Stretch* and *Dynamite* and *Peer* always have pictures of all the parties at the Faune, and *Time* took a picture of him in front of the Lurline and maybe are going to use it in their big article on the beach.

And Mom has been doing pretty well, too. In addition to selling the Lurline to Glenn Elliott she has been doing some somewhat more major deals. The Germans are evidently handing her name around, so when new ones hit town they call her looking for apartments and even some buildings. So we were all rushing around doing our thing.

So what can I tell you about the pilot? Finally, it was never terribly exciting. You get your script. You go to your room and memorize the lines. Maybe you do some private rehearsal with whoever's playing opposite you. You go to rehearsal and you shoot it. It gets a little complicated when you're busy learning your lines for tomorrow's shoot and you're shooting the scene you memorized yesterday, but everybody's pretty cool about it. And if you get stuck on your lines they put up the idiot cards behind the camera so you can read it if you just can't get it into your head.

We were doing a lot of the shooting at my high school, which was a little weird. Acting a role in the same hallways and rooms where you are *really* going to school.

I was the only Miami Beach person in the cast, but a lot of the extras are from school. That was the hardest part, acting in front of those people I saw around all the time at school. They cast some of the teachers, too, as extras and my favorite, Mr. Korman, who taught my English class last year, was there. They should have given him a part. He's great in his own bizarre way. He looks like Jacques Tati. You know, *Mr. Hulot's Holiday?* Like some great looming bird about to sweep down upon you, always kind of leaning forward.

We always had lunch served by caterers and we all ate together and I always went over and hung around with the kids from school if they were working that day. And I talked to Mr. Korman often, too. He said to me one day, "Hugo, are you keeping a journal of all this?"

"What do you mean, journal?"

"A kind of diary. You write very well, Hugo. You should be writing this all down. It's a unique experience and when you go to college this could make for some very interesting papers."

"Maybe I won't go to college," I told him. "Maybe I'll go to Hollywood to pursue my acting career." A lot of kids from school were impressed with the fact I had this part and talked about when I started making movies and how I could become a big star. I wasn't taking it seriously but I kind of wanted to bait the trap for Mr. Korman and see what he'd say. "Why don't I think you're going to do that, Hugo?" he said. Looking at me like a big parakeet with a sense of humor. "Why do I think you have other plans for yourself, Hugo?" He ended most of his sentences with the name of the person he was talking to. I guess it sort of keeps you alert. More likely from talking to so many different kids in class. "You're quite good, you know. You're quick. I watch your scenes and the director doesn't have to tell you twice to do something. But I think that's your brains at work. Acting is very easy for you, Hugo. This kind of acting. But I don't think you're very excited about it. We had a governor of Connecticut like that once. Lodge. He had been out in Hollywood in the 1930s and had done some leading man parts in movies. And then became a lawyer and went into politics. Acting wasn't enough to hold his attention. Even though he was good-looking, he wasn't vain. The idolatry part didn't interest him. Quite an interesting guy. Had a beautiful wife, too. That's how you can tell if a good-looking man is vain. The self-centered ones don't want the competition of a beautiful wife. They're always paired up with some plain lady who can't believe her luck."

I love this kind of talk. First, it's about me. And second, it's contradictory to all the stuff you read and hear everywhere else. I hear this kind of thing from my mom but we understand each other so well that we don't often speak about it.

I said to Mr. Korman, "Since we're talking about me, tell me more."

He said, "I think you're a smart kid, Hugo. I always think it's kind of interesting if you can encourage somebody to skip some of the mistakes the rest of us make and, if they're smart enough, I think it can be helpful. I'm sure you know that being rich and famous isn't the point. Learning something and passing it on to others isn't a bad overall plan."

"But isn't acting doing something like that?" I asked him.

"Ooh, I don't think so," he said. "Actors are kind of paper dolls to demonstrate someone else's ideas, don't you think? And then they don't even want to do that. They want to stay themselves, which is what people want to see anyway. How much is there to learn from seeing Mel Gibson being Mel Gibson? Now, writing for the movies is something different. But I don't know how different. What kinds of movies do you like, Hugo?"

"I liked *Damaged*."

"You did? That's interesting? Why?"

"Actually, it was the idea of obsession that interested me. I thought Jeremy Irons wasn't hot enough. That's a movie that Mel Gibson would have been great in, but he would never have had the nerve to do it. And Juliette Binoche was *it*. She was just an obsessive object and that was enough for her."

What would you have called Mr. Korman's expression? Quizzical? Not a word I'd ever heard anyone use but suddenly it went exactly with that expression. "You surprise me, Hugo," he said.

"I surprise myself," I told him, and went back inside where the AD was screaming himself hoarse trying to get us together for the next scene. And I continued to think about what Mr. Korman had said and even a bit about Mr. Korman himself. Obviously gay, but no come-on. A real good egg. I was going to have to talk to Mr. Korman some more.

There were some other people to talk to around the set. Not many. But some. There were eight principals on the show. In addition to Ferdy Bach, Missy, Alan Axthelm, and me there was Andrea Bellemere, who played the bad girl; Filomena Gorse, who is English and plays the intellectual transfer student; Mitzi Vanderbilt, the little cute one who is everybody's best friend who is a real Vanderbilt and actually quite okay; and Milton Weinstein, who is black and Jewish and in my book really, deeply, truly sexy. Milton always says they cast him because they got two token minority groups in one and could save on salary. He also always claimed that they didn't pay Mitzi at all because she already had so much money.

Milton was tops to work with. He was the other principal from Miami besides me, although he had been out in Hollywood working when they cast him.

Milton is from across the bay. Like me, he only had his mother, but never ever saw anybody who might have been his father. He told me his mother knew who it was but that he disappeared and his name was Milton Weinstein. So my pal is really Milton Weinstein, Jr. Cool, huh? Milton knows he was a gambler and somebody in that family was very good-looking because Milton is mucho good-looking. When I talk to Milton I feel like I've been nowhere and seen nothing. He's been through the mill at twenty and it hasn't fazed him a bit as far as I can see.

He left Miami when he was sixteen and went to Chicago to live with an aunt. I kept trying to draw some comparisons with what's going on with Glenn and me but it was quite different. Quite. Milton was out hanging around in the streets picking up guys for money and this older white guy picked him up and took him home and sent him to school and then sent him off to the coast and kept an eye on him financially. Still will, I guess, if he needs help.

I asked him, "But Milton, didn't it make you feel kind of creepy going to bed with an old guy?"

He said, "Mr. Arno isn't that old, and besides, you know, he's just a nice guy. He's Jewish, too. And I think he got a kick out of having a little Jewish friend who was black. I mean, let's face it, Hugo. What are you going to do with another guy? It's suck or fuck, right?" Nobody had ever put it quite so neatly before, but I couldn't tell him he was wrong.

He went on. "And Mr. Arno was so nice to me. Most guys the second they've sucked you off or whatever just hand you some cash and open the car door. Fred wasn't like that at all.

He was really fun and always wanted to make sure I had enough to eat and had warm clothes. Chicago is cold, you better believe it.

"The first night I spent with him he took me right out the next morning and got me a good coat. In a good store. I knew he was totally cool because it didn't bother him at all when the clerks saw us together. He told the clerk I was his nephew. It was a blast. And you know, I think he kind of thought I was. He was shocked when he found out I didn't go to school and he insisted I go and helped with my homework. And I zipped right through it. He wanted me to go to college but I went to acting school and his friends helped get me an agent and here I am, two hundred crowd shots as an extra later, back in my own hometown."

I asked him, "But do you love Mr. Arno?"

"Look, Hugo, there's these two kinds of love. No, he doesn't turn me on. At all. But I love him very much for being concerned about me. . . . It's like a parent with a little sex thrown in. And he knows that. He finds me a big turn-on, for whatever reason. I like him so much I want him to be happy. I suppose it's what a lot of women feel when they get married."

"That's all very well for women," I said. "All they have to do is lie there."

"Well," said Milton, "maybe all you have to do is lie there. And if someone wants to give you a blow job, Mr. Penis knows no reason.

"And on the other hand there's that kind of love where you just go crazy over how someone looks. Who can say why? It's not the size of their penis or how big their arms are, it's just *what* they are. Awful, isn't it? But if it wasn't for that there wouldn't be any movie stars. They look like something that rings a lot of people's bells. Tom Cruise . . . nobody cares how he acts. And if it wasn't for him there'd never be a Jeff Stryker. He's a Tom Cruise stand-in going all the way."

"But have you ever been in love like that?" I wanted to

know. "Can I afford to be?" Milton said. "My mother was, and look what it got her. Me and a lifetime of cleaning houses for a bunch of creeps. I want to be one of the creeps who hire other people to clean their houses. And I want my mother to be in that house being nice to whoever is cleaning in a way that practically nobody has been to her. Well, yeah, I have been in love like that a couple of times. But you know, nobody wants to just throw it all over and go somewhere and just be in love for the rest of their lives. At least in L.A. Oh, it's very complicated, Hugo. I'm black. I don't want some white guy paying my bills in exchange for a little ass now and again. And I don't think that's a very modern idea. Even women don't want that anymore. It's too boring.

"And everybody knows too much. They know that love wears off after while, so they just wait until it's worn off, and then they ditch you. That's the modern way."

"So what's your plan?" I wanted to know.

"Oh, basically I'm a silly fool, like everybody else. I think I'm going to be successful and make enough money to take care of myself. And also going to meet somebody whose exterior packaging gives me a jolt and whose interior personality is good and faithful and loyal and all the rest of that shit. One thing I can tell you, unless they're superior to me we haven't got a chance together, plus remember I'm talking about another man."

I had noticed with both Milton and Mr. Korman that they talked to me assuming I was gay. I mean, is it stamped on my forehead or something? So I said to Milton, "Milton, why do you think I'm gay?" and he said, "I don't know you're gay. I just sure as hell hope you are because you are one cute guy. And smart. And nice. You've got a lot going for you, Hugo, whether you're AC or DC or a switch-hitter. You must have excellent parents."

"I have an excellent mother," I told him. "And then there's AIDS," I added.

"And then there's AIDS," Milton said. "And then there's

102

AIDS. God, I hate the taste of rubber. But that's how it goes these days. As if it wasn't hard enough to get laid, let alone fall in love. You have to mar the magic by stopping and suiting up as though you're going scuba diving. But whatever you do, Hugo, be careful. No matter what anyone tells you, there is no-body to be trusted." I thought about Glenn Elliott. "Nobody. When guys get a chance to sink a little peter they just hate to pass it up. It's a rare bird that can say 'No, thanks.' Even these days."

I wondered if I was going to be as knowledgeable as Milton when I was his age. I asked him, "Milton, are you involved with anyone on the show?"

"No."

"Are you going to be?"

"Well, like with who, or should I say whom?" Milton said.

"There's Alan Axthelm."

"What are we supposed to do together?" he said. "Bump pussies?"

mr. korman

So we finally stopped shooting the television pilot. Which is okay because I really wasn't interested. Acting really isn't me. If I had written a book I'd be down at the bookstore all the time to see if anybody was buying it. That I would really want. But the show, it never really captured my interest.

And I was still interested in school. Particularly Mr. Korman's English class. At our last counseling conference he asked me, "So, Hugo, who are your favorite authors?" I told him, "Well, I guess Charlotte Bronte and Jane Austen and Muriel Spark. And I like *The Wide Sargasso Sea* by Jean Rhys. And I love M. F. K. Fisher's *Map of Another Town*."

I wasn't trying to give him a jolt or anything. I was just thinking about the books I like best.

He said, "The Fisher book, that's kind of an unusual selection. But excellent. How about Hemingway and Fitzgerald? Don't you like them?"

And I told him, "Don't you get the impression when you read books like Hemingway that they're really kind of mythical stories and Hemingway himself is the hero? That's the feeling I get from a lot of these men writers. That they dream up this story and it's really about them and how they would do things and how they would behave. You know like the James Bond books, and most of these spy thrillers."

"Well, of course that's not really great literature," Mr. Korman said. "How about John Updike?"

"Well, he's good," I told him. "But the things I like best are when he writes about his mother and his real life. Then you feel something good there. The rest is interesting, but you get the feeling he wants you to feel a certain way about him. I'd like to meet him. You know, once you see somebody an awful lot of things become clearer. Like why they're trying to peddle a certain idea about themselves. But women aren't that way. When they write they don't seem to want you to think they're sexy or beautiful or wonderfully brilliant. I just get the feeling they're trying to let you know how they feel or what they think about something."

"You have a point," Mr. Korman said. "But there are some men writers I think you'd like, even if they'd be a little heavy going for you right now. Like Proust. Proust wrote all these books with hundreds of characters and he himself is hardly present. And Gertrude Stein is like that. So self-centered, but when she wrote she wasn't in there herself. Except for *The Autobiography of Alice B. Toklas,* which she wrote."

"She wrote someone else's autobiography?"

"Well, it *was* someone she knew very well," Mr. Korman said. "But you know, I just discovered that even though she lived in France for many, many years she never learned French. That was a big disappointment to me. She was just like an American man. Wouldn't put herself in the embarrassing position of having someone be better than she was. So she made the woman of the family do the speaking in French. I've known so many people like that. But maybe I tell you too much."

"No, no, no," I said. "I know about Gertrude Stein and Alice B. Toklas. Alice wrote a cookbook with a recipe for marijuana brownies in it, did you know that?"

"As a matter of fact, I do," Mr. Korman said.

"Do you speak French?"

"As a matter of fact, I do."

"I'd love to," I told him. "It's my dream. That and to live in France."

"Have you been to France?" he asked me.

"Last summer my mother took me. She knew Paris and France pretty well because she used to be a model and worked there. It was great."

"Your mother was a model?" Mr. Korman said. "What was her name?"

"The same name she has now," I said. "Iris Carey."

"*Your* mother is Iris Carey?" Mr. Korman looked surprised. He wasn't using his schoolteacher voice. "I know who she is. I worked as a copywriter in New York in an advertising agency before I became a teacher. I remember seeing her pictures all over the place. Even in the newspaper when she danced on a platform at the Chez When."

"My mother danced on a platform in a bar?" I said. Mr. Korman laughed. Really laughed. "She wasn't a go-go girl. In the days then if you were *anyone* in New York you went to the Chez When and danced on the platforms. If you were good-looking enough. But you must have been born then. How old are you?"

"Sixteen," I said.

"Sixteen. Well, I guess you can handle that your mother went to clubs. Of course, dancing on platforms is something else." I couldn't help but wonder if Mr. Korman was putting me on and knew very well that I had danced down at the Bomber Club. I'd never seen him there but I felt pretty certain he knew people that went there.

"Oh, well, no, I'm not *shocked* by that," I said. "It's just from what she's told me it was all limousines and cigarettes and black cocktail dresses."

"Oh, Hugo, Hugo, Hugo," Mr. Korman said, cocking his head at me, sort of looking like a huge parakeet in horn-rimmed glasses. He's really cool, Mr. Korman, but he's no beauty. He does look like a parrot or a parakeet or something, with this big stalk of hair on the front of his head and those beady, bright eyes and that beak of his. But a nice parrot. "I'd like to meet your mother," he said.

"That's not the impossible dream," I said. "She's right here, not ten blocks away as we speak. I'll tell her you remember her from her modeling days in New York and I know she'd love to see you. Maybe you could come over for dinner." I really meant it but I wondered if this sounded like overwhelming brownnosing or what. I decided I shouldn't get too palsy-walsy. Mr. Korman is very astute.

He must have been thinking the same thing I was because he said, "That would be very nice. But I'd like to get back to your liking women writers better than men. That was very interesting. You think men writers often are writing with themselves as the star of the movie of their life?"

"Not all. There's *The Assault* and *The Tin Drum*. They're not really about the author as the leading character, you know. Maybe they are, but they don't make the main character to be some sort of super-sensitive, super-wonderful person you're supposed to feel a lot of sympathy for. Maybe I'm just talking about American male writers. You know, like Jay McInerney and all those young guys. You're supposed to read them and think 'so cool,' you know what I mean."

"Yes, I know what you mean." Mr. Korman was kind of looking down at his desk and fiddling with his pencil. "So what do you want to write about, Hugo?"

"I don't know exactly, but I know I don't want to write things to make people think things about life that aren't true. I want to write things that I think are true, and maybe I'll dress them up a little, or maybe just the way I think about things will dress it all up and be different, but at least I'll be trying to write about things the way I really think they are. Don't you think people pretend a lot about their lives, Mr. Korman? That they pretend they're happy or they pretend they like what they're doing because it's what everybody says they should be happy doing, and they don't even know they're unhappy because they've never done what they'd really like to do?" I was really getting all worked up and saying things I'd never said before, even to Macha. I kind of surprised myself; I wasn't even sure I'd ever thought of all this stuff before. Maybe I was being seized by an evil spirit and would have to go home and be exorcised.

"And you're not going to go to Hollywood after having done your television pilot? You were quite good, Hugo. They didn't give you a lot to do but I thought you were interesting to watch." Mr. Korman was maybe a little impressed with me, I thought, and I didn't like that very much. I kind of counted on him to keep some perspective.

"That was just a TV show for kids, Mr. Korman. That wasn't anything much and I don't think it's for me. I can tell that the other people on the show were a lot more into it than I was. I sort of feel that once people see me on television I'll look like someone different to them, and if I went along with it I'd become that someone different and I wouldn't even have any say about it. I don't mind becoming someone different but I want to be the one that makes me that way. Besides, my mom has a friend who says he never met a famous person who wasn't an asshole."

"Who's that?" Mr. Korman asked me. He looked interested.

"A friend of my mother's who used to be a makeup artist. He's retired here now. His name is Jean de Jehan. He's French. He told me that he once worked with Gloria Swanson and at first he didn't think she was, but finally she was. I'd hate to have people say that about me after they met me."

"Well, you can't control what people say about you," Mr. Korman said. "Maybe they're just jealous."

"Yeah, and maybe they're right, too," I said.

"Maybe there are worse things than being an asshole."

"There's always Hitler, I know. But even so, it's not too cool knowing people think you're an asshole."

"Maybe that's what you kids think about me," Mr. Korman said.

"We think a lot of things about you, Mr. Korman, but that's not one of them," I told him. I felt this whole meeting was getting a little out of hand. I certainly wasn't going to tell him we all thought he was gay but we didn't care. People of his generation like to think that nobody knows just because they haven't been caught in some porno theater with their head under somebody's raincoat. Weird, weird, weird, huh?

Mr. Korman is very okay. He didn't ask more about what we thought of him. He's a real gentleman because he realized that this little conference was about me and he was not going to turn it into a conference about him.

"Thanks, Mr. Korman," I said, getting up and pulling my books together. "You made me think about writing more than I usually do and straightened out a lot of my thinking. I really do want to be a writer. I want to go to Columbia University in New York and study English and see what happens."

"You're okay, Hugo. You're going to be just fine. Where did you run across writers like Jean Rhys and M. F. K. Fisher anyway?"

"Around the house. My mom reads a lot. Wait until you come over to dinner. Then you'll really get an earful."

"It sounds like you have a pretty interesting home life, Hugo. We weren't all so lucky. My mother never read anything but the *Ladies' Home Journal*. Well, it would be a great pleasure to meet your mother, and I'd be delighted to take you both out to dinner if that's easier for your mother. You never mention your father so I'm guessing there isn't one around."

"Never has been," I told him. "He's in South America, I guess. Mom is completely out of touch with him and I've never seen him."

"And your mother never remarried?" Mr. Korman asked.

"Not so far," I said. "But maybe, maybe. You never know. Maybe when I go away to college she'll get lonely and grab off some unsuspecting guy."

Mr. Korman was leaving, too. He had another class to teach. "You wouldn't mind?"

"Oh no," I said. "I'd like that. Sometimes I think I'm going to have to go and get one for her." Mr. Korman got a little nervous. Maybe he thought I was talking about him. Some people really don't get it, even if they're smart.

"Good-bye, Mr. Korman," I said. "It was really great talking to you." And it was. He waved good-bye and headed down the corridor with that kind of shuffly walk of his and slumped shoulders. He is really okay.

hugo thinks about france and other things

I rode my bicycle home slowly from school. One of those Miami Beach winter end of the days. The sky lavender, the clouds pink, the water in Indian Creek sometimes turquoise, sometimes lime green. Wiggling under the neon falling on it. Palm trees shaking their heads stupidly this way and that, as though somebody just socked them. The wind coming off the ocean not smelling salty but sweet. I wondered if Mr. Korman thinks it's pretty here.

And then I thought all of a sudden of how when we were in Europe last summer and in a restaurant in Milan there was this very well-dressed young father at a table with some other people and his baby sitting in a high chair beside him and he sat there and talked about stocks and bonds or something and sort of absentmindedly fed the child with his own fork off his plate. And the baby sat there like a little bird with his eyes fastened on his father, opening his mouth when that fork came swinging over. It was kind of loving in such an easy way. That's my idea of a father's love.

And then we were in France. Because I've always been so interested in Marie Antoinette, we looked for her tomb. It's in a little square not far from Madeleine Church. It's in sort of like a stone tunnel kitty-corner on the square, crossways on an angle from corner to corner. Strange, there's no real front. And inside on one end is a statue of Louis the Sixteenth and at the other one of Marie Antoinette.

These statues were done long after they were guillotined. And the bones were identified by some person living beside the burial ground who claimed to have seen where their bodies were buried. Seems unlikely, doesn't it? Particularly when all those headless bodies were just thrown into one big pit together. Sort of like the Tomb of the Unknown Soldier really. It could be anybody. Or any woman at least. I suppose they could tell that much. Pelvis bones and all.

Anyway. When I saw the statue of her it really stopped me. She wasn't even pretty. I always imagined this little blond doll in hoop skirts and a high wig, covered in diamonds. At Malmaison we'd just seen the carriage she came to Paris in, from the French border. When she arrived at the border from Austria the French officials bathed her, changed her clothes, sent all the Austrians back to Vienna, and put her in this little gold carriage filled with royal blue velvet cushions. She was like a precious little jewel in a beautiful jewel box. And only fourteen. Younger than me.

Her statue showed her with this long jaw, beaky nose, and one of those skulls where the face kind of hangs off the front end and the skull itself is rather small. No wonder she needed all that hair. Right then and there I got this completely different picture on her. She wasn't this spoiled little beauty at all. She was like the new girl who arrives from a not-so-good school and a lot of the girls in her class are prettier than she is, but she's determined to make it and she's rich. So she wears fancier clothes and lots of jewelry. And acts wild.

I'm sure Marie didn't think she was so hot. She was a German, for God's sake, in Paris! So she went all out to be liked. And probably went to the guillotine thinking it was just what she deserved for trying to put it over on them all those years. Trying to convince them she was the most beautiful of all.

When she was just a big-jawed kid from out of town. She was the first big glamour girl, and probably always thought, just like all the models you see around here, this really isn't me.

Another thing surprised me in France. About me. We were driving down a little, winding road in the country and I saw three men on bicycles ahead of us. In all that professional gear. Tight stretch shorts, bright-colored team shorts, little helmets like halves of cantaloupe, and nice legs, churning along.

But when we passed them I saw they were all old, gray-haired men. I don't mean old. But beyond that kind of funky, early middle-aged look that can be kind of cute. And I had this fantasy that they're cycling along, feeling like young studs. And a young woman in a car passes them and waits for them at a country intersection and asks them if they want to go off into the woods with her. One of those real porno scenarios.

And would they? If she called their bluff would they try to act like young studs and go in the woods and peel down those shorts and have at it, sucking and fucking? Or would they feel embarrassed and ashamed because they were too old and cycle away, never being able to pretend again that they were in the marketplace as horny dudes. It being France, they probably would have done it. I'd love to have been there. I guess I'd love to have been the young woman.

mr. korman visits

When I got home, Mom was already there. She was feeling good because the big 1950s house up on Pine Tree Drive she has been showing looked like it was going to go to some people in New York. She looked real good. She was wearing her navy blue skirt and white linen jacket that always looks so great on her. And her hair was a little shorter. She has bangs and straight hair. Kind of that Louise Brooks look. But she always had that. When she shows me pictures when she was modeling she wore her hair like that then, too. And she has wonderful eyes, my mother. They are the kind of eyes that look like they should be brown, but they're blue. You know how most people with brown eyes often have big round eyes? Well, she has these big, brown eyes, but they're blue. Kind of a dark blue and sometimes in some light they look like they're made out of metal. They kind of shine like the finish on a new blue car. I'm very proud of her. I only wish I had those eyes. I know it's unusual to be a blond with brown eyes, but even so it would be nice to have the eyes that she has. So we could look back and forth at each other out of the same eyes. And no matter how much I might love Glenn—I will never love him more than I love my mother. Call it sick if you will. She's the one person in the world I know I can always count on.

I told her about my talk with Mr. Korman. She said, "Korman, Korman? I don't remember ever knowing anyone named Korman. But I met so many people in those days."

I said, "He never met you. He only saw pictures of you. He said you were very famous. And he remembers seeing pictures of you in the newspaper dancing on a platform in a nightclub."

"Doesn't it sound wonderful?" Mom said. "Just like you'd always wanted to be remembered. Dancing on a platform. It really wasn't all that great. My friend Monique—I used to model with her in Paris—opened this club and asked us all to come on opening night and it was so crowded you couldn't move. I got very exasperated with all the crowd, and I decided if the only place to dance was up on a platform, I'd get up on a platform. I was wearing trousers. It wasn't as though I was stripping or anything. Did you ever hear of Frances Faye? She used to come out and say, 'Shall I sing or shall I strip?' She was quite plain and everyone would shout 'Oh, strip, strip, strip.' I wonder where she is now. I loved her. She used to say, 'I'd like to dedicate my next number to my ex-husband, who's the drummer here in the band. We were married for a couple of years out in Chicago. I was a little heavier then, but always a swinging chick.' So great. So great."

I loved it when Mom would wander completely off the track talking about things she'd done, places she'd been. I asked her once if she was happy and if everything was okay and she said, "Sometimes I look in the mirror and I can't believe I still look as good as I do. I'm surprised I don't look seventy. Sometimes you wake up at night and you realize you're all alone in the bed and you say to yourself, 'Thank God I'm all alone in this bed.' And you think of who you could be lying there with and you count yourself lucky." That's all she's ever said on the subject.

I said, "What about the picture in the paper?" She said, "Imagine my surprise the next day when everyone started calling me and were talking about my dancing on the platform over at the Chez When. Some dope from *The New York Times* was there and I guess I was the closest thing to a celebrity Monique had there. It was nothing."

"Mr. Korman remembered it," I told her.

"Well, if it was so thrilling a memory for Mr. Korman we'll have to invite him over and let him see what remains of the real thing."

And we did. But he insisted we go out to dinner with him at Tiberio's.

"So," my mother said, "What do you think about love, Mr. Korman?" She was being provocative. Mr. Korman stared at his fettuccine Alfredo and said, "What do you mean?" stalling for time. He was already in love with my mother. Not *that* way, but the way everybody is when she sets out to be fascinating, which she definitely was tonight. "I mean, what do you think about great love, like a love of the century, like the love between the Duke and Duchess of Windsor, when he gave up his throne for her."

"Well," said Mr. Korman very slowly, "truth be told, I think she probably gave a great blow job."

"Not even great," my mother said. "But you hit the nail right on the head." Mr. Korman looked pretty pleased with himself. The people at the next table looked around real hard for their waiter.

"Have you thought a lot about this, Mr. Korman? I think I'll call you Bill. Otherwise I'll feel as though I'm one of your students, too."

"My name is Harold," Mr. Korman said.

"Harold? That doesn't suit you at all. Too studious. Too academic. I don't see you that way at all. I see you more weird. More hidden depths. More surprising." Mr. Korman blushed with pleasure. I wondered how this was going to affect my grades. Either really well or really badly. "I think I'll call you

Mr. Korman, like those Victorian wives who always called their husbands Mr. so-and-so. What do you think? What did your mother call you?"

"Do we really want to do this?" Mr. Korman said. "This is going to get back to every single student in school." He looked at me knowingly. "No," I said raising my hand. "I swear, Mr. Korman, your secrets are safe with me. Totally."

"You're quite a pair," he said, looking back and forth from my mother to me. Do you ever have those moments when you wonder what the person you're talking to is seeing? If you were inside his head looking out, what would you think of this nice-looking lady and her teenage son? Does Mr. Korman glamorize us because my mother was a famous model? Do we look sleeker and slicker and more fabulous than we really are because of what he's bringing to the party? Or does he see us looking even worse than we think we look? Does he notice there's a button off Mom's blazer? Or that I have the beginning of a zit on my neck under my right ear? Maybe our act of the attractive witty mom and her intelligent, good-looking teenage son really isn't being bought. Actually, I think Mr. Korman is pretty smart and he probably can have his little rush of being with the once well-known and still be able to see us as we really are. I wish I could see us as we really are.

"My mother called me Harold Teen, actually." he said. As though he had decided to go for it. "After a comic strip when she was young. I was always kind of flattered that she thought I was like that, a little goofy and running around with average kids doing average things. I think she wanted that kind of life for me and that calling me that wove us into the American middle class a little tighter. So that was me, Harold Teen."

"I don't know. I think you're a little too mature for that." Mom said slowly, staring at him. "I think I'll call you Kor, sort of a caveman-type name, completely confusing for people when they overhear it."

"Whatever you like," said Mr. Korman, now sort of suave and in control. Mom had momentarily pushed him off balance but he was recovering himself now. "Let's talk more about love and the great romances. That's a subject that has always fascinated me. I mean, if you're going to fall in love shouldn't it compare to the romance of the century? And what were those romances like in fact? Think of Emma Hamilton and Lord Nelson, and the Austrian Archduke and his mistress Marie Vetsera in their suicide pact at Mayerling, and Clark Gable and Carole Lombard, and the Duke and Duchess, of course. What was really going on?"

"And Demi Moore and Bruce Willis," I said. They both gave me looks that would have burned holes in the tablecloth if they'd landed there. "Of course," Mr. Korman said. "Of course, Demi-clothed and her hair-losing hubby, of course."

"Of course," my mother said, as though she wasn't sure who I was.

"But let's get serious," Mom said. "Imagine the poor Duke of Windsor. He's the King of England. He's not too smart. He's always had girlfriends who looked like skinny boys, and probably there were any number of skinny boys thrown in there for good measure, too. I saw highly suspicious pictures of him sitting on Lord Mountbatten's lap during some kind of cruise in the South Seas. All in fun, yes, but! And then he meets another skinny little thing with a big head, sort of like himself, and she's very self-confident and bosses him around and probably in bed he doesn't have to climb on top and act like a man, she does all the work, and he can relax. At last he's found someone who's just his type. People forget how small he was, and she was. They were minuscule. And she was coached through the whole thing by Lady Mendl, who was another one of those little large-skulled folks who clawed their way to the bottom in those days."

"Is Hugo old enough to hear all this?" Mr. Korman asked.

"Oh, Hugo could give lectures on this kind of stuff. He's a big reader, you know, and I'm not about to edit what he reads." She looked at me quizzically. "What he does, I'm in no way of knowing, but what he knows I'm sure is pretty much everything. I think he should hear this kind of thing so he doesn't advance into adulthood or adultery without knowing what really goes on out there." I was trying to look modest but at the same time I was sort of startled. Mom and I had never really talked about sex directly as pertained to ourselves and this was the closest we'd ever edged on it. I wasn't sure how much closer I wanted to come to the whole thing. That I slept with guys I think she could handle if she thought they were my own age. Glenn was something else altogether.

"What you're saying, if I understand it correctly, is that great love affairs may be based on somebody's presence solving some of your problems, more than a great overwhelming drive to share their body," Mr. Korman said.

"Very much so," Mom said. "I was rereading some Hemingway the other night . . ." Mr. Korman looked very surprised. "That's right, Hemingway," my mother went on. "I think he's very interesting but not for the same reasons men do. He was always married to these little, wizened-up, bad-tempered blondes. You could just tell by looking at him that he was the kind of big guy that just gets drunk and goes into the bedroom and falls on top of whoever is there. Then rolls over and goes to sleep. No subtlety. None. Afraid of sex, but felt no big guy could admit he'd rather shoot animals. And his much-talked-about affair with Marlene Dietrich. You *know* that had to be largely fantasy time for both of them. She said as much. No, he obviously was very drawn to those tough little ladies that saw marriage to him as some kind of penance. He called his last wife Poor Old Mama. That says it all. No June, moon, spoon there."

"But yet, you do still call that a great love?" Mr. Korman asked.

"Oh, I think so, yes," Mom said. "But it's not the kind of great love that would work for me."

"And what about people who have never known great love?" Mr. Korman wanted to know.

"That's everywhere," Mom told him.

iris counts the bodies

Our talk tonight at dinner with Mr. Korman has made me think about love. What do I really think? The conversation was all right for Hugo to listen to. It was more about being witty than anything else. But our Mr. Korman would have been surprised if I had told him what I really thought. Maybe not. Those kind of studious, inexperienced types are always surprising. A lot more has gone on in their lives than you might think. I guess a lot more has gone on in everyone's life than others might think.

However, there was that night years ago, on location in France, when the director was talking about Grace Kelly. She was still alive then. His father had been a director in Hollywood and he had been raised there. He said Grace was known as "old mattress back" out there in those days. And I said, "Well, who is there among us that doesn't have a story to tell?" And that nice producer, John Greene said in a woeful voice, "I don't." So perhaps some people don't.

But to get back to bodies. Yes, bodies. When I fell in love with someone it was always their magical person that I loved. But after the initial excitement, it's their body that keeps you in love with them. And every man's body is so different. The skin, the muscle underneath, the color, the way they smell. I've never seen two exactly alike, although a lot of Italian men seem to be quite similar. It's probably the interbreeding of the races. Probably in the days before people traveled around the bodies in one region were pretty much the same.

But when I think of Baby, his body was sort of naturally hard and rather muscular. He didn't exercise very much. His body hair was coarse on his forearms and legs, although he didn't have a lot of it. He had very nice hands and feet, you could see the bones and muscles in them and his skin was smooth, but not particularly soft. And he had a clean smell and when you kissed him he never had bad breath. And his body was quite warm. I used to rub his back sometimes, he liked that, but I never thought a man's body was extraordinarily beautiful. It was sort of what I expected a man's body to be like. Different from mine. But my fascination and feeling were really for his overall presence. When he wrapped that warm body around me it was the feeling I liked.

But Fred, the man I loved in New York when Hugo was little, was an entirely different thing. He had a big, white, athletic body with almost no hair at all. And he had kind of fleshy thighs and buttocks. Big arms and his pectoral muscles were almost like breasts. I loved the feel of all that smooth skin. My lesbian side coming out I suppose. And he did like to be on the bottom a lot. But when he raised the big arms over his head and his chest lifted, it was like making love with a big statue come to life. He had nice hands and feet, too. Just thinking about that body used to turn me on. Made me want to get on top of it and dominate it, control it. Maybe I was growing up, too, and wasn't just a little poupée for men to play with anymore. And I liked to play with his penis, which I never did with Baby. I used to give Baby blow jobs, but I never really looked at it. It's so curious how a real sexual relationship unwinds so differently with each person. Maybe that's why men like one-night stands. They can just climb aboard and do their thing and they don't ever have to go on and find out what the other person's body is like and might like to do. Bodies, bodies, bodies. I have to believe that people are just as much their bodies as their minds. Because you can be very involved with someone's body and have very little to do with their minds. Such a mistake to live with someone because you think alike and get along together. That's just a roommate with some meaningless sex thrown in. I sort of get the feeling that's what most young people's relationships are like. Someone to fend off the world with and sex that doesn't move you any more than masturbation. Maybe not as much.

Well, I certainly missed Fred and his big body when he left me to get married. He was studying French in the evenings and lo and behold married his French teacher. She wasn't even French. I have often wondered how good her accent was. I was too old for him. And too inappropriate, being foreign and having Hugo. Too glamorous maybe, in his eyes. He went back to Kansas City and good luck to him. He wrote me once and told me he had never told his wife about me and never would but he thought he had learned a lot about life from me. He could have learned a lot more.

Why do we fall in love with the people we do? Or sleep with the people we do? I learned my lesson early on not to sleep with someone just because they're nice and they want to. I've never understood the French and their "baise de santé"—for your health. Sleeping with someone when I didn't feel like it certainly has never made me feel healthier. It's like going to the gym. Somehow things that can be very exciting when you're in love with someone only tickle when you're not. And make you want to laugh. And trying not to laugh just makes them think you're in the throes of passion.

Because that nice guy George I used to see after Fred ditched me was physically much the same. Even better looking. But his skin and flesh were all wrong. Kind of rubbery when he was going to the gym and sort of saggy when he wasn't. And he had a stale smell. And there was always something impersonal about

123

making bamboola with him. He always used to say, "Ooh, that's good, baby," which really isn't at all the kind of thing you say to someone like me. You might curse and say foul things but you wouldn't say "baby." All my friends used to think I was crazy not to get more serious with him, so good-looking and all and so crazy about me. But I used to tell them he wasn't really so crazy about me and I'm sure I was right. His body was not thrilling in any way to me even though everyone seemed to think he was such a hot ticket.

And that hunky young kid I thought I was so interested in last year. Very muscular, tiny hips, big shoulders, but he had curious skin and muscles. He had been a swimmer and there was something fishlike about him, or maybe a sea otter, with that straight almost Oriental-like body hair, even the bit on his chest. When you're massaging someone's back and their buttocks suddenly look like a baby's to you, they must be too young for you. At least he didn't remind me of Hugo in any way. No one I've ever been attracted to does, thank God. Hugo is a real combination of his father and me. That blond hair comes from my mother's side of the family.

It's all sort of Zen-like I suppose. Zen people believe that we aren't separated into mind and body. I remember hearing a Buddhist abbot say one time, "Your thoughts aren't all up in your head, you know. Your liver could be having a great idea right at this moment." So I guess if you're all wrapped up in somebody it's all right to be crazy about the way their back fits into their ass. That's just as much them as the fact they can talk about Proust. I guess that's why women are always so crazy about scholar-athletes and poet–mountain climbers. You get some sensitivity and some real physical beauty in bed.

Like Donald. I slept with Donald off and on right through all the other involvements because he was really great to be in bed with. You could spend hours with him because he'd made the sensual exploration of his own body a real art. He was technically crazy, I suppose. Well, I'm here to say crazy people

124

can be great in bed. What's that quote, from Aldous Huxley I think it is, "Love-making: two maniacs struggling in the dark." Not always in the dark. Donald had that long dancer's body with large thighs and really beautiful skin and he always smelled of Lilac Vegetal. He loved being massaged and fooled around with. I guess in many ways I was more the masculine aggressor and he was the female recipient, but we certainly both enjoyed it. Sex was really his most important product. But he wasn't a great kisser. Baby was a very good kisser and I can really get carried away with that. I didn't really mind not kissing Donald. Our mouths got quite a workout, even so. Well, time has torn them all from my arms.

Oscar Wilde was walking in a garden in Paris after his disgrace with a friend who said despite everything he still had so many friends. And Oscar said, "Friends? Friends? I don't need any more friends. What I need is a lover." Honest, that.

glenn elliott's worst date

"So, what was my worst date?" Mr. Paul and I were lounging around on his bed, which we did from time to time after our sordid physical maneuvers. I actually should have been out of there and at my final period gym class, but I figured I had already had my gym workout in a manner of speaking. And my gym marks didn't affect my overall average anyway.

Glenn had heard me talking about how the guys and I down at the Bomber Club used to play "My Worst Date" between numbers and evidently he'd been thinking about it. And I didn't bring it up. "My worst date wasn't really a romantic one. It was a date with my father. I was eight I think. About." I can never express surprise when I should. I always take these surprise statements very coolly. Only later do I realize I should have asked something like "Your father? You've never mentioned your father before." Glenn went on.

"It was here. I bet you didn't know I was brought up here in Miami Beach, did you? We lived up on Twenty-fourth Street and Pine Tree Drive. I went to Beach Grade School at Fifteenth Street."

Another chance for me to have a reaction, but I just react cool again. Like I'm an analyst or something.

"Yeah, my old man was a professional gambler. I think he

had connections with the Mafia probably. Not big connections. My parents were divorced and he had visitation rights. He used to take me to the movies every Saturday. Usually to the big movie house down on Washington. The place that's the disco Prince owns now."

He turned to me and pulled me to him. Mr. Paul is very cuddly. He likes to hold me a lot and frankly, I have no objection.

"I hated my old man. He was really a drag. In his fedora and his gabardine suits and his two-tone shoes. I don't think he liked me very much either. I think I bored him. He had married my mother because he thought she was classy, with her college degree and her sweater sets. And when he found out she objected to him boffing other women on a regular basis, he was out of there.

"And when she discovered he wasn't an accountant with a night job, she was glad he left. A poor gambler he was, too. He didn't play cards for shit, but I think he just liked the big-guy image of himself gambling. And not having to get up for a nine-to-five appealed to him, too, I'm sure. I'm like him a lot in that way.

"Anyway, this must have been about nineteen sixty-four. No, more like nineteen sixty-two. I was born while he was in the army and stationed in Florida. The Korean war had just ended. That's probably why they got married. He was in uniform. She fell in love. They screwed. And then he did the right thing. You can say that for him anyway.

"Anyway, by the time I was eight years old my mother was tired of Miami Beach and wanted to move back to New York. She was from Short Hills, New Jersey originally. That wouldn't mean anything to you but that is a good address, for Jersey. You know what they say about New Jersey. Three-quarters of it is underwater and the other quarter is under surveillance. All of this means nothing to you. And I digress."

Mr. Paul snuggled me closer to him so he was talking into my ear. I put my head on his chest. He could be really funny in his own deadpan, nonfunny way. I think lots of times these handsome guys with no sense of humor actually have quite a sense of humor. It's like they belong to a very exclusive club and they only occasionally let us see how funny they think the rest of less-handsome us are.

"My mother's family was still in Short Hills and I guess she got tired of having a tan. So she was planning to move north, even if it meant my not seeing the old man. And making it a lot harder for her to get her alimony payments out of him, too. He was a tight bastard, and of course he never really had any money. Plus he had this girlfriend, Sharon Cherie, who had been a dancer at the Villa Venice. Pronounced to rhyme with 'grease.' During the war. Before the Civil War probably. I really hated her. And she was actually there on our movie dates.

"But this Saturday, my old man decided he was going to kidnap me and disappear. He was really a sorry case. So dumb. He was going to take me somewhere, I think primarily so he wouldn't have to pay alimony anymore. He told me this while we were having a soda after the movies. We'd just seen Dorothy Malone in one of those cowboy movies she used to do. Never heard of her?"

I just looked up at him, all woo-woo eyes, from where my head was resting on that wonderful chest of his. He kissed my forehead. Really an affectionate guy.

"I think John Derek was in it, too. Never heard of him either, I'll bet. Very cool. I think maybe that's when I realized I liked guys. I used to get this very little hard-on thinking about John Derek.

"So. My dad had this place that we were going away together to. We were going to stay in an apartment in the same building Sharon lived in over in Miami Shores. Some friend of hers was out of town and she had the keys. Like no one was going to find us there, right?

"I told him I didn't want to go and he told me it was just to keep my mother from moving away because he would miss me so much. I can see it now. Him sitting in that booth at Wolfie's and Sharon beside him in her kind of Lauren Bacall side part nodding and smiling. She had pink fingernails. This was when nobody had pink fingernails. She was terrible. You'd hate her."

"Now, you mean?" I mumbled into his armpit.

"Oh, yeah, she's still around. So is he. They're still together. Two very old farts. Out in Hialeah.

"I was a tough kid. I didn't cry or make a break for it. Hell, we were only about five minutes from Mom's apartment. But he kind of buffaloed me into it. And you know how kids are. They love being the center of attention.

"Now get this. He and I were going to cross the bay in a boat. Who knows what movie he'd seen. *Key Largo* maybe. Sharon was going to take the car and pass by a girlfriend's and say she had left us at the restaurant and that would be the last anyone would ever see of us. He was going to rent one of those stupid little boats up there on Indian Creek and we were to putt-putt away on that. And then he was going to abandon it somewhere and then no one would know where we were. Is this boring?" I mumbled no, not at all of course. I could feel he was beginning to get hard again. Me, too, of course.

"We take this dumb little boat and we putter across the bay and somehow wind up in one of those little inlets over at Miami Shores. We just get out of the boat and let it drift away. And walk, more skulk, along those streets until we got to Sharon's building. I was really dragging my ass by this time. I didn't think it was fun—I hated Sharon and when I saw the apartment I really hated being there. It must have been some ex-showgirl friend's of Sharon's or some drag queen's. It was all in fake leopardskin. Even the lampshades. I shit you not. And red lacquer. Lots of mirrors. You've got the picture. Someone who had a very strong identification with Maria Montez. You don't know who she was either. To move along.

"We're sitting around in this hot, stupid apartment. Remember this was before air-conditioning was everywhere. Fans.

Nothing to eat in the refrigerator. Nothing but cologne in there. Blue Grass by Elizabeth Arden. God. How well I remember it. And finally Sharon shows up and she has forgotten to go shopping, so there's really nothing to eat and I throw a fit. I cry. I scream. And instead of trying to calm me down the old man loses it and starts throwing me against the wall and Sharon is screaming and so I shot them."

I try to pull away. This time I don't have any trouble having a reaction. Glenn doesn't let me go. He hangs onto me real tight and he pushes his certainly not so teensy-weensy cock between my legs and starts moving it slowly and steadily. I say in a steady voice, trying to play it very Sharon Stone, "You shot them?"

We are on our sides and while he's talking he is definitely fucking me. "That's right. My old man always kept a gun on him. Not in a shoulder holster but in his coat. A small gun. In his wallet pocket. And his coat was over a chair. And I knew how to shoot that gun. He had taught me. I grabbed it out of his pocket and he yelled, 'Hey, wait a minute.' And I let him have it. I was really pissed off. It wasn't that I wanted to kill him, I just wanted him out of my life. So I blammed him a good one. And he went over. And then Sharon made a grab for me and I let her have it, too. Pow. I had had enough. And then they were both lying there howling and carrying on, screaming, 'Get a doctor,' and stuff like that. I went over and called my mother and told her where I was. I didn't know the address, but trust her. She knew where Sharon Cherie lived."

Something was going on here. I squeezed my legs together as hard as I could and held him to me very tightly, too. He was moving very rapidly and his breath was getting shorter.

"Was there a lot of blood everywhere?" I asked him.

"No, you know how bullet holes are, a little hole with black around it. And then the blood oozes out. Really.

"I went out and closed the door and left them in there squealing. They'd heard me so they knew someone was coming. And in about ten minutes there were sirens howling and policemen stamping up the stairs. A mob. 'Where are they, sonny?' I remember the first cop said. I told him. He threw his shoulders against the door. I said, 'It's open.' He gave me a dirty look, walked in, then stuck his head back outside. 'Who shot them?' he said. 'I did,' I told him. 'I might have known,' he said. From inside he yelled out, 'Where's the gun?' 'Over by the telephone,' I yelled back. By this time there were medics running in and stretchers and all of that stuff. I just stood there. They carried them out past me on a stretcher. My dad had his fedora on top of him, I remember. He looked at me and said, 'You little bastard.' I said right back, 'You're the bastard.' Sharon wouldn't even look at me. Then the head cop said, 'I guess you'd better come along with us.' And I said, 'Can't I wait for my mom?' And right then she showed up."

And right then Glenn came. I mean came. Turned me over on my back and really thrust that thing down and shuddered and groaned for about five minutes. He always enjoyed his orgasms but this was special. And for once, this was rare, he didn't seem to care if I had come or not. I hadn't. This whole thing had been much too fascinating to get sexually worked up. He really got off on shooting his father. Freud or Jung or one of those guys would have had a field day with Glenn. He certainly wasn't repressing anything. Hated Dad. Shot Dad. Wow.

As he kind of returned to the land of the living I said from where I was lying half-smothered under him, "So, what happened?"

"Nothing much. They lived. You know that. They didn't press charges and that was before the press got hold of things and made them into a circus. My mother took me to Short Hills the next day and left me with my grandparents. Never told them what happened. And I didn't see my father again until I came back here. About the time you met me."

He sort of shook his head, pulled himself out from between

my legs and sat up on the edge of the bed. I crawled over and hugged him. "This must be love," he said, "When we feel like hugging each other one minute after we fuck."

"I don't know about you, but this *is* love as far as I'm concerned," I said. He pulled me around in front of him and kind of held me in his arms as though I was a very large baby. Which I loved of course.

"No. It never got in the papers. My mother and I hardly spoke about it. I think she was kind of proud of me for taking things into my own hands. It sure said a lot about how much I wanted to stay with her. I think as soon as the police heard kidnapping, they didn't give a damn about my father. And here he is. Still in Miami Beach. Still gambling. Wearing all these old clothes that are kind of yellow with age. Bell-bottom pants and those kind of plastic loafers. With matching belt. He didn't ever really care for me. Nobody could ever break up that big love affair he was always having with himself. Now he just hits me up for money from time to time and I just pay his rent so he doesn't throw it away on those card games that are still going on."

Now I really had to go home, and I felt kind of bad getting dressed and leaving him there by himself. But he had some sort of business date and was heading into the shower when I left. He gave me a big hug and really kissed me. And right. It did make me feel terrible. It wasn't so much that we were guys as that I was just too young. If I was maybe ten years older this might have been the great love affair of the century because we did love each other. To prove it, only when I was going down those varnished yellow wood stairs of his did it pass through my mind, my boyfriend is someone who shot his father when he was eight years old.

hugo sees magenta

The next time I went to Glenn's apartment I really had something to think about. The magenta lipstick I found in his bathroom. You wonder if it's your mother's and you open it and you see it's magenta. A color she never wears. And your little mind goes click, click, click. And out comes Estelle. Our little office secretary. This is really boring.

A couple of weeks ago when I ran past the office to do a little cleaning and Mom was out, Estelle cornered me. She said, "You know that Mr. Paul your mother is going out with?"

"Yes, Estelle, I do know Mr. Paul. We call him Glenn." I wondered if she was going to ask me if I was going out with him, too. I wouldn't put it past her. She is very smart, our Estelle. You can count on her to notice everything.

"Mr. Paul is trying to get me to see him."

"So," I said.

"I don't think that is very, should I say, correct."

"Well, he's not married to Mom. I don't suppose there's any law against him going out with more than one person." That certainly was true. And I could swear to it.

"Even so, I wouldn't like it if the situation were reversed. If I was the boss and your mom was my secretary, I would not like it at all if my boyfriend was coming on to her."

"I can understand that," I said, "but I'm not going to discuss this with Mom. This is the sort of thing that has to sort itself out." I'm so, so wise. I must have seen all this stuff on daytime TV. "You have to decide this for yourself, Estelle." Is there anybody in this town he doesn't want to fuck?

"Well, I've been telling him no. Besides, he's not Hispanic, you know."

"Well, gee, Estelle, you wouldn't hold that against him, would you? You must have gone out with someone who wasn't Hispanic before."

"Once. I didn't like it."

"Was he as cute as Glenn Paul?" I can really be a bitch when I want to be.

"No." She was getting ready to drop the subject. She went back to her desk. Estelle is very pretty and she was looking particularly pretty in a new magenta blouse. She had bought lipstick that matched it exactly. Her hair was kind of piled up on top of her head false carelessly. Her nail enamel didn't match exactly. You had to give her that, she's not a floozy.

"This is between Mr. Paul and you, Estelle. If you think he's cute, go for it. Of course, if you do, and I ever find out about it, I'm going to hate you both forever." She looked up at me to see if I was kidding. I wasn't sure if I was or not and I thought I'd just let her think about it.

And here I was leaving that shithead's apartment with her magenta lipstick in my pocket. Nothing is by chance. Even if she didn't mean to, that lipstick was left behind for *somebody* to stumble upon.

So what do I do? I go straight to Mom's office hoping she's not there. She isn't. But Estelle is. She's wearing a white linen dress. No magenta, obviously. As I pass her desk I put the lipstick down and say pleasantly, "This must be yours." Silence.

She's typing. She finishes what she's doing without even looking up. Then she says, "What were you doing at his apartment?" and I realize I have made a big mistake. Huge. Hugo the huge mistake maker. "I was just passing by."

"I'll bet." Estelle got up from her desk, straightened the papers on it, looked at her watch. "I'm going to leave a little early today, Hugo. I'm not feeling all that great. I'm not going to quit. I wouldn't do that to your mom. I really like her. Nothing has happened that she needs to know about. You know, the fact that he's not Hispanic is a very big problem. Too big for me." She left. Then came back in and said, "Hugo." Then said nothing. And she was out of there again.

Leaving me to sit at her desk and think about how dumb I was. How could I have possibly thought she wouldn't immediately figure out I was in Glenn's bathroom? That's elementary. And now she was another one who had a clue I was fooling around with Glenn. Plus Macha, plus Ken. This whole thing was getting tense. Then Mom came in. She was looking very cool in a dark orange linen jacket and a brown linen skirt. With brown and white shoes. Spectator pumps. So adorable. So Italian. I love my mom.

"Where is the ever dependable Estelle?"

"She had to go home. She was feeling a little under the weather."

"But she never feels under the weather. That's so unlike her."

For a minute I considered telling her the whole thing. That Estelle was sleeping with Glenn Paul. That I was sleeping with Glenn Paul. For all I knew half of Miami Beach was sleeping with Glenn Paul. I really wanted to burst into tears and sit on her lap and crumple up all her linen and have her tell me that everything was going to turn out all right. I almost did. But then I thought of Glenn and I knew that would be kaput for all of us with Glenn. He was the wedge between my mom and me.

And suddenly I was somebody else. I really left the womb once and for all sitting there in her office looking at my beautiful mom. "Let's go home," I said. I had that hard knot feeling at the back of my throat like you want to cry and you can't.

new york

It was spring. The rainy season was coming nearer. I was going by Mr. Paul's apartment from time to time to get laid. My grades were pretty good. And Macha and I were talking about going to college. We had to make some decisions now if we were hoping to get into a decent school in a year from next fall.

Macha's father was taking her to Harvard, where he had gone to school, as well as Brown and the University of Pennsylvania. She wasn't so determined to be an actress anymore and was talking about being a lawyer.

"You could come with us, Hugo," she said. "That would give you some idea of what these colleges are like."

"I don't know," I said. "I think I'd like to go to school in New York. I could be a writer or a journalist or work in advertising or something. I don't really want a career. I just want to live in some sort of romantic wild way."

"Should I work in a bank?" I said.

Macha said, "I think that's quite a reach, considering you're so terrible in math. And besides, it would be too fascinating. You don't deserve it. So go ahead, be a journalist. Or a fashion writer. Or something like that." Macha was getting bored with this conversation. She was trying real hard these days to be conventional and see herself as a high school junior. I know my life, which she knew all about, was making her wonder if she was getting a slow start in life. But we both knew it was dumb to let older people just use you up because you're young and nice-looking. And without an education we'd never get to be one of those older people trying to use up younger, nice-looking people. Which seems to be the whole point, doesn't it?

I asked Mom what she thought at dinner that night. I guess my whole idea of living in New York came from her talking about when she lived there as a model. Sort of the center of all that was glamorous and exciting. Where everything came from that the rest of the world used as ideas.

She knew more about going to school there than I thought she would. "You could go to Columbia. It's sort of ratty but it's a good school. And after you've been there a couple of years you could decide if you want to study journalism or just do a degree in English literature. That could be good, too. Or you could go to Parsons School of Design if you think you might want to go into fashion. But I think you're probably too intel-lectual for that. You could probably work on Seventh Avenue tomorrow and do just fine." I noticed how much she got the picture on me. Probably a lot more than I realized. And I always thought I was being so foxy.

Glenn Elliott came by to take Mom to the movies and she started talking about it with him. He was looking particularly hot in a blue blazer. Linen. Kind of lightish blue that made his eyes really bright. "I could take Hugo," he said. "I've got business to do in New York. We could go up in a couple of weeks. Figure it out, Hugo, and we'll go. When's your spring vacation?"

"The end of the month, but I don't want to miss work," I told them.

"We'll go in the middle of the week. Like a Monday through a Wednesday or Thursday. How does that sound?" Mom thought it was a great idea.

I got the picture right away. He wanted to go somewhere and

really get down, which I didn't disagree with. But I wondered how Mom could possibly not figure it out. I suspect that fold-out couch bed at Glenn Elliott's must be seeing plenty of activity. Mr. Glenn Elliott Paul. Providing sex to an entire family. Sort of a Florence Nightingale of sex. What a great guy.

So I called Columbia and Parsons and they asked me to write letters, which I did, and they answered them and it was set for me to go up on my spring break. I was beginning to find the whole thing kind of boring and I hadn't even gone yet. I stopped by the Bomber Club, but the guys at the club were really excited at the idea of my going to college. They all wanted to go and had all kinds of plans about what they could do with their lives.

When I told them I was interviewing at Parsons, that really got them going. Myrtle Beach wanted to be like Bob Mackie and design for the stars. Coco wanted to be an interior decorator, which surprised me. He knew all about Memphis in Milan and Philippe Starck and the Paramount and the Royalton in New York, and Ian Schrager had almost bought the Eden Roc to do the same thing in Miami Beach. Maximum Shell, who doesn't talk much, admitted that he was going to night school preparing to be an architect. Could any of these things happen? Could be. This is a tough little bunch of characters here at the Bomber Club.

Glenn Elliott took care of where we would stay in New York. He said he knew a little place in the Village and it would be quite inexpensive and we could share a room to save even more money. Uh-huh. Ugga-ugga-ugga. Yuk-yuk-yuk. I bought my own ticket from my savings account.

It turns out we were staying at a kind of bed and breakfast without the breakfast called the Centra. It was a couple of old houses put together with rooms and staircases running off in all directions. Our room was sort of down a few steps from the street. It was called the Tack Room as it had been originally part of the stables of the old house. A double bed, of course.

Mr. Gawain was the owner. He looked like he'd melted a little bit. His blue eyes sagged slightly at the corners, his face was slipping slightly off the front of his head, and his body was slipping slightly off his skeleton. The baseball cap worn backward didn't help a bit. And the shorts and tank top were definitely negatives. What is it with those tank tops? The only people who look really good in them have great builds, and they never wear them. But it's kind of the official summer uniform of the aging raver. Why is it people think if they show it, it must be good? There's something so vulnerable about where the arm meets the torso. It always looks so sort of babyish unless you're in peak form, and that's in the front where the pecs hit. In the back it always looks like a rag doll. It's the one spot where nature couldn't get the design right.

Mr. Gawain had that kind of floppy toy look. He seemed to know Glenn Elliott and was very roguish with him as he showed us our room. But then I suspect that half the Eastern Seaboard knows Glenn Elliott. Mr. Gawain exited from our room through a door at the back. He said this led to his dining room.

"I'll lock it on the other side so you don't have to worry about being raped or anything," he leered.

"It's the 'anything' I worry about," I told him. His bleary blue eyes looked mystified and he fled.

I saw his digs later. He had a bedroom and dining room right next to our room. Upstairs was the living room that also doubled as the sort of boardinghouse lobby. It had a grand piano. I could occasionally hear Mr. Gawain playing snatches from the *Moonlight Sonata*. I think he saw himself as a kind of Blanche Dubois–style hostess and let his assistant, Theresa, take care of all the real work of booking rooms and collecting bills while he carried on his fantasy of living in a large house where he entertained hordes of wonderful guests, all there to amuse him. The wonderful guests weren't much to be seen but the steady scurrying of feet on the stairs and murmuring of voices passing the door testified to their presence. The few I saw looked like provincial gay guys from Toronto out on a fling. Or the occasional tortured type, staring soulfully at you as you passed, hoping to be taken right there on the hall parquet, I suppose.

As soon as Mr. Gawain pulled the door shut Glenn Elliott wanted to tussle and I was sort of in the mood myself. It was kind of exciting being there on that rickety old Victorian bed with all our clothes off while people's feet passed by just outside the flimsy casement curtain by our heads. Tackiness is sexy, no doubt about it.

Glenn Elliott seemed to know his way around this part of town. We ate down on Hudson Street at The Sazerac House. A dark cavern kind of place. Our waiter was a flighty kind of person who said to the bartender, "Oh, don't talk to me that way, George, when you know I'm so vulnerable right now." He wasn't someone you'd really want to sleep with, but he looked like he'd be fun to know.

Then we went back to the Centra and fell asleep in each other's arms. I don't think Glenn Elliott really had anything to do in New York at all.

At least there didn't seem to be anything on his schedule. He went up to Columbia with me the next morning and everybody seemed to accept him as my young-looking father. I talked to the people in the registrar's office and they seemed to think if my SAT scores were okay I'd have no trouble entering a pre-journalism course. We walked around the campus and visited a dorm and it seemed pretty cool. I had this idea that everyone would have short hair and look like something out of a 1950s movie. But they looked fine. Or *not* fine, if you know what I mean. Lots of ponytails and black jeans. Actually, I could kind of see myself there.

We were scheduled to go down to Parsons in the afternoon and that was something else altogether. The girls looked good but a lot of the boys were really swishy. I could tell Glenn Elliott was not at all enjoying himself. A lot of the boys were eyeing us, and I don't think a lot of them got the father-son picture. Why should they?

We walked back from Parsons to our room. It was very pretty, the Village, at that time of year. The trees had little tiny leaves hovering around the branches like swarms of little green insects, throwing pale, broken-up shadows across the red brick houses, the iron stair railings, and the heaving, broken sidewalks.

"Thank you for bringing me up here," I said. Glenn Elliott put his arm around my shoulder and said, "I wanted to do it."

"You didn't really have anything to do here, did you?" I asked.

"I just sort of wanted to look around," he said. "I used to live here and I wondered if it was still the same. If I would want to live here again."

"Would you?" It made me a little frightened to ask.

"No, not really. My life is in Miami Beach now. With your mother and you."

I stopped to look at him. His arm dropped off my shoulder. "I don't get it, Glenn. What gives? You can't be in love with both of us."

"I'm not in love with either of you. I don't fall in love with people. I never have. But I want to be with both of you. Not at the same time." He turned and started walking again. I followed him.

"But what's going to happen? What's the plan?" I said to his back.

"There is no plan. Why does something have to happen? Maybe we're just going to go along like this for a long time. Don't you like what's happening?"

"Yes, but it seems strange. Like I'm two people. There's me that's planning to go to college and preparing for my SATs and all that stuff kids my age do. And then there's the me that's dancing at the Bomber Club and sleeping with you and knowing that I'm never going to wake up some morning and be called Betty and be married to you." I hated the way my voice sounded. All whiny.

"Would you want to get married to me?" Glenn asked, looking at me sideways.

"No. I don't know. No. How could we? I'm too young. Yes, I'd like you to run far away with me somewhere like South America and we could just screw all day forever. That's what I'd like. But that's what everybody who's crazy about someone else thinks. And what about Mom?"

"Yeah," said Glenn. "Yeah, what about Mom?"

Now we were in front of the rooming house. Mr. Gawain was looking out the window. I didn't want him to see me looking all frantic.

"Let's go down to that café on the square and get a coffee," I said.

At the café I decided to change the subject completely. "Tell me what you did before you came to Miami Beach, Glenn. I don't really know."

"I used to be in import/export," he said looking down at his cup.

"In Miami Beach that means you sell drugs," I said. Everybody's in import/export around Miami.

"It sounds like it, doesn't it? But not really. That's kind of a tacky business and it's real easy to get killed. If somebody doesn't like you. Particularly around all those Cubans. Actually, I sold guns and stuff."

"To collectors?" As soon as I said it I knew it sounded dumb. Hopefully he thought I was being a smart-ass.

He looked at me with a funny expression around his eyes. I could tell he was deciding whether to tell me the truth or not. And whatever he told me, I'd never know. I was surprised he was telling me anything at all.

"No, more major league than that. I used to be in the Marines. In Beirut. I met a lot of people out there. I stay in touch with them and they ordered stuff through me. Still do.

143

I don't get orders very regularly but I make a good percentage when I do."

"Is it legal to do this?" I know I really sounded like a kid.

"I guess so. I never really ask. I guess sometimes it is and sometimes it isn't. I guess I don't really want to find out in case it isn't.

"But I'm getting out of it. Completely. That's why I'm in Miami Beach. Seeing what else I can do. And then I saw you. I'm really not into kids but you're a real cutie, Hugo, whether you know it or not. And your mother is something quite special, too. And here we are. Kind of up in the air." He was looking around for the bill. He obviously had said a lot more than he had planned to and didn't want to go on.

When we got back he said he wanted to take a nap. I wanted to say all kinds of things, about how I didn't care what he did and how I wanted to stay with him the rest of my life. I wanted to cry and have him hold me and tell me he wasn't ever going to let me go. But instead he went down to take his nap and I went up to say hello to Mr. Gawain, having nothing better to do.

I really don't think Mr. Gawain had been drinking when he told me his story, although it sounds like it. When I came in he asked, "Mr. Hugo, would you like a cup of tea?" I said I would and we began to talk about nothing in particular and I asked him how he happened to be running the Centra. He said, "Oh, I hadn't been doing anything for a while after Charlie died and it just occurred to me. I had some money and I need to do something that wasn't very complicated and that would require a lot of attention to detail."

"Because you missed Charlie?" I said. Obvious question.

"Missed?" he said. "Missed? It was much more than missed."

"I know *something* about love," I said.

"I'm sure you do," said Mr. Gawain. "I'm sure you do. I never stop thinking about it. And I don't talk about it a lot. I don't tell everybody who passes through the parlor. Really I don't. I've worked hard at not being just another dizzy old queen. Have I been successful? You'll have to judge, Hugo. That evening I lost Charlie was like none other I've ever seen since. It looked rather like a movie set at the Morrison house when I went to pick up Charlie. They'd been sailing. When I got out of the car it was like a Magritte. Light in the sky, little clouds, darker down below but you could still see the green in the lawns. It looked like a set for a play. I entered stage right. They entered stage left. I don't remember anyone telling me Charlie had drowned. It was just that suddenly everything began to compact into squeezed-together chunks. They'd left all the picnic things out on the lawn and they all at once looked all crushed together and I thought of the sandwiches and the mayonnaise soaking into the white bread. And the lawn chairs looked all crushed together. You know, like those sculptures where they crush a car into a cube. Everywhere in the shrubs, the people were scrunched up cubes. Or like pieces of club sandwich.

"I imagined them all stacked up on each other like a child's fortress. And I'm sure you've read about people being in some extreme situation and hearing a voice crying out and it turns out to be theirs? It was just like that. This voice screaming, 'You let him die,' and it was mine. Charlie's boss was there and his wife. She's the one who grabbed me. She was wearing a royal blue silk dress and had on some little rings with red and blue stones in them. And her ankle was in a cast. Why I don't know. But she dropped her crutch and pulled me down to the ground. There we were on our hands and knees, like two dogs, me slobbering and bawling, her holding me. Finally my father did something. He took me in his arms and dragged me into the backseat of a car and I cried and cried in his arms. You know, my father never touched me. Never. But he came through when I really needed him. I cried like that for days and days."

"But you finally felt better, didn't you?" I asked him. I really wanted to know. "When was this, how long ago?" "Oh, over forty years ago now," he said. "But you're all right now, aren't you?" I really did want to know that he was all right. Mr. Gawain's little story had me real shook up if you want to know. "Well," he said, "what I tell people when they ask me how I am I tell them I'm fine, now that I'm dead. I'm fine now that I'm dead."

Leaving Mr. Gawain, I went down to our room where Glenn Elliott was sleeping. He was lying under the beige and white bedspread on his stomach, clutching a pillow. I think our conversation made him sad. I lay down beside him and pulled his arm off the pillow and put it around me. "I love you, Glenn," I said in his ear. "I love you, too, my little Hugo," he said, and tightened his arm around me, and we both slept.

When we woke up it was getting toward seven o'clock, that sad time of day, and especially when you're just waking up from a nap in a cheap boardinghouse. I wished Macha was with us. To say something wise-ass and make us laugh so I wouldn't feel that life was a lot more than I could handle.

Glenn Elliott was lying on his back staring up at the ceiling. I jumped up and said, "Let's get out of here. Aren't you hungry? Let's go eat somewhere really good. How about a steak?" I was talking a mile a minute, pretending I was Macha. I put on my new blazer that I wore to the interviews.

He laughed at me jumping around the room and said, "Okay, okay, okay. There's a French restaurant just a block over, on West Fourth Street. The Belle Étoile. It used to be pretty good. Let's go give it a try."

The restaurant was sort of romantic for a father and son, but the people there couldn't have cared less who we were. In the Village they just don't think about that stuff. I guess they figure everybody's up to something weird so it's nothing to get excited about.

Two sailors came in and took the table next to us. They didn't know what to do with their caps and finally put them under their chairs on the floor. The restaurant was paying a lot of attention to them. The Village isn't so blasé that two cute guys in tight sailor pants can't arouse their interest.

They were confused by the menus and asked Glenn if he could help them, so he explained what might be good. They introduced themselves. The blond one was Ben and the dark-haired one John. They were from a ship that was in port and had never been in New York before. They said they'd heard that Greenwich Village was kind of a wild place but so far it seemed old-fashioned and quiet. But certainly different from where they came from.

Glenn said, "I thought you guys could wear civvies off the ship?" They explained that usually they could but the captain had ordered everybody to wear their uniforms in New York, so people would know they had a navy. They laughed and said they thought it was because the captain thought maybe they would get into less trouble.

Ben was from California and John was from Iowa or some-where like that. Glenn introduced us. He said, "My name is Glenn and this is Hugo." They reached over and shook hands. They were both very polite and didn't ask us anything about ourselves, except where we were from. By dessert we had pushed our tables together and they were telling us all about the aircraft carrier they were on. How they'd been to the Mediterranean. Glenn Elliott told them some stories about when he'd been in the Marines in Beirut. He took a couple of glasses of wine from their bottle. I didn't drink anything or say very much, but they were having a good time together and didn't seem to care.

We all left together and since it was pretty early Glenn El-liott suggested we stroll around with them and show them the Village a little. We walked down to Sheridan Square and then across to a very busy street with a lot of shops still open. Eighth Street.

Glenn and Ben walked up ahead and John walked with me.

took my clothes off and hung them in the closet. Glenn lay down on the bed and I sat down on the other side. Ben sat in the rickety easy chair.

"I'm not going to be able to sit here very long without getting a hard-on," Ben said. "Hugo and you are both pretty good-looking guys."

"That's fine," Glenn told him. "I'm getting one myself thinking about what we might do here. Why don't you come over to the bed and let me get you out of those encumbering navy undershorts?" Ben got up and came to the side of the bed. Glenn undid the buttons and pulled his shorts down with some difficulty as his pretty sizable cock was on its way up and had to be extricated. Glenn put it in his mouth and Ben shut his eyes, swaying slightly.

Pulling back, Glenn said, "Let's see, what'll we do here? How about . . ." He put his knees up toward his chest and pulled his own jockey shorts from under his butt and off his feet. Pulling a pillow from under his head he put it under him. "How about condoms?" Ben said from where he was kneeling on the end of the bed, steadying himself with one hand and holding his hard-on with the other. "Hugo, look in my bag," Glenn said. "There are some condoms there and some KY." I thought, wait a minute, this little party wasn't entirely by chance.

I found the condoms and Glenn unrolled one down Ben and squeezed some KY into his hand and slipped it under him. "Here, Hugo. Come here. Sit on the head of the bed and hold me." I slipped under him and held his head and shoulders in my lap. He pulled my head down and kissed me and grunted slightly as Ben pushed his way into him. Ben groaned, too. Pulling Glenn down a little he pushed my Calvin's down and slipped me into his mouth. Glenn wrapped his legs around Ben's waist and put his arms around his neck. Ben and I came at the same time.

I pulled away and went into the bathroom. When I looked

back Ben was straddling Glenn Elliott and putting a condom on him. They were smiling at each other. Before I looked away he was sitting down on him. Glenn had his hands on his thighs and was pushing up. I closed the door and looked into the mirror. This is quite an evening, I thought. I looked at my watch. It was only 12:30. I sat on the toilet seat and waited until the bed stopped creaking. It took quite a while. Then the refrigerator across the room shuddered to a stop, too, at the same time.

When I came out Ben was pulling on his underpants and Glenn had the bedcover pulled over him. "Thanks," he said to Ben.

"It was my pleasure," Ben replied, very politely and as though he meant it. "You've got quite a dad here, Hugo," he added. He didn't sound as though he was kidding. I didn't say anything. Then after a while I said, "Yeah, isn't he something."

Glenn asked Ben if he wanted to stay overnight but Ben said he had to be going and besides he thought three would be crowding that double bed. He put his sailor hat on at a jaunty angle and came around the bed to kiss me good-bye. He smelled good and felt warm. He leaned over the bed to kiss Glenn. When he was at the door I said, "Ben, do John and you fool around?"

"We have a couple of times," he said, "but we're really not into each other's types. But, yeah, sometimes if we're in a hotel together and we haven't scored, we'll get it on."

"He's good-looking," I said.

"Very," he said, opening the door. "Well, see you guys around."

"We're in the phone book in Miami Beach," Glenn Elliott said from the bed. "Call us if you're ever in town."

"I wouldn't miss that," Ben said and was out the door. Glenn looked up at me from the bed. "Are you okay, Hugo?" he asked.

"Oh, very okay, Glenn Elliott," I said. "Very okay."

"Well, what did you think?" he wanted to know.

"What do I think?" I slipped into bed. "What should I think?" We put our backs together and he patted me on the hip.

"Whatever you think," he said.

"I think you're quite a trip, Mr. Paul," I told him and went to sleep.

The next morning we dressed, had greasy eggs and bacon at the little restaurant next door, and left for the airport. On the plane I heard a man behind me say to another man, "If we can avoid the problem, we don't have to find a solution." Mom met us at the airport and was very glad to have us back.

the bomber closes

The Bomber is closing. I think somebody wants to open a boutique in the space. It's just down the block from the Versace store so it makes sense. And it's summer. There aren't many out–of–town gay guys around and the locals have been to the Bomber so many times the dancers probably look like their cousins. I'm glad it's over. Too much fantasy time on the part of the clientele. The guys who are dancing aren't really such hot tickets. Just guys. I don't think anybody when I was there loved the attention from the crowd all that much. Maybe Maximilian a little. But I don't think the rest of us think we're such beauties the world owes it all to us.

When I worked there the chance the news would leak out to Mom always worried me. She'd feel bad for a lot of reasons. That I'm in such a bad environment and that I'm working to get money for college, which makes it look like she couldn't handle it. There were a lot of reasons that it's good the club is closing.

There's a club up on Lincoln Road, the Winter Palace, that's doing good business with stripping and drag acts, but that's not Louie's thing. I wonder if inside that fat body somewhere he doesn't like guys himself. Because that's what he wants for acts. "Drag queens," he says. "Equal rights for drag queens. Not

He asked me where I was in school and I told him I was in New York interviewing for college. He said he wanted to go to college when he got out of the navy and was thinking of doing some kind of engineering course or computers or something like that. Probably out in the Midwest somewhere. He was getting out of the navy in a year and probably would start school the same time I did.

He was almost twenty-one. He seemed like a real grown-up to me, even though he was only about three years older. He was quite handsome and lifted weights on the ship so he had a bodybuilder's kind of body, but not overly so. Pretty groovy-looking guy in fact.

Glenn said when we'd walked down below Washington Square, "I can't invite you guys for a drink in a bar because of Hugo, but maybe you'd like to come back to our place. I've got a bottle of Scotch there."

They looked at each other and John said, "No, I think I'll head back to the ship. I've got duty tomorrow morning." But Ben said he'd be glad to, and putting John in a taxi, we walked back up Bleecker Street to Mr. Gawain's place. I wondered what was cooking exactly, but knew I'd find out soon enough. Ben thought our room was a great place. Glenn took a couple of glasses from the bathroom and pulled a bottle from his suitcase. I'd never really seen him drink before. He'd never suggested that I drink anything with him. The bottle said "Grants's." Ben was impressed. I'd never heard of it.

He handed Ben his drink and said, "What do you say we get out of some of these clothes and get comfortable?"

"That sounds like a good idea," said Ben, cool as a cucumber. They stripped down to their underpants, Ben folding his uniform carefully over the back of the chair. He must have lifted weights with John because he had a great body. Tan. I guess they let them lie out on the deck on that ship of theirs.

"How about you, Hugo? Want to join us?" Glenn asked me. What was I supposed to do? Scream or giggle or what? So I until they get rid of those terrible shoes. Whoever saw a woman who looked like that? Some of those religious revivalists on TV maybe. Tammy Lee Whatever. What guy would ever want to sleep with that? If a guy wants a woman there's plenty of real ones around. Those guys just do drag because they're too lazy to go to the gym." He may have a point. I talked Fred/Myrtle into dropping his Carmen Miranda number and doing a straight act, if you'll pardon the expression. We did that Karan layered look. So Fred had a lot of stuff to take off before he got down to his skivvies. He's been coming to the gym with me more, too, so his body is getting really buff.

Louie asked me if I'd perform one last time closing night. For old times' sake. And I agreed I would. I had the idea for Fred and me to do an act together where we take each other's clothes off. Louie loved it. Am I cut out for this business or what?

We did this thing, coming on in leather jackets and doing our hair James Dean style. Kind of '50s gay look. Tight T-shirts. And then, like we're cruising each other, meet and start taking each other's clothes off. When I pull his leather belt off, nearly tearing his belt loops away, the crowd goes crazy. I got the DJ at Glam Slam to mix me a cover of "Strangers in the Night." Very corny and very cool at the same time. Maybe I should become a director. No kidding. Very creative. Me.

So that was our closing act the last night. When the guys rushed up to stuff money in our knickers I noticed this cute Latino type, small, stuffed a note in with the bill folded into it. $20. Back in the dressing room we pulled out our money and I read the note. "We want to meet you. Roberto and Eduardo." Lots of luck, guys. There were actually guys hanging around after the show but I'd never gotten a note before. "Let's split," I said to Fred. "Some Latino maniacs want a late date after the show."

"Are they cute maniacs?" Fred wanted to know.

"Who invited you?" I said. "Well, how many of them are

there? Did they look like they thought you could handle a gang-bang?" he asked.

"Two," I told him. "And I don't want to have to explain to them I don't screw around." I took a breath. "And you, for all your willful ways, don't screw around either, so don't give me that Miss Slut routine."

"For a high school junior you have a very fast mouth, Hugo. Okay, we're out of here."

Easier said than done. There they were as we ran out the back door. Mutt and Jeff. The little Latino and a tall guy with him. Older. Kind of French looking, kind of devilish looking. A dark Keith Carradine but older? "Hi, I'm Eduardo," says the short one. He *was* pretty cute and he spoke English just fine. "This is Roberto." We nodded. Fred and I didn't smile. And we didn't speak. "We thought you might like to join us for a drink."

"I can't." I said.

"Oh, sure you can. We thought you were very interesting. And since we're in the film business, in a way, we want to get to know you better. Your *friend* is included of course." This is the tall guy, Roberto. He leaned on the "friend" just enough so it was quite clear he thought we might be a couple. I wasn't going to shatter his illusions.

"No, it's not that. We're not old enough to drink."

"Oh, really," the tiny one said. Fred, to his credit, didn't bat an eye. He just stood there trying to look simple and young.

"Well, a Coke maybe?" Tiny Tot added.

"Sorry, we really aren't supposed to mingle with the clientele," Fred said. Genius.

"This really is a special kind of gay club," the older guy interrupted. "You're not afraid of us, are you?"

"It's not that," I told him. "It's just that we're both still in school and we have tests tomorrow and we've got to get home."

"Tomorrow is Sunday," Tall Roberto said.

"Right. I meant Monday. We've both got a lot of studying to

do." I thought we were making it pretty clear that we were not interested.

"This is some town." Tall Roberto turned away. "Schoolboys working in gay strip clubs. Even in Rio we don't have that."

"We really appreciate your interest. Maybe another time." Fred was being polite. I grabbed him by the arm and we beat it around the corner and into the parking lot toward Fred's car. As we were jumping in I looked back and they were standing at the corner of the building under the streetlight watching us. Pretty mysterious goings-on for them. Down in Rio they probably never ran into anyone who turned them down.

"Film business. I can imagine what kind of film business they're into. Dirty Polaroids in motel bedrooms I'll bet. With lots of close-ups," Fred said, hunching over the wheel. He's a terrible driver.

"You've seen their type before," I said.

"Creepy. Older guy has the money, his little boyfriend goes out scouting for new flesh. Can this be love? At least they've got each other."

As I got out of the car I said to Fred, "It's over, Fred my friend. No more Bomber Club. A chapter in my life, over."

"If it's not good enough for you it's not good enough for me," Fred said, gunning the motor. Waking up Mom, I'm sure. "Besides I was really beginning to find drag a drag."

"You and Louie," I said. And I slammed the door just to make sure Mom knew I was home.

I crept into the house and all the cats came running. Their idea of morning and food was every time anybody came in the house. I slapped some cat food down for them in the kitchen. Hell, it was Saturday night. Why shouldn't they have some fun? Tails up and noses down they quickly ignored me as they ate and I walked as quietly as I could up the stairs. I was beginning to feel like I didn't care if I never went out again. Working in a club sure kills your interest in going to them.

armani

It's summer in Miami Beach. It's a different town in the summer. I like it better. The models are pretty much gone. The
South Americans are pretty much gone. We're just here by
ourselves. The Miami Beachers.

Now I'm selling clothes at Armani Exchange. The manager,
Bert, was pretty excited when I went in and asked for a job.
"But you're the model I see in the Versace ads," he said. "Why
do you want to work here?"

"Because modeling is dead in the summer and I live here."
I told him. "I don't want to go to New York or Europe and go
to all those casting calls and go-sees and all that stuff. I'm just
planning to go to college and am getting some money together
to do it."

Well, of course they hired me. Bert thought it would look
good in the store. He even made me assistant manager, which
means I still sell jeans but I watch the store when he goes to
lunch.

I even got Fred/Myrtle a part-time job here. Myrtle lost his
job over in Miami making dental fixtures, or parts, or whatever
you want to call it. He said that proved the city is getting
younger all the time. Younger people don't need so much dental repair work.

Myrtle is a very presentable young guy as a sales clerk. He doesn't twirl and twitch around the store the way he does backstage. I often wonder about that sort of wrist-slap gesture gay guys make, and that settling into one hip that goes with it. Do you think it's genetic? I mean, you never see women making those gestures. My theory, Doctor, is that there's this kind of stewpot of human energy boiling away somewhere, and we're just bubbles on the surface. We bubble up, pulling with us whatever mix there is of other people's personalities from earlier lives when we pop after seventy years or so. Settle back down into the glop, and bits and pieces of us bubble up into other people.

And guys like Myrtle bubble up with bits of women from some other century, when they wore bustles or hoopskirts and carried fans and Myrtle keeps snapping somebody with that imaginary fan, and twitching that imaginary bustle.

I like to think that maybe that's the punishment for being a beautiful woman in another life and having been cruel and thoughtless to people who loved you. You come back as a gay guy and really pay your dues.

And what about guys like Glenn Elliott and me? In the straight-looking, straight-acting category, as the little ads say. At least I like to think so. What's our punishment for? Maybe we're the people who were so obsessed with ourselves we never could really care about anyone else? Because I don't really feel like a girl. I kind of want to feel in love with somebody I'd like to be like. Falling in love with myself, only older. And for Glenn Elliott, it's falling in love with himself, only younger. Curious, isn't it? I have the funny feeling I want to be part of him, so when he's inside me it's sort of like we're one person and coming is like glue. For a few moments we are. Heavy. But I don't know what he thinks. If he feels the same way or not. I have to ask him.

It's less mysterious and less frightening to make love with another guy. You know what he's feeling. When you put his cock in your mouth, you know what it feels like, so you know whether he's enjoying it or not. Somehow it's much easier to know another guy. Anyway. I really haven't had much trouble with guys coming into Armani who come on to me because they've seen me at the Club. Lots of people seem to know me from being in ads. Once in a while somebody says, "Didn't I see you at the Bomber Club?" And I say, "I'm too young to go to the Bomber Club, and besides it's closed." Which is true. And they forget it.

ken and hugo lunch

It's really not hard to sell clothes. You just have to know what's in the store. One look at the person and you know what's going to look good on them. Here in Miami Beach, of course, there are no normal bodies. Everybody is either overweight or so splendid their shoulders are five times wider than their waist. Women included. So many fatties. Poor things. Dreaming of love but unable to stay away from those nacho chips. As Macha said to her friend Nicole, "You're very smart, Nicole. Unfortunately nobody wants to fuck brains." Tough but true. It's only the package that turns you on. I asked Macha once when we were at Gertrude's having lunch and all the tables were full of rather ugly people staring deeply into each other's eyes, "Is it possible to fall deeply in love with somebody who is not attractive?" She looked around the room and said, "Not for you and me, not for you and me."

And as I'm standing there leaning against the counter waiting for either a fatty or a dreamboat to walk in, in walks dreamboat Ken. He's looking good. I don't know what's happening with Macha and him. I haven't talked to Macha seriously in a long time. We've kind of drifted apart, largely because I really don't want to talk to her about Glenn Elliott and Mom and me. Quite a little pickle we're in.

"Hi, Hugo," Ken said. Shook my hand, very manly. He was looking very handsome in that kind of Patrick Swayze, what's his name, that guy who lives with Goldie Hawn, Kurt Russell style. "I was wondering what you were doing for lunch?" What am I supposed to say? Ken, I think whatever you want to talk about is going to be very embarrassing for both of us and having lunch is a terrible idea? No, all I could do is smile and tell him I took a late lunch and I was on until the manager came back. "When's that?" he asked, and as luck would have it the manager walks back in ten minutes early, and has no problem with me leaving right away. I introduce them. Ken Weitz. How do I remember that? Thank God. It would look pretty dumb to be going out for lunch with someone and you don't even know his last name. Or more like you're having lunch with someone who just walked into the store off the street and picked you up. Very cool.

We went to the News Café. I looked okay. Working at Armani you have to dress a little. At least I didn't looked wrecked. The News Café people think I'm some kind of minor celebrity because of the TV pilot, so they kind of fussed around a little bit. It was pretty late so there wasn't any great problem getting a table.

I didn't want to venture anything. This lunch was Ken's idea. He was going to have to do the talking. He said, "Macha's a really interesting person."

"She's been my best friend since second grade." I ordered an avocado salad. Ken ordered a BLT. The waiter was wearing very short shorts and an attitude that suggested he was not interested in men or women or children or dogs or anything at all. The world deserves disdain, but it was probably going to get avocado salad and BLT. Weird guy. Probably all clingy and emotional once you've slept with him.

I wasn't about to give Ken a break. Whatever he wanted to talk about he was going to have to bring it up.

"Macha and I aren't really involved emotionally." Ken said.

"Are you sure?" I asked him. "I think Macha likes you a whole lot."

"Well, yes, I guess so, but I've told her that I'm too old for her." And too gay for her, I thought. Let's see if he brings that up. He did. "And you know that I'm bisexual." I wondered how Myrtle Beach would have played this one. I just continued on with my nice high school student number. I nodded. What next? Now he's going to tell me that he's in love with *me*.

"Well, practically everybody seems to be bisexual these days," I said. The table of Brazilians next to us perked up when they heard that. Maybe they didn't speak English but there was nothing wrong with their sex vocabulary.

"Ken, I've never discussed you with Macha. When you showed me that tape I never talked about that. Not even with Glenn. I figured Macha is a grown-up. You're not her first boyfriend. And whatever is cooking between you is your business. And if you're just seeing her to keep some kind of contact with Glenn, that's kind of crazy but that's entirely your business."

I was on a roll. The Brazilians didn't really get it but they were loving it. Not a word was spoken at their table, just little heads bent over their plates with those little ears standing right straight up. "It's the same with Glenn. If he's really the shit you say he is then I'm going to have to pay the piper myself. It's too complicated, Ken. Why don't people just speak up and say what they want?" I really wanted an answer. So did the Brazilians. I'm sure they went right back to Sao Paolo and enrolled in English courses. They were missing some good stuff.

"Because they don't now what they want," Ken said. "Or they want a lot of things and they can't have all of them, but they try anyway." I was sort of beginning to like Ken. That was a good answer. "Anyway. I know it's ridiculous, but I wanted to make one last try to steer you away from Glenn. You and I are sort of alike, Hugo. We're kind of nice guys. And Glenn isn't like us at all. He sees something beautiful or interesting or new and he wants to have it. He's sort of like a television set. You flip the switch and the show goes on, and you flip the switch and the show goes off without any trace it was ever on the tube. The tube doesn't change. Maybe someday it blows out. You and I think the show is going somewhere, that all this love counts for something. That it's appreciated or maybe you think someday it will be something like being married or at least you'll be remembered and have been a part of someone's life. But it isn't like that. I'm sleeping with Glenn, too, Hugo."

I burst into tears, which surprised me. "I'm sorry, Hugo, I'm sorry." Ken was reaching across the table holding my shoulder and kind of patting it at the same time. I just had my head down and was soaking my avocado salad. The Brazilians were really looking now; this was too good to be polite about. I took my napkin and blew my nose good and wiped my eyes. "I've got to go back to work, Ken. Don't worry. I'm not really crying about Glenn. I'm crying about a lot of things. I've got to figure some of this stuff out. Can you pay for this? I'll call you."

So I stumble away from News Café, my eyes red and no sunglasses. I'm pretty okay by the time I get back to Armani. The manager doesn't say anything. And I have to think. Why did I start crying when Ken told me he was sleeping with Glenn? That wasn't such big news. After that trip to New York, Glenn was a pretty open book to me. Do I love him that much? Do I love him very much and I don't even know it? You'd think if you were crazy about somebody that you'd be the first to know.

So when I get home I call Macha and I ask her straight off, "Are you in love with Ken Weitz?" I guess I was planning to warn her to use condoms and all that gross stuff they're always talking about at school. She hardly needs to hear it from me. "I think I'm in love with his legs," she answers. And then we both laugh and laugh and laugh.

henry rollins band

It's June and it's my birthday and to celebrate Myrtle (now Fred) and I went to the Henry Rollins Band concert at the Bayside Amphitheater. Glenn is out of town coming back tomorrow and Mom and I will have dinner with him tomorrow night. You have to like Henry Rollins because he's so handsome and has that great body, even if it's covered in tattoos. He can't sing, of course. But he gets pretty het up all the same. He does this funny kind of upstage strut between numbers flexing his back, maybe to relax, maybe to show off that "Search and Destroy" slogan across his shoulders. He has quite a shtick, but I like his little conversational asides between numbers. This kind of sly, not too deep voice that makes you think there's another Henry Rollins altogether from the rowdy roughneck tearing up the stage. Of course, that's exactly what he wants us to think. He said, "I know, I know you want me to throw myself off the stage right onto you, don't you?" And all those bikers and their chicks scream their heads off. "Last time I did you tore all my clothes off [more screams. He does have a great body . . .] and beat me with my microphone. Nothing doing. I love you but you hospitalize me." Much screaming.

And he does one great song, "Liar." In it he sings, "You give everything you've got but that's all right because it's to me." I don't think all those guys in their goatees and Charles Manson T-shirts and their ladies with the tons of awful red hair really get it. They just like all the noise and that crashing and cursing and howling he does.

As we drove away in Myrtle's wretched old salt-worn Lincoln convertible, Myrtle said, "What's cooking? You seem kind of blue tonight." And I asked him what you're supposed to do when you find out the person you think you love is also sleeping with somebody else. I didn't feel like telling him that that person is also going out with your mother. That's maybe beyond most gay guys' experience.

"Hmmmmm," Myrtle said. "Hmmmm." Then sang Billie Holiday, "It's the same old story that's been told much too much before." Then he said, "As the song says, it's the same old story but it's all new to me. Or to you, in this case. Well, let's see. Men are no fucking good. We know that. As that other song goes, 'He may be good fucking but he's no fucking good.' You can say all those things but it all boils down to, do you really know this other person at all? Or are you a complete asshole for getting all wrapped up in somebody who's just fooling around? Oh, Hugo, there have been many, many songs written on this subject."

"I know, I know, I know," I said, feeling very much like an asshole myself.

"Is this the good-looking older guy I see you hanging around with? That kind of Paul Newman type? The young Paul Newman." I admitted it was. We were parking behind Books and Books on Lincoln Road now. I guessed we were heading for Gertrude's, where Myrtle likes to hang out.

"Are you really in love with this guy?" I said I didn't really know. That I thought that I was, although my subconscious seemed to be keeping a certain amount from me.

"Well, I like finding out that you are only human, Hugo, my dear. Although you are only seventeen today you are a very composed young man, and seemingly close to faultless. And for an older guy to want to make out with someone besides you is pretty hard to fathom, but who can figure out the mind of man? Having known the best, he had to go and treat himself to less than the best, right?"

"It was somebody he had been having an affair with before he met me."

"The guy you had lunch with today," Myrtle said, not asked.

"You don't miss much, do you Fred?"

He looked up from his piña colada. "I like it when you call me Fred. I'm thinking of putting Myrtle Beach away for a long, long rest. No, I do *not* miss much. Least of all when you come back from lunch all red-eyed and stand around like a wet chicken all afternoon. That is not the Hugo we all know and love. Maybe the guy's lying."

"He could be, but somehow I don't think he is. Actually, I think he's quite a nice guy. It's all mixed up. I think he's jealous and at the same time I think he's trying to steer me away from a bad situation. But I don't think that's even very important. It's more, what am I supposed to do about . . . with . . . to Glenn. I mean, it isn't like he's ever said he loved me and wanted to stay with me forever or any of that kind of stuff. If I say anything to him he's probably just going to say, 'so what?' "

"Well, look, you can just drop him. Do you want to do that?"

"No, definitely not. I can't." For one thing I was going to see him all the time at the house when he was with my mom, so saying I didn't want to see him anymore was kind of out of the question. "Look, Fred, the big question is, where does all this stuff go, anyway? Have you ever known two guys who really stayed together?"

Fred said, "Of course. You see them all the time. Short. Overweight. A pair of fussbudgets. Shopping. Looking exactly like their mothers. A pair of dowdy lesbians, except they're men. I don't know. There must have been dashing male lovers. Alexander the Great loved his boyfriend all his life, through marriages and all. Tyrone Power and Cesar Romero must have been a great-looking couple when they were together. Marlon Brando and Wally Cox? No. It's a tough one to answer. Maybe the best way to start out on an affair is not to be discouraged and to plan it as the first great one. The first one where both people are attractive and loving and intelligent. And determined to stay together. Intelligence is very important, Hugo. I think most people aren't smart enough to look around and not make the mistakes they see everywhere. And I think they're lazy, too. It's easier to ditch the loved one and start in on a new project. Until your looks go and then nobody wants to start again with you. And you're all alone on the telephone."

"You're pretty intelligent yourself, Fred," I told him.

"Want to marry me?" he said.

"Well, it seems to me a person could do a whole lot worse."

Fred seemed embarrassed. "Back to your Paul Newman lookalike."

I said, "I'd just feel so dumb asking him if he loved me and accusing him of betraying me by screwing around and all that stuff. Our relationship really isn't like that. I sort of pursued him in the beginning. Sort of. I pursued him. I got him. Now he's getting bored. It's so stupid. I feel like my life is on daytime TV."

"Let's just take it a step at a time," Fred said. "Do you want to still see him? Let's not talk love. Let's talk lust. You still want to hop in the sack with him, right?"

"Right."

"Number one," Fred said. "Never do what they expect you to do. The running, screaming, crying routine never works unless you really don't care and you're trying to get rid of them. Oh, God, it is really easy to tell someone else what to do. So hard to do it yourself."

"Are you in love with someone, Fred?" I asked him.

"I'm always in love with someone. Yes, I'm in love with someone up in Fort Lauderdale who is about to get married to his girlfriend and then a divorce and several kids later will be back, having proven to the world that he's quite a man. It's so bizarre. If they weren't quite impossible you wouldn't be interested. Programmed for stupidity. He is. And I am.

"I'm just giving myself over to the tropical rhythm of the moment. I could be wrong. Maybe one of these nights he's going to show up and say 'It's you, it's you!' " Fred laughed. "Look, your guy is going to know that his old boyfriend spilled the beans to you. You can count on that. So, he's going to expect you to come on the run. So you don't. I guess if you really love him the best thing to do would be to let him think he's free to leave at any time. Be mysterious yourself. Don't tell him if you love him or don't love him. Don't tell him to go or stay. Just sit tight. But you probably can't do that, can you? I know you, Hugo. You act cool but there's a little Mexican spitfire under all that Teutonic exterior."

"It's my Brazilian father cropping up, I guess," I said.

"Your father is Brazilian?" Fred said. I think it actually surprised him. I told him yes but didn't think it was necessary to also tell him that I'd never seen him. No point in explaining my entire history to him.

"Well, my little blond bombshell, you've got your work cut out for you. At best, you can keep this guy on the string for awhile, Hugo. But let's wake up and smell the cappuccino. You're going to college. You're going to meet all kinds of different people. You are going to change. Even if this romance was to last forever, would you want it to? Do *you* want to miss all the fun by going out of circulation when you've hardly stepped in? *But,* of course, Hugo you must do as you feel. That's the best advice I can give you. Don't be sensible."

But I was. Mom and Glenn Elliott and I all had supper together. The next night. At the Strand. Which wasn't bad.

They brought out three pieces of cake with candles. It was nice. My gift from both of them was a huge beautiful book on Tiepelo, the 18th century Venetian painter. My new craze. The last of the Renaissance painters they called him, even though the Renaissance was long over. I must say they both do pay attention. At least Mom does and drags Glenn along.

I wasn't working the next day and Glenn asked me if I wanted to go to the beach. I could tell by that "nothing is wrong" style of his that he was expecting trouble. So I told him no but that I would like to go to Viscaya. I've been there for school projects of course, but I've never been there just by myself and it struck me that a really weird place like that might be just the place for a really weird conversation.

viscaya

Do you know Viscaya? It's the only house I've ever seen in the United States that was built to look European that actually looks European. Or perhaps it's that the houses in Europe it resembles that I saw as a child were built to look like some kind of fantasyland, and Viscaya inhabits that same fantasyland. On both continents they tried to make magic. And they did.

Viscaya is Italianate. As though it were in southern Italy somewhere. Or more Sicily. A big grand villa. When I first came to Miami when Hugo was small we visited it, and the central court was still open to the weather, and the big loggia facing the sea still had gigantic canvas draperies looped back, to be dropped in bad weather. Very dramatic.

I would have loved to have gone there in its heyday when yachts actually tied up to the giant stone gondola just offshore from the landing terrace. How did they ferry those lavish visitors to the terrace with all their trunks and dogs and jewels?

Like the woman who sat across from me at dinner years ago when I was modeling. Deedee something. She had planned to cross on the *Andrea Doria* but at the last minute had flown to attend a party in New York, leaving everything on the ship. "I lost everything," she said. "My jewels, my furs, my dog, my maid. I lost everything."

Those were the kind of people who came to Viscaya to party. They *had* to come by boat. There were no roads. Just a village of Italian artists to do the building, stucco work, frescoes, sculpture. It's a very elaborate house.

And there must have been other kinds of guests, too, because the owner was gay. Confirmed bachelor I suppose they said in those days. The guide book is very discreet but they did admit that there were torchlit parties in the gardens and dryads and nymphs were to be found in the grottoes. More dryads than nymphs would be my guess.

There's something about that house that suggests liaisons. Stealthy creeping up narrow staircases to small bedrooms, beautifully done in First Empire Yellow.

There's nothing spic-and-span about Viscaya. It's not like those terrible Williamsburg places where everything is so fresh and clean. You just know those poor old Colonials never lived like that. Not with all those smoky fireplaces.

But Viscaya has slightly frayed upholstery, worn silk at the windows, crumbling edges to the sculpture. Now that it's air-conditioned they'll probably put a stop to all that, but for the moment there is still that feeling of rich men indulging themselves, good-looking young men of no background advancing themselves, lechery and sneaking around and no guilt. That's what probably makes it feel so European. No guilt except for that poor guy who built it. His family made tractors to allow him all this excess luxury. He probably tossed and turned some nights in his painted Venetian bed, unable to forget that Grandpa had marched through the furrows behind a mule until it struck him how to improve upon the plow.

Some famous names were attracted to the isolation and sex shenanigans at Viscaya. I remember going there before the renovation and seeing reproductions of Sargent drawings done at Viscaya displayed along an upper wall. The most obscure one showed a naked black male in the sand under a low branch of beach grape, the villa scarcely to be seen in the distance across the water, a little sketch beyond the curving buttocks in the foreground. This sketch you never see in the collections of Sargent works. And I've looked. Nobody wants to add any further fuel to the feeling that Sargent must have been homosexual. I certainly hope he was. Horrible to think of that uptight guy hanging around all those rich people and never having any kind of romantic life at all.

Hugo and Glenn Elliott are there today. I wonder if they'll pick up on that little quiver of illicit romance that hangs in the air there. It is quite fantastic to think that this large and beautiful house, filled with beautiful furniture from France and Italy, the paintings, the silks and satins, was here in the mangrove swamps when the best that the rest of Miami had to offer was wooden boardinghouses and coconut plantations. A true Xanadu. When those yachts unloaded their passengers from New York and Boston and Philadelphia and perhaps even directly from the Continent, they must have felt it was almost a mirage. A mirage filled with beautiful Italian boys. And of course, I'm Italian. So I would like these feelings of beauty and magic first, morality second.

Viscaya 2

I decided I wasn't going to talk about anything. Anything I planned to say was just the kind of thing I'd never want to hear. And I certainly didn't want to hear *myself* saying them.

So I decided on deep pleasure. I love Viscaya and being there with someone I love.

From the parking lot we walked into that leafy reception court, hanging heavy with jungle and those stone half-statues, half-pillars, where all the faces have a kind of smart-ass look. As though they know something. That you are going to find out.

Then down that inclined road with the streams trickling on each side, the jungle still heavy around us. That smell of rotting things and watery plants and heat. Pulling you in, wrapping you up.

And then that big stone house with its tile roofs and shutters, showing up too soon, looming over you. So big and heavy, but not scary. Inside, thick tile floors and dark walls and little delicate lights set on the walls. I heard the ticket seller say to Glenn Elliott, "That's ten dollars for you and your son." An older man, maybe an ex-policeman. Where's he been, I wonder? Glenn caught up with me. He looked a bit sulky, not liking being thought of as my father, I guess.

As you first come in there's a little dressing room. Where ladies used to go to repair their face powder, I suppose. The small silk-covered chairs, mirrors you can hardly see yourself in, the lights are so low. You peer in and you're floating there, almost underwater. Blond hair. Brown eyes. Sort of like yourself, sort of not. Glenn behind me. Even darker, murkier. He looks at me in the mirror. He puts his hands on my hips and pulls me tightly against him. No one is there. We have a little paper guide sheet to tell us what we're looking at.

The big empty drawing room. I can imagine entering it. No ropes to keep out tourists in those days. Trying to decide where to sit, with dozens of choices, none of them comfortable. And so much cloth. Upholstery, draperies, rugs. Now we would never think of being in the tropics with all those yards of cloth around us. And all this frail, inlaid wood furniture. Waiting to split and fall apart in the heat and humidity and become sad ruins for people to see later and think, How did they ever think such delicate wood and painted flowers and woven shining fabric could survive? But it did. Long enough for air-conditioning to rescue it.

The angular, toppling dining room. Like a dining room in some giant stone castle in Scotland. High, huge vases standing up above, ready to fall on you. High stiff-backed chairs, row facing row. People trying to be amusing. Laughing, raising their glasses. You'd have to be awfully drunk to make a go of it.

Outside in the hall there's a portrait of Mr. Deering, who had the house built. Just as wrapped in cloth as his drawing room. A white suit, a shirt, a stiff collar, a tie right up under his chin. Little glasses on a round face with round eyes. Slicked-down hair, a neat part. I wonder if he was short? He must have been. Hard to imagine this big sprawling house his choice. But I guess all that rigid dining room furniture, all that prissy upholstery fits in.

He must have wondered if *he* really fit in here, all this sun and tropical flowers and beating sea.

Now the center courtyard is glassed over, but I remember being little and looking up as it rained down on me and the plants in their big, round pots. We were all looking up and sopping up the rain. Mom in the breezeway toward the sea calling me to come to her, to come out of the rain.

Behind her the big, square porch with enormous draperies filled the arches. The wind blew through, and looking out across the gray bay, I saw a big stone gondola raising its ends just offshore. That's the most magic part. Supposedly when people arrived by boat they tied up to the gondola. But I wonder. It's more like a statue, or a stage set. Looking over the stone gondola to Key Biscayne in the distance you can imagine that Key Biscayne is the mainland of reality, and here we are on an island of unreality.

Today the sea is very blue, the distant key very green, and the gondola very white in the sharp, sharp sun, carved more deeply with black shadows. The clouds are piled up higher and higher in twirling peaks. Everything is green and blue, white and black.

Glenn and I stand on the porch looking out, the draperies tugging in the wind, huge wicker furniture covered in big chintz flowers. Perfect for cuddling and nuzzling. And casual nookie upstairs in the afternoon with the sun slanting through the blinds. Perfect for everybody but Mr. Deering in his collar and cuffs.

Many beautiful bedrooms upstairs and Mr. Deering's large glassy, glossy tile and mahogany bathroom. I imagine him lowering that pale, white body into his bath. Only his valet around to hand him towels. Sort of like a snail out of its shell. Then bullying and tying itself into the shell of clothing and crawling slowly through the even more gigantic shell of this house.

There are two beautiful little bedrooms up separate small flights of stairs to the third floor. So exquisite with their screens and ornaments and small drawings and gathered silk daybeds. Here seems to be the real heart of this house. Those secluded sets for sexuality. You can just imagine someone on all fours on the counterpane, hanging off the end of the bed, upside down on the floor, legs supported by the side of the daybed, the lover probing down from above. Naked, sweaty, spunky in all this pretty decoration, all a little too small for full-size fucking.

The gardens are the most beautiful part. Formal low hedges, paths moving straight ahead at right angles. And the cascades at the far end. It's as though some ballet was about to be performed all the time. Walking up the steps at the sides of the cascades there is a kind of fresh, dripping feeling. Centuries ago when they first began creating these things, it must have been a wonderful treat in hot weather. For the upper classes, of course. The poor folk were struggling around outside in the dust.

They were so locked into their clothes in those days. I wonder what Queen Elizabeth wore in the summertime? All the pictures you ever see of her she is in ruffs and massive skirts sewn with jewels. In really hot weather I wonder if she permitted herself a little white robe to blow in the breeze. Women seem to have smartened up sooner than men. Back in Mr. Deering's time you see photographs of women in little flowery dresses with bare arms. And men still in their three-pieces with a straw hat.

Above the cascade is a terrace with little card rooms at each end. They probably came up here to catch the afternoon breezes. Below a little cliff is the canal where the gondolas waited to take guests through the jungle that lay beyond the garden. Now it's a trailer park. Quite a sight, those sun-cooked trailers without a tree or a bush, sitting there in front of you. Behind you the cascades trickling down over mossy stones to the gardens, a checkerboard of flowers and shrubs and hedges.

Glenn Elliott said nothing and I said nothing on the whole visit except things like, "Let's go here" and "Look at this."

Above the cascade he said, "I've never seen a house like this, have you?" I said, "I've been to this one quite a few times. And I've seen similar places in France. But not really like this. This is like the palaces in Italy."

"Do you find it sexy?" he said.

"Sexy, how? Do I want to crawl up on one of those beds and get down? Yes. Definitely."

Glenn turned to me from looking out over the gardens. "That's exactly what I mean. Don't you get the feeling that there's been a lot of fooling around in this place? It kind of hangs in the air. It's like it was built for fooling around."

"It could have been," I told him. "When it was built you could only get here by boat. There weren't any roads. It was a real hideaway. If you got here and didn't feel like fooling around I guess you had to swim out."

"And leave your luggage behind," Glenn said, and laughed, as though he was thinking of someone upstairs trying to decide if they should abandon their new shoes or let some old fart have a go.

We went back down the stairs beside the cascades and passed one of the grottos. I said, "Someone told me they used to have wild parties here and there were naked boys in the grottoes."

"I'd like to have a naked boy in the grotto right now," Glenn said and dragged me in. He pulled down my shorts. Elastic waistband, of course. I felt behind me. He was very hard in his pants. He's pretty amazing. From neutral to full speed faster than a Ferrari. He had his hand in my underpants.

"Think of the naked boys, Glenn," I said. "It's pretty cold and wet in here. Besides, I don't want to get arrested."

"I love to fuck you, Hugo," he mumbled into my neck.

"You love to fuck a lot of people," I said. He stopped. Tucked me back into my underpants and pulled up my shorts. Like a parent dressing an awkward child.

"That's true," he said over his shoulder as he walked through the garden ahead of me. "That's true, but it doesn't take anything away from you, Hugo."

"It doesn't make me feel very special." We were already talking about Ken without even bringing his name up. I knew we weren't talking about Mom, except maybe I was speaking for her as well as myself.

He turned around and it was the first time I had seen the cool Glenn Elliott look angry. "Give me a break, Hugo. Who could feel more special than you? So beautiful, so smart. I've seen those guys at the Bomber Club. They'd give ten years of their lives just to get a crack at you. What's that navy expression, 'They'd eat a yard of your shit just to get to your ass.' You are too special, Hugo. You're so special and I'm so lucky to be fucking you there's nowhere to go from here but down."

Myrtle-Fred had been right. "So you decided to start down all by yourself," I said. He looked at me admiringly. We were walking up the jungle incline now.

"You're really something, Hugo. Hard to believe you're only seventeen. I'd like to punch you right in the eye. But instead I'm going to take you home and punch you right in the pants. Come on."

I didn't put up a fuss. This was where the whole afternoon had been heading anyway.

When we got to his apartment he pushed me down on the bed and undressed me very slowly and carefully. When I lifted my hips so he could pull off my shorts he said, "Don't. I want to do this myself." While I lay there he slowly and methodically undressed himself and hung his clothes carefully in the closet. His erection stood straight out from his body. It was like a drawing of what a perfect penis should be.

He pulled a condom from his drawer and unrolled it on himself and then straddled me and put one on me. A tube of KY and a towel were under his pillows. Always ready for an emergency fuck, this guy. He pulled a pillow under me and slipped his fingers and some KY between my cheeks. Slowly, firmly, steadily he pushed himself in. He lowered those perfect pectorals onto my chest and just before his mouth closed over mine he said, "I do love to fuck you, Hugo."

Isn't that love?

miami by night

Miami in the middle of the night is a world all its own. Empty and windy. I can remember when we first came here and we were staying in a hotel. I would wake in the night and hear the wind. I still do. And I would have to get up, Hugo asleep in the other bed, and look out at Miami. Miami Beach. At our hotel you could see down onto the front porch of the hotel next door. This was back when all the old people were here. One night I saw this old lady sitting on her chair at the end of the porch, looking out over the ocean. The streetlight, the palms moving the way they do in the wind, over and back, over and back. I wonder, all in black and white in the starlights, what she thought, the old lady on the porch? Was she lonely? Did she feel sad, all alone in the high winds in the night, all the other old people all snuggled up in their beds upstairs, smelling of musty sheets and apple cores?

Was she sitting there thinking, "And it's come to this, it's come to this?" Or maybe she still felt young inside. As young as ever. And she loved being there in the high wind, looking out at the ships anchored at sea, waiting for dawn to enter port. No person, no car, no sound on Ocean Drive, except that end-less rustling of the palm trees, the tick and tack of the wind moving things. What things? And she would still be ready for romance to come along and whirl her away on one of those freighters. Or maybe, just being there, still alive in a world of romance and excitement and night magic. Maybe that was her fun. Maybe that was why she was up in the night, buttoned up in her sweater, her hair tugging in the night wind. I hope so. I hope I will be, too.

eavesdropping

The roller hockey game was kind of a bust. The Tampa Titans
sort of cleaned up on the Miami Hammerheads. They're only
a few years older than I am, those guys. And sort of nice guys.
You can tell that at the breaks their coaches are telling them to
rough it up more so it's more like ice hockey. What can they
get paid? Zilch. But it's exciting all the same when they get that
little puck into the net. Macha and Fred wanted to go hang out
at the Marlin but I had them drop me off home.

My shower was blocked up so I was taking a shower in the
guest bathroom. That's how I heard Mom talking to Glenn Elliott on the front porch. If I'd been in my own bathroom I
would never have heard them. I was just drying off when I
heard them coming up the walk. Glenn was saying, "I hate to
talk about love and being in love and what love means and all
that stuff."

Mom said, "All men do, but you brought it up."

"I was just asking how you know when you are in love,"
Glenn said.

I dropped my towel and just stood there. What's this, what's
this, I thought? You're always hearing about how you shouldn't
eavesdrop and you never hear anything good, but I felt no
guilt. This definitely concerned me and I wasn't about to scut-

tle back to my room feeling all good about myself. This I definitely wanted to hear.

They must have sat down on the porch because I could still hear them. Mom was probably sneaking a cigarette, the butt of which I would find in the flowerpot when I watered. It was our little thing, her sneaking a cigarette from time to time. I'm always keeping up the pressure so it won't get out of hand.

Mom said, "If you don't know if you're in love with someone or not, you are not in love with them. Real love is that brief period when you would follow them to the ends of the earth. When you would crawl through the Sahara on your hands and knees for them. And there would be plenty of things about them you don't like, but whatever that connection is, you can't *not* be there for them. I suppose it's like a crash course in how you love your child. I would throw myself in front a train for Hugo. And I suppose he would do the same for me. But that's something that builds up over a long period of time, and he is the flesh of my flesh. When you fall in love with someone it's pretty much the same thing but it crashes over you all at once."

Glenn Elliott interrupted her. "But that's kid stuff, Iris. That's puppy love you're talking about."

She said, "Well, yeah, but don't you think puppy love *is* love? Anything less than that is just kind of watered-down, talked-yourself-into-it kind of emotions, don't you think? Have you ever been just crazy in love like that, Glenn?"

I was very interested to hear his reply.

"I think I might be in love with you, Iris."

Mom answered. "You can't be, Glenn. Or you wouldn't think you might be. I'm nice. I'm not ugly. I think you're very interesting. Maybe we could be in love with each other someday. But I don't think either of us has to be in love to be enjoying our lives, so we both get along fine without it. Because if I *was* in love with you, Glenn, you would certainly know it."

"Do you think it can happen with someone you've known for a while?"

"Oh, yeah. It can drop from the skies at any time. But I don't think it slowly creeps up over you like rust. Why I'm telling you all this, Glenn, is not that I'm such an expert. But because if things go wrong later, and they always do, you know why you got mixed up in all this mess. I know so many people who are being emotionally wrestled to death, or are in a really ugly divorce, or just being abused generally. And they were never even in love with the other person. Doesn't make sense, does it? Here you are, having your life ruined by somebody you never even cared for very much. How can you think of yourself as anything but a real asshole?"

"Hummmm, hummmmm, hmmmm." Glenn sounded kind of stunned. Of course you could hear Mom all the way down to Arthur Godfrey Boulevard. That last "asshole" really rang out.

"What about companionship?" Glenn asked.

"Hire a housekeeper," Mom said. "You really want someone around so you're not alone? Hire somebody. They'll fix meals, do the shopping, keep the place clean. And when you can't stand them, you fire them. If you've got somebody around for companionship you're probably not going to like the sex anyway."

"So if you never fall in love you should stay single," Glenn said in a kind of sulky voice.

"Why not? If nobody ever got married or had children unless they were really in love, don't you think it would clean up a lot of the mess around here?"

"Miami?"

"Life."

"But then so many people would be alone."

"Is that such a terrible thing? I remember the first time I was lying in bed all alone and feeling sorry for myself and I said, Wake up, Iris. Wake up. How often have you been in bed with someone who was making you feel bad? Unconfident, unloved, or constantly having to hustle to *deserve* to be loved. Or being cheated on. And I thought, this is definitely better than any of those real-life situations. I was just trying to con myself into remembering romantic situations that, in fact, hardly ever existed. No. If I can't go first class I don't want to go at all. And it's me, if I'm being honest, who knows what first class is."

"No accommodations. Is that it?"

"Oh, I could accommodate a lot. I can handle a missing limb. Or someone who's not brilliant. Or not a great money-maker. Those things are not a problem. I might very well fall in love with someone in one of those categories. What I don't want to do is fall in love with someone I don't really know. Someone I've given a personality to, and later I find out they're someone completely different. And I'm fucked, in more ways than one. Life goes on, Glenn. Life goes on. I don't want to waste any time giving really heavy emotion to someone who doesn't get it. Doesn't appreciate it. Doesn't even know what it is I'm feeling. Doesn't that make sense?"

"Is Hugo home?" Glenn asked. I split from the bathroom on my tippy toes and fell on my bed. Mom called in the front door, "Hugo?" I yelled back. "Yes, Mom. Are you all right?"

"I'm great. Have you been listening to us?"

"Who's us?"

"Glenn and me."

I lied. "I'm in my bedroom. You'd have to have been talking pretty loudly for me to hear you."

Mom was on the stairs now. "We were. At least I was."

She was at the door looking pretty in her white dress with the green trim. I asked her, "Were you swearing?"

"Only a little."

"That's good. I hate to hear you swearing."

She said, "What are you reading?"

The Age of Innocence." I held it up.

"I'm going to say good night to Glenn."

"Say good night for me."

She went downstairs and I heard Glenn's car pull away. She

was wandering around downstairs. Putting some cats out. Bringing some cats in. I never really got the program. The girl cats stayed in, the boy cats stayed out, I think.

I turned out the light and lay there, waiting for some great thoughts to come to me. What I was kind of thinking about is what people want from other people. It seems to me that there are two kinds. The kind of people who play with other people. Other people are just there for you to sleep with and take out to dinner and take care of you. Cook meals. Make beds. Like Mom just said. If you want that kind of person in your life you should just get a housekeeper.

And some people want somebody to really do things with. Somebody they can take care of, who will take care of them, too. Sort of like your own child. Each person being the parent and the child for the other person.

And both men and women are like that. All those guys who are out cruising chicks in bars and trying to get laid all the time, and not particularly interested in who they're laying, they are exactly like those gay guys who hang out in gay bars and are always trying to score. So there isn't really any great difference between heterosexuality and homosexuality with people like that. They ought to create a new division called ono-sexual or something like that. People who just want to get laid and really don't want the other person to bother them by having any personality.

And then there are people like Mom and me, and I suppose Macha. And actually I think Fred is like that, too. Who want some give and take and want to really be interested in that other person and who are very sexually attracted to them at the same time. And I guess that's love. As we know it today.

And that makes me wonder about Glenn. He's kind of hanging there between ono-sexuality and this other thing. But when you're good-looking, ono-sexuality is just so much easier. Except I wouldn't want to be running around trying out this guy's prick and then some other guy's. Except maybe out of kindness. But then, good-looking men don't really need kindness.

Mom called up the stairs. "Hugo, are you asleep?" I called back, "Not now, Mom."

"Just wanted to tell you I love you," she said.

"Not as much as I love you," I called back, just to bug her. She came running up the stairs and hit me a good one in the behind. "What do you mean by that?"

"Just kidding, Mom," I said. "Just kidding."

butterfly world

We were driving on I-95 heading towards Butterfly World. Glenn was driving. I had read in the Herald about a Saturday morning seminar that taught you what plants to put in your garden to encourage butterflies to congregate there. Glenn isn't all that interested in butterflies, but Hugo will like them.

After our talk the other night I had been thinking. About Glenn. Looking at his profile I said as much. "Glenn, I've been thinking about you."

"What have you been reading?" he asked me.

"The usual. No. This hasn't been prompted by reading *Cosmopolitan*. Maybe by seeing *The Piano*. No, it's this. I want to be in love with you. So much in love I tear at the sheets just thinking about you. I don't like this business of kind of holding part of myself back in case you dump me so I don't feel bad. We've been seeing each other for about nine months. We're sleeping together and that's great, but it's not like we're sleeping with 'each other,' you know what I mean? We're sleeping with somebody, but is it really us? Am I making myself clear?"

"I don't really think about these things, you know."

"That's why I'm telling you." I said. "To make things clear. I'm half in love with you. It's not too late to get out. And I don't like it. If I don't take a stand, this whole thing could kind of drift along indefinitely. Until my looks are really shot. And then inevitably someone younger will step in and look good to you and you won't really break it off with me, you'll let me find out and then I'll be really unhappy and I'll break it off and you'll be guilty of nothing. It's sort of like two lionesses tussling over a water buffalo carcass."

"Nice image." Glenn said.

"No, really. You guys are all alike. You're too nice to break a woman's heart, but you can hang in there forever until she breaks it all by herself on your refusal to make a decision. That's why I'm taking the bull by the horns. I don't think there's another woman on the horizon yet, and I want to speak up. I mean, here I am, someone heading towards forty on their last bombing run and I'm willing to risk it. I want to be crazy about you. I want to be nuts about you. I want to cry. I want to fall down and pull at the draperies. So win or lose, if you go or if you stay, I know something happened."

We were passing the Atlantic Beach Motel, really sleazy, smack on I-95. Glenn pulled into it. I said nothing. I could see his pants full as he got out of the car. He pushed down at himself to get his crotch in order as he went into the office. He came back with a key and as I got out of the car he went into a ground floor room almost directly in front of the car.

As I pushed the door shut behind me he turned and loosened his belt. I fell to my knees in front of him and pulled his pants and jockey shorts down his legs and put his cock in my mouth. I pulled him down on the scruffy wall-to-wall. He groaned and rubbed his hands repeatedly through my hair. I stuck a finger up his anus. He struggled to open his legs and couldn't with his ankles stuck in his trousers. Still holding him in my mouth I moved over and with one hand pulled off his loafers and trousers and underpants. He pulled up his legs to help me. God, I thought, What am I doing? I crouched between his bent legs and pushed up his striped polo shirt with both hands and ran my hands over his smooth torso. I gripped his pectorals and squeezed. He groaned some more.

He pulled me up on top of him and rolled me over onto the floor. His hands were tearing at my pantyhose. He didn't seem to understand they came down. He wanted them off. He tore. They gave. He got in. Very deeply in. He was pushing hard, not pumping. As though he was looking for something. I opened my legs very widely and kicked over a side table. The big ugly chartreuse lamp on it went over with a sick plonk. It didn't sound so much like it was breaking, more as though it had collapsed. I seemed to be registering these things at the same time that my stomach seemed to be melting and I seemed to be opening up more and more and more. As though I was offering myself up and it wasn't enough. His mouth was very tightly on mine. As though he was trying to get into my body as profoundly as possible at both ends.

Why am I wearing shoes? I thought. Particularly black suede pumps? And pantyhose? Where did I think I was going? Did I know this was going to happen?

I felt for his buttocks. I put my finger as deeply into him as I could. I was curled up now, my chin on his shoulder, reaching as deeply into his ass as I could as he plunged and plunged.

"Almost ready?" he mumbled into my ear. A question? A statement?

"Yes, honey, let's do it." I said.

"Oh, My God, My God, My God." he said, his arms pushing him away from the floor, his head pushed towards the ceiling, his face twisted. He shuddered and shuddered again, his head whipped right and left, right and left. I held tightly to his body at the waist. He sank down upon me and held me very tightly. He kissed me again and rocked his body slowly back and forth from side to side as he pulled his penis out. He rolled off and put one arm over his eyes and the other companionably under my shoulders. He pulled me over to him. I put my head on his chest and one arm across his mid-section. It felt warm and sweet.

"Well," he said, "Are you really in love with me now?" I sat up and looked at him, my hair falling down around my face. I lifted his arm off his eyes. They were closed. He was smiling slightly to himself.

"You can certainly let yourself go when the spirit moves you, can't you?" I said.

"Not with everybody," he said. He opened his eyes and looked up at me quickly and then closed them again. I turned away and pulled what was left of my pantyhose off and wiped between my legs with them. Then I reached over and wiped his groin, too. Stumbling over my shoes I went into the bathroom and squeezed out a washcloth in warm water. Gently I wiped him. He winced a little, still shading his eyes with his arm. His body looked very beautiful lying there on the ratty gray industrial carpeting. Sweat socks are a great thing for a naked body to wear. His polo shirt bunched up under his armpits made me think of the Michelangelo statue at the Louvre called The Slave. That statue looks like it just had an orgasm, too, I thought.

I sat down on the edge of the bed, my legs stretched in front of me, looking at him. He turned and rested his head on a bent arm. "Do you still want to go to Butterfly World?" he said.

I looked at my watch. We had only been in the motel room fifteen minutes.

"I think I begin to understand Einstein's theory of relativity," I said.

"What?" he said in that way that requires no further explanation. He sat up and looked for his underpants. They were over by the door. His trousers had half gotten under the edge of the bed. He crawled on his hands and knees to recover his underpants and stood up to put them on. The sun, creeping under the heavy draperies was making a long rectangle on the floor near him. I noticed the door was unlocked.

He picked up his pants and ruffled my hair with one hand. I pulled him to me and put my head against his hip. He pressed it to him even more tightly. "I love you, my little weird one." he said. I didn't say anything.

I just pressed my head against him more and tightened my arms around his thighs. "Well," I said, "let's be on our way to Butterfly World. I'm sure we missed the lecture on how to attract butterflies but we can still see them." Glenn pulled on his trousers and pushed his feet into his loafers. He looked into the mirror and ran his hand over his hair. "I look a wreck," I said, looking over his shoulder into the mirror. I touched him slightly as I put on my pumps. My hair was all over the place but it looked good. I stuffed my torn and messy pantyhose into my purse. "Somehow I think the maid has enough to put up without finding my pantyhose in the wastebasket," I said.

"At least she doesn't have to change the bed," Glenn said.

"I'll bet she does anyway. They probably always do, no matter what." I looked at the lamp. "I've got to go to the office and pay for that lamp."

"I'll do it," Glenn said.

"No, I want to do it," I said. "I kicked it over. It makes it more real—that something happened if *I* pay for it."

"Well, something certainly happened," Glenn said as he looked back into the room before he closed the door.

The motel clerk was a young Hispanic girl. She looked up as I walked in. "That must have been great," she said.

"I broke the lamp," I said.

"Forget it," the girl said. "They get broken very rarely. It's the sheets and towels that take a beating and nobody ever pays for that. I'm sure it was in a good cause."

I turned to go and then I said to my new friend, "I'm caught in an irreversible tide of love. Next week, a hurricane of tears and regrets."

"I'm jealous," the girl said.

We went to Butterfly World. It was small and the lecture was over. In the screen-covered butterfly house, frilly black and white butterflies from the Philippines looked like floating bits of old lace. Tinier butterflies winked here and there in shades of turquoise and fragments of scarlet and black. A gray haired lady in a pink shirt told us that these were not the kind of butterflies I could hope to attract as they only existed in the Butterfly House. And the local butterflies only lived for a week or ten days after their three month caterpillar and chrysalis phases.

"It's hardly worth it," Glenn said.

"Oh, no," the little gray haired lady said. "Each one only lives a week but they keep being born and being born. You will never be without them."

In the plant department I bought the recommended plants for attracting the local butterflies, mostly yellow, and left. "These plants look like weeds," Glenn said.

"I guess butterflies figure they are beautiful enough in themselves. The plants they like to feed on and lay their eggs on don't have to be beautiful, too."

When we got home, Glenn said, "I'm going to stay here tonight."

"That would be nice," I answered him.

In bed that night as we lay in each other's arms Glenn said, "You didn't come this morning did you?"

"I think you came enough for two people, don't you?"

"No, I mean it. I'm serious. You didn't, did you?"

I sat up. "No, but I had a very thrilling time all the same. You have to realize that women are very different from men. Men have to have an orgasm or the whole thing is a disaster. Your orgasm was very exciting to me. Really exciting. I have never known you to let yourself go emotionally so much. It was very exciting and very flattering and I felt I had really been through the mill when we got done, even without an orgasm."

"But you said you were ready."

"I was ready—for you to have an orgasm. The experience was you screwing the daylights out of me, see?

"Maybe it has to do with domination. Or control. Or winning you over. Who knows? All I know is that I wanted our relationship to feel like it was really happening and that certainly felt like it was really happening. And you know all this *Cosmopolitan* magazine bullshit about women deserving the same orgasms as men and men being insensitive to women's sexual needs, and so on. I mean, what kind of woman knows what's going on sexually and what she enjoys and doesn't manage to have it happen? We're not all alike. Some of us get a great deal of pleasure out of the fact that the man who is sleeping with us is getting a great deal of pleasure out of it. Men and women are really very different sexually. You're just lucky if the person you sleep with is really interesting to you and you're interesting to them. It's so American. Thinking there is some kind of system that we should all follow. Because we're all alive we must be all the same. Very silly."

"Sticking your fingers up my behind was a little different. Where'd you learn to do that?"

"I didn't. I don't know where that came from," I said. "Out of the woodwork. It just happened. And then I wondered what it felt like."

"We could try it. You might even like to see what it feels like for me to put little Larry up there." Glenn said. "For one thing, I wouldn't call that thing *little* Larry," I said, straddling him. "And for another, I think we should just let nature take its course."

hugo thinks about stanford white

Now Glenn is staying here nights. Not with me. With Mom. Which is cool.

Sex is such a complicated thing. You think things are going in a certain direction, and then voom, suddenly they go off somewhere else. Or they disappear. Or go underground, like those rivers that disappear in the desert. I don't know where I thought this thing with Glenn was going. I thought he knew. And then suddenly there's like two Glenns. The one who sleeps with me and the one who sleeps with Mom. Except the one who sleeps with me is on vacation.

Here's my question. Why do people have it all wrong about sex and how it works? Obviously men like to run around. Obviously it's sort of a trophy sport. What's important is that they can lay claim to it later. Like scalps. Or hood ornaments. I mean, the sex thing is probably like not much. He slips the little minnow in, squeezes, feels good, it's out and over. She wonders what's the big deal. And he goes running back to his pals and say, "I did it! I did it!" How many people really have a great time in bed together? That's my question.

I'm reading about Stanford White. Very important architect. Built lots of beautiful buildings in New York. And then the husband of an old girlfriend shot him in the head in an outdoor

194

theater on top of the old Madison Square Garden, which he had built. When you read about it and look at the pictures there's his wife, this big sort of battle-ax lady. She lived in the country. He lived in town. And you think, they probably had terrible sex together. He just popped on occasionally, she didn't mind if he never did. So he wanders off with some sixteen-year-old sexpot. And she doesn't see that it's her fault in any way. Because nobody ever said it was supposed to be fun. Or that you shouldn't marry somebody if it wasn't fun. Mrs. White lived until 1950 and he was shot in 1906. I'll bet she never thought once that maybe she should have given him some better shagging.

And the last *Esquire* had this article on unfaithful husbands. It's like nobody ever says, "Look, men like to screw around. It's good for their ego and keeps them from getting too bored at their dopey old nine to fives. So maybe steps should be taken to relieve the pressure." No, they marry some dame and live in the suburbs and you get the feeling they never had this big romance in the first place. I really don't get it. How can you climb into bed every night with someone you really don't care about all that much? I mean, sleeping in the same bed is a very intimate thing. It's like sleeping with your dog, otherwise.

Just reach over and give old Fido a pat. What are people thinking of? To me, most marriages are living with someone you don't particularly care about, but who makes it impossible for you to meet someone you might care about.

People think that all this stuff about romance is a lot of hooey. I don't think they make enough out of romance. Basically women have it right. The big deal is that other person. And if you hold out until you find that other person, is it such a big deal if he never shows up? Getting married and having a family and all that stuff is just keeping busy.

If people weren't just killing time replicating themselves, what would they be doing? Funny idea, isn't it? All these bored people doing the same things over and over again because they just can't find something else to do. Maybe we'd be better off if we were like bees. Just one woman has children and everyone else in the tribe runs around taking care of everything. Servants. I could kind of get into that. Serve, serve, serve. It's real clear. Except we have the problem of being able to think and then there'd always be somebody who wanted it to be their turn to be Queen Bee.

And now if I step out of the picture, what gives with Mom and Glenn? I think she really loves him and she deserves to be in love with somebody. I'm much younger and I've got time to be in love, I guess. Or I could run into the house screaming, "But I love him! He's mine!" Can you picture it? Mom would die of embarrassment. Me, too. Except old Glenn would give us both that great stone-face treatment of his and walk out, like he'd been stuck with a couple of crazies who imagined something was going on that wasn't even happening. I'm sure that's how he deals with this stuff. Who, me? You must have me confused with some other handsome, well-built, well-hung guy. No, this hand is going to go to Mom. And she won't even know I was ever in the game.

father

Glenn Elliott had picked me up after work at the Armani Exchange. I had kind of planned to work out but when your lover wants to see you you can't say no, can you? Ha, ha. I have never thought of him as my lover or even my boyfriend. He doesn't seem to think of me as his lover either. Doesn't seem to think about it at all, matter of fact. Mom is channel 1, I'm channel 2. No prob.

In the car I told him that if he was thinking of marrying my mother he ought to wait for a while. At least until I finished high school.

He said, "I don't know that I want to marry your mother. But I have to admit I've been thinking about it. What would be the problem?"

I looked at him. We pulled up in front of the house. "You don't see a problem being my father?"

"I wouldn't really be your father, Hugo. You have a father somewhere. And you're a big boy. A very big boy." I was about to tell him that we seemed to heading dangerously toward the kind of stuff that's on *Oprah*. Right behind me my mom's voice was in my ear. She was at the car window. "Having a little argument, are we? I hope it's not about me." She was kidding so I knew she wasn't getting the picture.

"Actually, Mom, we were talking about fathers."

"Yours or his?" she said.

"Neither one. Just fathers in general. How necessary are they? You know."

"Funny you should bring that up. Your father called me today. He wants to see you."

That really stopped my motor. Glenn's too. He started getting out of the car. It was sort of as though she had been rehearsing this for a long time. "He's here. In Miami Beach. Actually, Fisher's Island. He said he'd been running into some of the old-time models like Sylvia DiMazzo in Rio and they'd told him I was here. He found the phone book and the rest is history."

"What about you?" I wanted to know. "Doesn't he want to see you?"

"Actually I think he could skip that part, but he's not going to. There's no way he's going to see you without seeing me."

"What about me?" Glenn said. "If there's going to be any trouble I'm at your service."

"There's not going to be any trouble. He's here visiting people on swanky Fisher's Island. Curiosity got the better of him. I told him we would meet him in public and so we're going to have dinner with him at the Strand. Tonight."

"What about me?" I said. "Don't I have any say in this? What if I don't want to see my father? This is somebody I've barely heard of. What if I don't like him? This could be traumatic." Actually I was very excited. I never really had missed him or fantasized about having a father. I just never seemed to have cared. But now one was about to appear before my eyes. I certainly wasn't going to miss it. I knew Mom was reading this. She knows me all too well.

"Trauma is your middle name, Hugo. If you can just step in and do a television pilot, you can certainly step in and say hello to your old dad. I cannot imagine what he's up to and my first instinct was to tell him to go fly a kite. But then I thought, this could be interesting."

"You know, Mom, to me he's just semen," I said. That stopped her.

"I think maybe we should go into the house to continue this conversation," she said. "I think it might be getting too fascinating for the neighbors. And we're already the highlight of their day."

Glenn Elliott said, "I should be going but I'm not going to. I'm coming in just to take lessons on handling dramatic situations. You two do make quite a fascinating couple. I'm sorry to have to agree with the neighbors. I wouldn't miss this for all the world."

This kind of surprised me. Coming from Glenn this was kind of droll. He doesn't usually display much sense of humor unless he's fucking you.

In the house I said, "First things first. What should I wear?" Glenn laughed but my mother knew I wasn't really being funny.

"The navy blue blazer I think. That makes you look like a little gentleman. And definitely a tie. Let's make it real clear, the real reason we're doing this is to show you off, Hugo my darling. I want to show that jerk what he missed."

"You'd never go back to him, would you, Mom?" I said. Glenn Elliott was sprawled on the flowered rattan settee. I sat down on the chair. Mom was kind of marching up and down from one end of the room to the other. "Go back to whom?" she said. "I haven't heard from this guy for fifteen years. Those were two other people altogether. We'll see what he's like. But if all your cells completely replace themselves every seven years, I am at least two different people away from the person I was in Rio." She looked in the mirror. "Although I don't look all that different."

"Better probably," I said.

"I think it's for the good, Mom." I told her.

"I think it's for the great, Iris." Glenn said. Funny, I felt like he and I were kind of a team, doing our little number to keep up Mom's morale. She was being a trouper, but having been on her own with me all these years, and then having this guy suddenly appear, a guy with plenty of money who had never even wanted to find out how she was, how we were, had to be heavy. I'm sure she didn't give a damn about the money. Or being ignored. Just figuring out how she should deal with it that was bothering her. He hadn't given her much time.

"What's my father's name?" I wanted to know. "Roberto Baroncelli. But no one ever called him Roberto. Everyone called him Baby," Mom said.

"Baby?" Glenn and I said together. I suppose we were thinking of the same thing.

"In Europe calling someone 'Baby' isn't the same thing as it would be here," Mom said. "Everyone was called Johnny or Harry or some kind of American name. It was the chic thing. I think someone was trying to call him Bobby and it just came out Baby. I guess. I suppose. Who the hell knows? He was Baby Baroncelli when I met him, but he wasn't much of a Baby. He was like a movie star. Like Robert Taylor. That look."

I drew a blank. Glenn looked a little miffed. Evidently Robert Taylor must have been very good-looking.

"Anyway, we'll see how much of those looks survived. You must be braced for anything, Hugo. He always lived very fast and he could be pretty much a wreck. I hope not, for your sake."

"For my sake, Mom? I couldn't care less." I got up and put my arms around her and we looked in the mirror over the fireplace together. I put my head against hers. We have pretty much the same face. She kept her arms down by her sides, so as to not encourage me. "*You're* my dad," I said to her in the mirror. "You're my dad and my mom and my granddad and my grandmother and the whole shooting match. And you're well up to it. I kind of hate to think what it would have been like if all the rest of them had been on hand. I'd be crushed to a little smidgen of dust from all the supervision."

"You're a very good boy, Hugo." She pushed her hands up through my arms and squeezed my face. "I'm going to give you a baby kiss." She put her lips on my face and rubbed them up and down in a blubbery way that left a lot of spit, just as babies do.

"Mom, you know I hate that," I said and tried to pry myself away from her, but she's strong. Glenn pulled himself up from the couch. "Nobody ever gives me baby kisses," he said, heading for the door.

"Count yourself lucky," I yelled after him as I headed for the stairs. In the door I could hear Mom calling good-bye and that she would call him tomorrow.

the strand

The Strand. You know the Strand. Where all the models go. Or all the people who would like to meet models. Or all the people who want to be models. Handsome Eric was at the door. So handsome I would think most other male models would have a sinking feeling of "what's the use of trying?" Eric was a famous model and now owns the Strand. Mom and he spoke French a little. That usual "Comment ça va" variety. He gave her that look that only French men seem to give. An "admiring" look. Not coming on, but that "how do you get so beautiful" look. If I were a woman I would think that would be a very nice reaction to get. Rather than that "let me touch your tits" routine American men do.

Eric was very nice to me, too. "You should model," he said. "He's already past that stage," my mother said. And we were shown to the Baroncelli table.

I could feel Mom kind of gathering herself. As we came up to the table the candlelight didn't make it too easy to see, but I could make out three people. Two men and a woman.

Mom walked up and said to the man in the middle, "Baby, it's me." The man turned and looked up. He had dark hair and a dark tan and deep lines on either side of his mouth and between his eyes. He was handsome like a Mexican movie star and there was something a little devilish about him. Long eye-brows, maybe. He was the guy who, with his little friend, had tried to pick up Fred and me backstage at the Bomber Club.

My father stood up. He was tall. A navy blazer and no neck-tie. He came around the table and I think he was going to hug Mom but she stuck out her hand and made him shake it. "Iris, darling," he said, "how wonderful you look."

"Do I?" she said. "I think I've looked more wonderful in my time. This is Hugo." I stepped up and shook his hand. It was large and a little moist. I didn't like the way it felt.

So this was my father. It was sort of like doing a scene from a show. I didn't feel what might be a genetic pull. It was hard to imagine Mom and him as a couple. It felt good that he wasn't my father now. Macha's folks wouldn't have liked him at all and they love Mom.

"This is the Count and Countess De Vecci del Vecchio," he said, turning to the couple. The count was kind of a little old man. He stood and shook mom's hand. The countess did not rise. She was a blond lady in a pink dress with a rather stiff face. She said, "Hi. It's wonderful to meet you. Roberto has been telling us all about you folks." Mom sat down beside the little old count. I sat beside the pink countess. Mom sat up very straight with her hands on the edge of the table. She spoke to the count in Italian. He said in English, "You are Italian? How very interesting. But we must speak English as my wife doesn't speak Italian."

"Hell," said the countess, "I don't even speak English, I don't know how anyone could expect me to learn Italian." She was like some kind of wind-up doll, the countess. Behind her sort of flat, expressionless face I got the impression there was an old ex–Texas cheerleader. "It would be impolite as Hugo doesn't speak Italian, either. I just felt like speaking a few words to see if I still could," Mom said.

"When did you come to the United States?" the count asked. "Oh, long ago," Mom said. My father, Baby, sat down between the count and the countess, sort of beaming at both of us, and occasionally at the count and countess. I wondered if he was on something.

I think just about then Mom doped out that my father hadn't told these people that this was his former wife and present child. "How do you happen to be here?" Mom said very politely to the three people facing her. "We have an apartment on Fisher's Island," the count said. "This is our first time, and we love it," the countess said. My father said, "The count and countess asked me to come with them. We've known each other for a long time, Enrico and I from Rio. And of course, Lorene for a number of years too, now."

"So, Roberto, you just happened to be in Miami and decided to look Hugo and me up? Is that it?" There was a little edge to Mom's voice. I could see that both Enrico and Lorene had directed their attention to her. I suppose in their world ugly scenes at restaurant tables were old stuff. And it would give them something to talk about whenever they went back to wherever they came from.

"Do you like Fisher's Island?" I asked Lorene. The menus arrived. "It's pretty much like all these places," she said. "The Costa del Sol, the Costa Smeralda, what's that place on the Mexican coast that Goldsmith girl has? They all kind of look like they're made out of plaster over chicken wire. But they gave us a great deal because of the count's title. What they forget is that I am the former Lorene Fogel of Lubbock, Texas, and I knew all those rich assholes when I was married to Gus Fogel." This was pretty weird coming out of that tight little mouth with the pink lipstick. I really did wonder what she used to look like before they stretched her face all over the front of her skull. I kind of liked that voice.

"Haven't you ever been to Fisher's Island?" she asked Mom. "I thought you were in real estate."

"I am," Mom said, "but not in that league. I sell houses

mostly here in Miami Beach. And Hugo goes to school at Miami Beach High."

"Are you a widow?" Lorene asked. Now the fat was really in the fire. Mom looked straight across the table at her and said, "I'm a divorcée, but I wish I were a widow."

"That bad, hey?" said Lorene, from that gash of a mouth. I was really beginning to dig her. I looked at the count. Enrico knew something wasn't going right but he wasn't quite sure what. Roberto, my father, was studying the menu very carefully.

Handsome Eric came to the table. "Is everything all right?" he asked. Mom smiled at him and said, "Eric, I'd like you to meet my former husband, Roberto Baroncelli. And his friends, the Count and Countess . . . del Vecchio? Did I get that right?"

"Close enough," Lorene said. "Did I hear you say that this is your former husband?" She gestured toward me with her menu. "Is this your son together?" She didn't wait for an answer. Poor Eric was standing by the table, cool and collected but realizing he's walked into some kind of booby trap. "I'm sure you'll excuse me," he said and glided swiftly out of sight.

The count looked like he had just had the face-lift. Not a speck of expression. And my father had the same look. Everything just smoothed away. Lorene was quite the opposite. What was left of her facial muscles were working overtime. In a completely different of voice, quite low, she said, "You shit. I'm going to say this for your wife—former wife. *She's* too much of a lady to do it I'm sure. You are a shit. You invite your wife and son to dinner. You haven't seen them in years. This kid probably never. And you ask us to come along? And don't even tell us?"

"I didn't know what to say, Lorene. I was going to explain later," this guy who is my father says.

"Not. You were going to just slip them in and out of your life like they were old acquaintances from the past. You are absolutely empty, Roberto. Empty. And now I know why Eduardo didn't come tonight. Headache, my ass."

I was really liking Lorene. My mother stood up from the table and I did too. We had finally gotten the attention of the table full of models and their Latin boyfriends at the next table. "Don't go," Lorene said, reaching out her hand. It was very scrawny and speckly, like a chicken's foot, with a great big diamond ring and bracelet on it. "Don't go. Or if you go I'm going, too. Really, Enrico, can't you say something?"

"Roberto is my friend," he mumbled down into his plate. I was figuring out that those diamonds Lorene was wearing hadn't come from him.

Lorene turned to me. "What do you think, Hugo? What do you want to do?"

"I think we should stay. We're all hungry and everything's out on the table," I said to Mom.

"But the food," Lorene said.

"Let's stay, Mom. You haven't seen mmmmh"—I nodded toward my father—"in a long time. Let's not just run away. Come on, sit down." And she did.

"Spoken like a little diplomat," Lorene said, clutching my hand with her chicken claw. I figured that Lorene and Mom and I could have a really good time together, and we'd fit the two stiffs in somehow. Lorene swiveled in her seat. "Waiter," she cried out into thin air and one magically appeared. She was used to that, I guess. "We must have some wine immediately," she called out, as though he was still halfway across the room. "Bring us a good red wine. Right now. Don't bother with the wine list. Just bring some wine right away . . . and some water"—looking around the table a little wildly—"and for God's sake some food."

And so we ate. I had swordfish. Don't ask me why. I don't particularly like it. I guess at least I knew what I was going to get. Mom had a Caesar salad.

There wasn't much to say, really, except to scream at each

other. There was no way I could tell anybody that it was my father who had tried to pick me up at the Bomber Club on closing night with his little boyfriend. For one thing, Mom doesn't know I worked there, and why bother since it's closed? Baby Baroncelli, my father, didn't look very fussed that the kid he had tried to pick up was his son. He hadn't flickered an eyelash when he saw me and he wasn't giving me any meaningful looks now. In fact, he wasn't giving me any looks at all, and few to Mom. Strange, huh? Here's your genetic father and it's somebody you don't like. Somebody you could never like. Somebody you wouldn't mind if you never laid eyes on again in your whole life.

All these stories about adopted kids who spend years trying to find their real mom, or look for a father who deserted them young. All that stuff. Like it was going to make a difference. The fact they stayed out of your life all those years doesn't exactly suggest a lot of loving, does it?

Thank God Lorene was at the table. She was really nice. Or at least she knew how to act the part of a nice person really well. Which is just as good.

She asked me about school and what I wanted to do. I told her I would like to be a writer. She said, "But you should be an actor, you're so good-looking!" She added, "But not at all like your father." Kind of to take sides, I guess. Mom told her that I'd done a TV pilot that perhaps was going on the air this fall and I would probably work in it some more if it was successful.

My father kind of woke up when he heard this. He asked Mom, not me, if I had made a lot of money. She told him I would make more money if the show was successful, and that, yes, I had made some money but didn't particularly like acting. "But why?" he wanted to know. "When he's off to such a good start."

Lorene picked up on it right away. She turned to me. "It's as though you're not even here, Hugo. Hugo the Thing." I had

207

to like her. I said, "Maybe it's because I'm only seventeen."

"Why only?" she said. "Seventeen isn't so young. Thirteen isn't so young. All this Michael Jackson furor. Where *were* all these people when they were thirteen?"

Mom had been listening out of one ear. She turned and said, "I was in a convent school."

Lorene said, "Well, I suppose that does exempt you, but I'm not even sure of that from all the things I'm reading in the papers lately,"

"This was in Italy," Mom said.

"Oh, I'm sure *that* made all the difference," Lorene said. She was kind of a hot old dame.

She took out her lipstick and her compact and redid her lipstick. She said, "It was the Duchess of Windsor who made it all right to redo your makeup at the table. She was right of course. Why spend a fortune on these compacts if no one ever sees them?" She finished and slapped the compact shut. Very pink mouth. I asked her, "Did you ever meet the Duchess of Windsor?" "I was at a couple of dinner parties she and the duke were at, yes. She was really rather terrible. She liked bawdy stories and I thought she drank too much. You certainly didn't get the impression that she was from anywhere but Baltimore."

"Is that bad?" I said. She really focused on me.

"Have you ever been to Baltimore? No. Of course not. No one has. Doesn't that tell you something? My husband knew her better than I did. And the duke. Before we were married."

I looked at the count. "But he loved her very much, didn't he?" He looked back at me as though he couldn't quite make up his mind what to say. "He counted on her. You know she outlived him by quite a few years. I think she saw that as her task. To always take care of him all his life. And that's what he wanted. He was never a celebrity, you know. He never had the temperament for that. She was a celebrity and he liked the life that went with that."

"And of course he was always faithful to her," Lorene the

countess added. She didn't say it in any special way but the count said no more. Then she said, "Don't you sometimes long to live a life in a cheap little flat with nothing of value? All Formica and puckered seams?" Mom said, "My life isn't so far from that." Lorene didn't even look at her but said, "I'm sure that's far from true, far from true."

Suddenly Mother straightened up. She said, "Hugo, you and I must go. Someone is waiting for us at the bar to see us home." I looked over in the direction she was looking and saw Glenn Elliott leaning against the bar with a drink in his hand, looking at us. He was wearing a black and white check jacket and looked very handsome. My heart jumped, just as my mother's had, I suppose. It was like seeing your real father when someone had been trying to pass themselves off as your dad and you know it's not true.

Everyone decided to leave at the same time and as we all moved into the bar on our way out Glenn Elliott came over. My mother at her politest introduced him as Mr. Paul to the count and countess and to my father, whom she only said was Mr. Baroncelli. Everyone shook hands very politely. "What a handsome fellow you are, Mr. Paul," Lorene said. She paused, looking at Mother standing beside him. "You make a very good-looking couple." She could really be cruel. The count and my father had on their lizard faces. Nothing showing. They were leaving. Mother shook hands with the count and countess and then she took me by the arm and pulled me up close to her. "I'm not shaking your hand good-bye, Roberto. I don't think it would be correct. We're just going to say good-bye, and leave it at that." She didn't really sound angry and the people around us didn't notice anything unusual.

The countess said, "You're perfectly right, my dear. Perfectly right. It was a great pleasure to meet you and I won't say I look forward to seeing you again, because I think that's doubtful. But it was a pleasure. I learned something tonight, and at my age that is not usual. Good-bye. Good-bye." She took the men by their arms and walked away with them. We saw them waiting for their car outside. They didn't seem to be talking to each other.

"I liked her," Glenn Elliott said.

"She was the good one," Mom said. "I used to know a lot of people like that. Good people in a world of not-so-good people, but they manage to hang on to their goodness. And all their little badnesses don't count for much."

"And that is your ex?" Glenn said.

"Oh, very much my ex. What did you think?"

"Still good-looking but what else? You wouldn't still want to be with him?"

Mom made a funny shape with her mouth as though she tasted something sour. "I wasn't going to shake his hand, Mom, no matter what you did," I said. They were going outside and we went out and waited for Glenn's car. The soft, sweet salt air was blowing. It was warm and I felt relaxed. We were all going home together. My family. My weird, weird family.

roberto shaving

It was curious seeing Iris again. It was curious and I was curious. She looks well. Capable. You never could shake her up very much. Of course she had every reason to leave me. I think I probably set it up to get caught with that American so she would leave me. She was very sweet and very beautiful and very famous when we met.

Not like Lorene. Poor Enrico. He tells me that she is still very eager to make love. He's got his work cut out for him. Twenty years ago he was a good-looking man. But always so polite. Even in bed. Always, "Sorry . . . If you please . . . May I." It's being Catholic that got him through all this. Duty, duty, duty. He must have thought he would outlive Lorene, she being so much older. I'm not so sure. She may outlive him. Then it would be my turn to marry her. Better Eduardo. He wouldn't mind the fucking part.

I think I'm jealous of Iris. She has a career. A handsome boyfriend. I did her a favor. But not much money.

I'm sure she doesn't know her handsome son works in a strip club. Even if it is the best one. I wonder what that's all about. That he's a vicious little boy with the face of an angel. Seen those boys before, haven't we? A vicious little boy who enjoys all the natives ogling his body. Or perhaps he just likes to get fucked. Or maybe he needs money? Americans are so difficult to figure out. They can take the most sinister kind of sex deviation and turn it into just another way to make money. And the bright light of moneymaking cleanses all. If you can make a good living doing it, can it be bad? I sort of like that idea.

My son, my son. What can be done with my son, the beautiful boy? A beautiful boy like that, there's certainly something better for him to do, some better way for him to make money than that dingy little strip club?

God, I'm going to have to have a face-lift soon. I look like hell. But where's the money supposed to come from? The vicious circle. No money if you don't look good. And if you don't look good there's no money to be had. I must ask Lorene who did her last three jobs. So I can avoid all of them.

My mind keeps running down all these little blind alleys like some half-crazed rat, and there's no money at the end of any of them.

And once Eduardo gets the picture he's going to be history. And who cares? Dull little twat. All he can think about is how large a cock he can get inside himself. And he's not even very careful about condoms. He's not going to be around very long, one way or another.

So Hugo, my thoughts keep coming back to you. There's got to be some way to make a bundle with a little cutie like you, my very own son. But how? I've got to put some real thought into this.

And where is Eduardo? He went to the pool two hours ago and no sight of him out there now. Probably being fucked by that guy in the cap who's been crawling around here ever since we arrived. He'd find somebody to fuck in the Antarctic.

the hooters

The Hooters, the Hooters, the Hooters. Macha wanted to go see the Hooters. Don't ask me why. But we'd been seeing so little of each other I felt like couldn't say no. I asked Fred at work about the Hooters. I said, "I thought the Hooters were those restaurants with the waitresses with the big gonzobs where men go to act macho. So this is women's football?"

"Yes, it's topless football. There's a national league. Who are they playing? The Toronto Tits? Or the Buffalo Bosoms?" Fred asked, sorting out the sale T-shirts, which the customer had thoroughly messed up without buying any.

"I can't believe this, Fred." I started helping him fold and pile. "Here, this is a medium. Football hurts. What happens when they get tackled? Why bother wearing a helmet if you're breasts are bare?"

"I know, I know," he said. "Why don't we put the navy blue down on the end? But when they come out of the huddle and hunch down the line, it's quite a sight."

"A: Fred, it would not be quite a sight for you. And B: I'm sure it's a sight you've never seen. And I don't believe you."

"What a wise young man you're becoming," he said over the armful of forest green long-sleeved T's he was moving around to the other side. "The Hooters are just a football team, spon-

213

sored by the Hooters restaurants. Eight-man team. Some guys who used to play for regular professional teams. We used to play eight-man in high school." Fred always had something surprising to pull out of his mysterious past.

"I thought you went to a convent school? That's what you tell everyone."

"Yeah, but the nuns were crazy about football. I was center. No remarks about bending over."

"Macha wants to see them," I said.

"I'd kind of like to see them myself," our Fred said.

"Let's go." And so we did.

Quelle evening. Turns out Macha wanted to go because she had met some girl who was a Hooters cheerleader for the team. And was very impressed. Her dentist's dental technician I think. In certain groups being a cheerleader for a professional football team is major prestige. What kind of prestige is attached to being a Hooters cheerleader I don't know. We were going to find out.

We were in the Miami Arena. Not great seats. We're in the end zone, behind a huge net that stops the ball when they kick it over the miniature goal posts. But as Macha pointed out, a great place to see the Hooter Girls in action. First things first. Macha seems to be into reverse snobbism. Her big concern being how she stacks up against a Hooter Girl. Hair, legs, face, etc.

On first sight, I knew poor Macha was hopelessly outclassed. She has the legs for it but she could never make the moves. The Hooter Girls are sort of like frantic wind-up Barbie dolls, life-size. A couple had good hair. Their faces, who could tell? They are nonstop movers doing a series of something between aerobics and chorus girl routines. With pom-poms. Great legs, we have to give them that. But zip this way, kick that way, hands on hips, shake that booty. Their backs were to the audience and grinding their buttocks in the audience's direction was a major part of the choreographic inspiration. At least they got to wear

Adidas. It would have been hell to be on the move like that all night in heels.

It was kind of nice, actually. It's kind of a future for ex-high school cheerleaders. It isn't all over after high school. You can take that pep and peddle it at the professional games. I imagine in time they'll have geriatric football and we'll have the pleasure of seeing frantic grandmas kicking over their heads. With all this Baby Boom chat it's got to happen.

Macha has never been a cheerleader in high school. That was far too enthusiastic for her. So I told her she was setting her sights pretty high hoping to be a Hooter Girl. Or Hootette, as I started calling them, which she said nothing about but obviously found irritating. Grace Kelly dreaming of being Marilyn Monroe.

The poor football players kind of got lost in the showbiz shuffle. First the Hootettes did a kind of chorus routine, grinding and shaking, stomping and kicking. Then the lights came down and lasers flickered as a herd of motorcycles came charging out of the lower depths and circled the field, carrying some biker girls who made the Hootettes look like debutantes. Spidermen came dropping out of the upper reaches of the arena on cables, James Bond style. Could these have been some division of the Miami Police? Or is this some new variation on bungee jumping, the Cable Club? Down they came, dangling by an arm, a leg, a neck. Got me. Once they hit the ground smoke began billowing out of the ramp entrance and out the players came, one by one, announced over the intercom, like showgirls. They raised their arms, they punched the air, they ran jauntily down the field. A couple of them had cute runs. Impossible to tell if anybody was good-looking or not. Not that I could care. Of course not.

The other team got the same treatment. The scoreboard showed us that the Miami Hooters were playing the Fort Worth Calvary. Could this be? I asked Fred. He said, yes, they used to bring them out nailed on crosses but religious groups objected. The announcer finally told us that they were in fact the Fort Worth Cavalry. But Calvary was what it was for the poor Hooters, for all their cute ways of running. There was lots of ball-dropping interceptions, throwing passes into the stands.

In desperation the announcer told the crowd that something very special was going to happen in the last quarter. Maybe my fantasy was going to happen in the last quarter. Maybe my fantasy of the Hooter girls playing topless was going to come to pass. It was about the only thing I could imagine that was going to keep the restless, sexy guys around us in place.

At quarter-time, four Hootettes, one wearing a hardhat, one an Indian bonnet, the others scraps of military uniforms, led the crowd in a chorus of "YMCA," the Village People number. The words were accompanied by gestures, which everyone in the Arena except me seemed to know. You stood up and opened your arms above your head for "Y," drooped your hands down to your head for "M," and so on. Macha and Fred amazed me by knowing all these things. I was pretty agog that this very white bread crowd was doing this big gay anthem number and loving it. I guess it just went right over their heads. Or maybe they got it just fine and it was their naughtiness for the evening.

There was a gang of really good-looking young guys right in front of us and they were moving their pelvises around to beat the band. These were guys who had never been in a gay club in their lives, unless I was sorely mistaken, and here they were making all the moves. Here they were. A night out with the boys. Is the whole world gay? I know. I just had to ask.

As though to answer my question, as everyone's gyrating around I see my father with his boyfriend Eduardo in the next section. They are not doing the YMCA maneuvers either. In fact, they are looking right at us. Eduardo sees me looking and he waves. Hey, wait a minute. Am I hallucinating, or what? I asked Fred and Macha to look over in that direction and see if they recognized anyone. Macha didn't of course, but Fred did.

"It's Rik and Rak, the night of the living dead come back to haunt us," he said. "Those guys who tried to pick us up at the Bomber Club are on our trail." He would have keeled under the seats if I broke the news that it wasn't just two gay guys from Rio. It was Dad. And his lover. To hell with it. If we run into them I'm not going to introduce him as my father. He doesn't deserve it. That's out. It will just be Roberto and Eduardo, the weirdos from Ipanema.

Of course, at half-time while we're getting hot dogs, they appear. I introduce them to Macha as Roberto and Eduardo and explain that Roberto is a friend of my mother's. He had his "don't blink an eye" number down cold, but I noticed that his little friend bobbled around a little, so he knows.

They decided to come over to our section and sit behind us for the second half of the game, the only interesting part of which was when they threw dollar bills down from the rafters to keep people in their seats. It was pretty clear that the Hooters were not going to get inspired. I got the feeling they didn't care very much. What with all the smoke-cloud introductions and spidermen and Hootettes, they probably don't feel a lot different about their show than the strippers did down at the Bomber Club. That's showbiz.

At third quarter Roberto and Eduardo got pretty insistent about our joining them after the game and we were pretty hooked because Macha kind of dug them. She would, with her taste for weird.

She even came up with the idea that we should all go to the Winter Palace on Lincoln Road. Seems that she and her friend Gale have been going there on weekends for the fun. "It's quite different from the Bomber Club and the Paragon," she said. "Quite different, you'll see. It's a little raunchier." Eduardo and Roberto perk up. "But it's quite a different kind of crowd. It's great!"

"Oh, Macha, Macha, Macha." It was three against two. I did say that it wasn't exactly that much of a treat for Fred and myself but she cried out, "You'll love it! You'll love it!" In high gear Macha is not to be denied.

When we got there Roberto insisted on paying the five bucks admission fee for everyone. My father, that is. I wonder if there has ever been anyone else whose father paid their admission to a gay strip joint?

The guy at the door recognized Fred and me; he used to work the door at the Bomber sometimes. "What are you guys doing here?" he wanted to know. And refused to take our tickets. "Refund, refund," he yelled out to the cashier. "Celebrities, celebrities." Everybody around us stared. Middle-aged gay accountants from Homestead. Which was exactly the crowd. Macha and I didn't have any trouble getting in, so they weren't making any big attempt to keep out people under twenty-one. But the under twenty-one crowd was definitely not on at the Winter Palace. Except maybe onstage. Like myself, some of the dancers looked pretty young to me. But their fans looked pretty old. This wasn't the busting-out-of-your-T-shirt crowd. There were even some guys in vests. And I don't mean over bare abs.

Macha disappeared as soon as we hit the inside and I saw her in a few minutes up on a dancer's platform over by the stage, hurling herself about. She seemed to be well-known and lots of guys were yelling, "Macha, Macha!" I guess she's some kind of mascot for the place. There were maybe half a dozen lesbian couples here and there about the place, and the rest hard-stomping teachers and bookkeepers. Eduardo asked me if I wanted to dance and I said, "No, no, I want to watch the dancers." The kids onstage were mostly Latin types and they went all the way with their strip. Which made it pretty hard to collect the money. Some of them had the money stuffed in their mouths.

The big deal were the shower booths on each side where the dancers took showers after they danced. Much soaping up, suggestive lathering, you get the picture. "I think we got out of this business in the nick of time," Fred muttered in my ear. "It's clean, but is it good and is it fun?"

Macha dragged Fred out onto the dance floor and left me to deal with the two wild guys from Rio. Roberto started, "I've been thinking about you, Hugo, and about your dancing in places like this." Whoa, I thought. Am I going to get the fatherly advice on such short notice or what? "I'm sure you're doing it just for the money, right?" I nodded. "And your mother doesn't know about it, right?" I nodded again. "I don't think you should be doing this. This is a tough way to get the money together for your education. And I think I know what kind of person you are. You don't want your mother to worry about things and you want to take care of it yourself, right?" That wasn't exactly insightful on his part, but it was surprising me.

"I have some background in making films, and I think that maybe I can help you." So. He's not going to offer to pay for my schooling after all these years. Eduardo was sitting perched over his margarita like a cat getting ready to jump on some poor little mouse. Something's cooking here, that's for sure.

Here it comes. "So, I had this idea. I have a friend in Rio who does very beautiful films. And it's excellent money. I was thinking of maybe doing the scenario myself, and Eduardo and you could be the stars. I think we could get you ten thousand dollars probably. And it's not a lot of work."

I was pretty well stuck to my chair. If some other creep had suggested it I could have laughed about it with Fred. Let's face it, it's a lot to handle. Your dad, whom you've never seen, wants to put you in a porno movie. Very far out.

He didn't seem to notice that I was pretty thunderstruck. "At first I thought we might do it with your friend. That maybe you'd like that better. But he's black and there's less of a market for that in Argentina. And Eduardo and you would make a beautiful couple. Eduardo thinks it's a great idea."

Eduardo said, "Some movie stars started this way. Stallone.

It could maybe lead to something. In Hollywood." Dream on, Eduardo. It might lead you to some pretty big peckers but I don't think it's going to get you to Hollywood. I finally said, "Well, gee, I hadn't even thought about it." I wanted to yell, "You fucking creep!" but didn't want to make a scene. Not in a swell place like the Winter Palace. I stood up. "I've got to go to the bathroom. I'll be right back."

I could feel I was kind of losing it as I dug my way through the three-piecers, looking for Fred and Macha. Macha was just heading up for another turn on a platform and Fred was heading back when I ran into them. I dragged Fred over to the men's room and kind of acted like I was freaking out on cocaine or something. This whole thing was getting to me.

"We've got to split, Fred. Right now. Macha will be all right. She'll get home. You've got to get me out of here."

Fred looked scared. His little Mr. Super Cool was crying and pounding the wall and generally coming all to pieces. He grabbed me and said, "Okay, okay, okay. Calm down. We're getting out of here. Come on. We're leaving right now."

He headed for the door. I really freaked. "No, no, no. I can't go back there. I can't see those guys again."

Got to hand it to old Fred. He looked around, tried the window, it lifted with a lot of effort on his part, and he looked out. "This is a piece of cake. No, it doesn't smell like a piece of cake. It smells like a piece of shit. But here we go, Bucko." And he pushed me out the window into the alley. There we were, standing among about forty-two garbage cans right behind Burdine's.

I was shaking and crying and shivering and stumbling. I was shot. Poor old Fred. But he got a grip on me and walked me down the alley toward the parking lot over across Meridian. "I should really go back and tell Macha we're leaving," he said.

"No, no." I was really yelling. We were getting toward his car. We heard, "Hey, Hugo!" and the Brazilians were under the streetlight. We weren't in that bathroom all that long but they must have gone to look and seen that we'd split. They were running toward us. "Oh, shit," Fred said, fumbling with his keys. He got that door open, pushed me in, and was around the other side, moving like he never did onstage. I got the door open in his side and we were out of there. I felt a thump on the back of the trunk but I wasn't looking. "Christ." That was all Fred said as we hit 17th Street. "Christ. Christ."

I wouldn't let him take me home because I figured they would go there to see if they couldn't intercept me. I was getting very neurotic. Maybe they were going to shoot me up with something and ship me off to Rio. I made Fred take me to his place in Miami Shores, figuring I'd call Mom early in the morning and tell her I'd stayed over because it got late or something.

So we went to Fred's. On the way, I spilled the beans. All of it. Not all of it. I didn't say anything about Glenn Elliott and me. Telling him that Roberto was my father seemed enough of a shock for one night. He was pretty knocked back by that news. And when I told him that he had a little plan to make me into a porno star he stopped the car and pulled off the highway. "You're not on anything, Hugo?" "No, life just seems to have gotten a little out of hand here, Fred."

He pulled back onto the highway. "Very Miami," he said. "Very Miami."

At his place, the standard mattress on the wall-to-wall and a TV. I just wanted to go to bed. And then we did the unwise thing. We slept in the same bed. There really wasn't anywhere else to sleep. Mom says nothing is by chance. So maybe I was setting this whole thing up. Who knows?

Anyway. I was feeling very much like a baby. Dad a porno magnate. Mom dating the man I love. And me only seventeen. I know, there's no excuse and I don't excuse myself. Fred for all his Carmen Miranda numbers is really very manly and kind. He held me tight and rocked me and I hunkered down and felt better. And of course we did it. Two healthy young fellas like us. In the morning I called Mom and then told Fred, "We shouldn't have done it, Fred. I'm sorry." From the bathroom he yelled back, "You're absolutely right. But it was great." In the night he had said he loved me but in the dawn Fred-Myrtle was back. I really appreciated that.

the fleet's in

This is really seedy. My double date with Glenn Paul and the two guys we met in New York. The sailors. Ben and John. I was riding home from school on my bike and Glenn Paul pulled up beside me at a stoplight. I think he was out looking for me.

"Ben called," he said.

"Ben?" I said very wittily. Blocking, I know, blocking.

"The guy we met in New York." We had never ever said a word about that trip before. Now it comes up at Pine and 24th. The light changed. I yelled, "Wait for me at home, I'll be right there," and Glenn zipped away.

He was there when I pedaled up. So cute in his blazer and short hair. You know that feeling, when you're kind of short of breath and nobody else in the world makes you feel that way? That's old Glenny.

"As I said," he said, leaning on the car door.

"As you said," I replied.

"Ben and John are coming to Miami and they would like to see us."

"I daresay."

He doesn't really like it when I indulge in smart repartee. Just looks at me, as though he hasn't understood what I said. Which he has, of course.

"Would you like to see them?" he asked me. Sometimes I feel like I'm in some kind of training course. How decadent can you get? He doesn't really want me to be decadent, except in his way. Quite a guy. "I'd say it's more like do you want me to see them?" I said.

"Yeah, I kinda do. I'm getting a little hard-on just thinking about it. Yeah, let's see them. It could be fun. They're showing up here Wednesday."

"Their ship is coming in? To use an expression."

"No, actually their ship is in New York. They're flying down."

"Just to see us."

"More just to see you, I think," Glenn said.

"No," I said, "I'm sure it's to see both of us." And the deed was done.

They arrived in a taxi at Glenn's apartment. We didn't go meet their flight. Enough is enough. They were pretty well dressed, actually. I thought they might be in polyester suits or something but they weren't bad.

Ben was wearing chinos and a blue blazer with a blue and white checked shirt. He's the blond one. And John, the dark-haired one, had on jeans and a white T-shirt. Loafers and no socks. And a navy blue sweater over his shoulders. Crew neck. Not bad. Also nice bod. They had these small canvas bags with them. Where were they planning to stay? Not my problem.

We decided to go over to Gloria Estefan's place, the Allioli. I like that place a lot. Tapas. I love tapas. We went over in Glenn Elliott's convertible. The boys were enjoying it. The top down. The tropical night. The streets swarming with handsome guys on bicycles, roller skates, skateboards, some were even walking. And there were some girls on the sidewalks, too. But the percentage of fab guys is so high here. If you're between the ages of sixteen and sixty in this town and not interested in women you wouldn't dare go out with less than that buffed look. Or you'd have to wear a bulky raincoat.

What would happen in Miami if all the gay guys woke up one morning and were straight? There'd be some frantic dating and some happy women, that's for sure. And all those gyms would close.

We sat on the terrace and the unending cavalcade of guys went on, back and forth on Ocean Drive. Ben and John were pretty blown away. I made sure they sat where they could see the sidewalk. Glenn and I really didn't need to. We see this stuff all day, every day.

After we ate, Glenn asked them if they'd like to go somewhere and have a drink and we decided to go to the Warsaw Ballroom. It was Thursday night, one of their big gay nights.

Eldorada met us at the door. I hate her. She always wears this big white wig and is very "Oh, darling." Bugs me. Drag queens. It's like they know any attractive guy would find them repulsive so they take it to the extreme where everybody thinks they're repulsive. Not amusing. But Ben and John seemed to get a kick out of it. Probably not a lot of drag queens on the USS *Sumter* or whatever they call their ship. And it's the usual. Except I realize this is the first time that Glenn and I have ever gone to a gay bar together as sort of a couple. And taken another pair of guys with us to boot. All the tired business queens from Dade County were there and eyeing us like alligators watching an unwary bunch of baby ducklings. Of course they always do. And of course it never does any good.

A couple of guys from the club passed through and I did get up and dance with Max Shell. He wanted to know who these fab-looking guys were and I said I didn't know, they were friends of Glenn's and I was just along to show them some of sights of Miami Beach and I had to go home and study soon. Which was a laugh since it was nearly midnight by now.

I was the one who said I was ready to go. I wasn't drinking anything but the big boys were. They were feeling fine. As we pushed our way out of the club Glenn said in my ear, "I'm right behind you." I said, "I can feel that." And I could.

So we raced back to Glenn's place. Do you ever have the feeling that the situation is out of your hands? It's like watching your ball bob around in a pinball machine but you can't make it land anywhere you might want it to. It's just going to land somewhere. That's it.

So we go into Glenn's flat. He goes into the kitchen and makes himself and the boys something to drink. They sit down. It's all kind of awkward. I think maybe this whole thing will just burn out from general embarrassment. Then Glenn says, "Here's my idea. I'll make some slips of paper; one will be shorter than the others. I'll mix them up in my hand and draw. Whoever gets the short one gets to ask anyone here to do whatever he wants." Glenn gets up, takes a notepad from near the telephone, and strips four pieces off against the edge of the telephone stand. Puts them in his hand and moves them around so nobody knows which is which. One of them he tore a bit off so it's shorter. We each draw. I had the feeling there must be a camera somewhere. This was like the beginning of a porn movie. Maybe it was. One Glenn had been in.

John got the short one. Maybe the night was getting to me but he was looking more and more like Bob Paris to me. Very macho with that shy edge.

He said, "I want a blow job from Hugo. And you guys can watch. Is that okay, Hugo?"

He stood up and was starting to lower his jeans. Stopped partway and stripped off his T-shirt. He was wearing jockey shorts. They were not Calvin Klein. Give him that.

He looked at me. And he had this frightened look in his eyes. Like he really expected me to say no. And I couldn't do that to him.

So I said, "Right on, John. Come over here." And I pushed him down in the armchair I'd been sitting in and knelt down in front of him. I pulled his jeans down to his knees and then his jockey shorts. He lifted his ass so I could get them out from under him. He had been looking forward to this. He was already pretty well pronged into those shorts and Wee Willie Winkie popped right up once that waistband set him free. Not so wee either.

Glenn sat down on one arm of the chair and handed me a condom. I took him in my mouth without the condom for a few pulls. "That's just to warm you up a little," I said. And then I tore the condom pack open and unrolled it down him. Ben had come over and was sitting down on the other arm. John was already stretched back with his eyes shut. So I did the sucking. Glenn was massaging his pectorals. Ben had his hand under his ass with a couple of fingers in him. He had his hands in my hair and was groaning and bucking all over the place. Pretty exciting even if you wish you weren't involved.

Glenn pulled the condom off and washed him up with a washcloth. Then he started undressing and said, "Well, what's next? Or should I say, who's next?"

I said, "I've got to go. School tomorrow." And started toward the door. Glenn said, "You're being an awful spoilsport, Hugo." I said, "I think you'll have plenty of fun without me. I played the game. Now I want to go." My voice was getting a little shaky so I knew I had to go.

Glenn was out of his clothes pretty much by now. Except for his sweatsocks. And Ben had everything off but his T-shirt. Sexy guys, no kidding, but not for me. John was pulling his jeans back up. I went out the door and down the stairs. John came down the stairs pulling on his T-shirt. Somehow he had his loafers back on, or were they ever off?

"I'm coming with you," he said. "You can't," I told him. "I'm going home and I've got my bike." I really felt like crying now. But big boys don't cry, big boys go home to their mother.

"Why don't you ride me over to the Kent Hotel, then?" John said. "The Kent?" I turned around and looked at him from my bike. "We have reservations at the Kent. We were going to go over there later. And I don't even know where it is."

"It's over on Collins. Come on. I'm not going to give you a ride but I'll go over there with you." And we trundled through the tropical streets of Miami Beach. Me pedaling slowly. Him walking beside me, touching me on my back from time to time. And he talked and talked. About how he had been thinking about me a lot. And how he realized after tonight that I wasn't really into this scene with my father. And I told him that Glenn wasn't my father, that maybe he was my lover, I wasn't sure about that, and I did not tell him that Glenn was my mother's lover. I didn't think the whole scene needed to look any tackier than it already did.

And I deposited him at the Kent. And let him go in and struggle with the desk clerk himself. Wandering in out of the night in a T-shirt. They couldn't care less. A lot of stuff had wandered in out of the night and into a bed at the Kent.

Home I went. Thinking about all this open relationship stuff and how Aristotle said, "Once is a learning experience, twice is decadence." And so on. Glenn just loves to get excited and then forget it. We are not the same people.

hurricane andrew

The storms have been circling us for days. Great piles of clouds rumbling, cracking in the distance. There are high winds in Fort Lauderdale. Drenching rains in Dania. Wind and rain and storm circling, circling, but here in Miami Beach the sun continues to shine, the breezes blow, trudgers move back and forth to the beach with their folding chairs and umbrellas, and towels. Hurricane warnings are long overdue.

It's sort of *Last Days of Pompei*-ish except that it happens every year. The big storms are reported out at sea. You can kind of imagine them raging over nothing, strong enough to push over buildings, with nothing to push over except waves. Brainlessly wandering around until they come in contact with something worth knocking down. Like us.

All the time we've been here, every hurricane season is like this. The storms are offshore. Everyone's nervous that something is going to happen, nobody believes that it really will. Los Angeles has its earthquakes. We have our hurricanes.

Nobody you run into has ever actually been in one. I saw pictures taken from the air over Miami Beach in 1925 when the last big one hit head-on. There were just a few lone palm trees sticking up here and there. There wasn't even much foliage left. Miami Beach was in its Venetian period then, so you can tell

the buildings that survived because they have a kind of plas-
tery Grand Canal look.

I read somewhere that then people knew so little about hurricanes that when the first half passed and the eye of the storm
was overhead everyone thought the storm was over and headed
back in their cars across the wooden causeway that connected
the beach to the mainland in those days. When the other side
of the hurricane hit, it just swept all those cars right off into the
bay. That's the main reason quite a few people were lost.

There had also been a train down to Key West built back in
the end of the last century. Down through all the keys. Another
storm took that out and killed a lot of train line workers who
were in a camp down on one of the keys. The sea went right
over their key and the only survivors were a few men who were
lucky enough to get caught in some trees.

It makes you think. And not think. Everybody's afraid. And
no one has any real plan. Only when the TV told us that Hurricane Andrew was heading directly for the beach did everyone get panicky. And of course the weather report was wrong.

I'd been out prowling around with Macha and Myrtle. The
usual night weather. Those winds that come and go. Clouds
pink against the navy blue sky, reflecting the city lights across
the bay. Something dramatic, something romantic in the air. But
it always is in Miami Beach. Drama or its potential is nothing
new to us.

So I was pretty surprised when Mom woke me up at 7:00 and
said, "This is it! That Hurricane Andrew we've been hearing
about will be here today. So up and at 'em."

Macha checked in early. She was heading over to Coconut
Grove to stay with Ken and wanted us to come over there. This
does not bode well, I thought, but Macha talked to Mom and
she thought it was a good idea. We should get off the beach
but she didn't want to go far away. And no use going north and
trying to find a motel. We'd have to leave immediately and even

then it was a question of whether we'd find anything. And Mom wasn't going to leave her house unprepared for the storm.

I called Myrtle, who of course knew little about what was going on, and told him to go down to Ken's also. He doesn't really know Ken so he didn't think much about it. He just thought it was cool that we'd all be together during the storm.

What surprised me was that Glenn Elliott didn't object. I think he likes to play with fire. The idea of going through the storm with his old boyfriend, his new boyfriend, and his girlfriend probably struck him as a good scenario. What I'm kind of beginning to pick up about Glenn Elliott is that he doesn't really project what's going to happen with anything. He lives in the minute. A storm is heading our way and we have to go somewhere else. Someone suggests we go somewhere else and that's cool. Is that dumb or is that smart? He's just a completely different kind of animal. Like Mom and I are cats and he's a dog. That's probably why we like him.

So we hauled everything we could upstairs: the books, the dishes, the rug, the smaller furniture. We packed up food to take with us, we pulled the mattresses off the beds and leaned them against the windows. Glenn Elliott and I took a run past the lumber company to see about plywood. They were staging the sinking of the *Titanic* there. The lumber company wouldn't dream of cutting wood to any size in good weather. Now they could really show disdain for the peasants. The fact that the lumber company employees are all Spanish speaking and their customers all Anglos has to have something to do with it. Not very often they can treat them like shit and have them come back for more. We decided not to bother. There was such a mob waving money around, it was almost better to let destruction roar over you than to be one of those hysterical assholes. On that much, Glenn and I agreed.

By this time we had stuff upstairs, the mattresses in place, the cats in the house and food and water out for them, and the kitty litter box freshly filled. It was really and truly time to leave. Mom said cats were great survivors and would climb up to the driest and safest place in the house, and she couldn't take all five of them over to Ken's and she wasn't going to play favorites. So they were left in the house.

I called Macha over at Ken's and told her we were on our way. I asked her if she had storm-proofed her place before she left. Her parents were still in the Grand Tetons, where they go every summer, and hadn't called. Or had she called them? She had put their four or five cats in the house with food, turned on the police alarms, and split. "What if they come home and find the place a wreck?" I asked her. "Fuck 'em," she said. Oh, Macha. So independent. So sassy. How I admire her.

It was after lunch when we left and we must have been among the last. The highways were completely empty. I thought about Mrs. Rasmussen, the old lady who lives behind us. We asked her to come with us but she refused. Maybe she's incontinent. Maybe she doesn't like to meet new people. Maybe she just figures that if the hurricane wrecks everything she'd just as soon be wrecked along with it.

There were no cars on Royal Palm. There were no cars on Alton Road. There were no cars on MacArthur Causeway, and nothing moving on I-95. It was like one of those movies where some kind of germ bomb has done away with all the people but left everything else. The sun was shining. The clouds were drifting about. The palm trees doing their usual restless thing. Maybe the weather people had dreamed the whole thing up. But when we got out of the car at Ken's place there was something kind of whiny about the wind. You could have easily ignored it, but knowing something was lurking you could sense a kind of light steadiness about the wind. It wasn't coming and going, it was there. Not strong, but sort of like the Chinese water torture, steadily pressing on without any letup.

There was no sign of any people around Ken's house either. He had a nice little house behind a bigger house. I'm sure the

Macha is the coolest of the cool. She doesn't know where Ken fits into this but she's sleeping with him, I would guess, so must have some sense he's not one hundred percent heterosexual. She's quick about this stuff and it well may be that she's sussed the whole thing out and is just sitting on it. If there's no solution, there's no problem in her book. It's just a situation. In the meantime she's going to fool around with Myrtle doing the jigsaw puzzle and not show the least bit of nervousness that the wind is really beginning to slam through the trees outside.

And there's me. Trying to be helpful. Making sure that I talk to Ken and tell him how great his house is and ask about his car (It's in the landlord's garage at the front of the house. They're gone.) and not be aloof. And not be too chatty with Glenn Elliott so no one thinks we know each other any better than the son of his girlfriend should.

It's not easy, subterfuge and deception.

iris's hurricane

So what do you say about a hurricane? It was as if we got smaller and smaller. Intimidation and diminishing I think would be the words to describe the experience.

At first we all sat huddled in the living room in the dark, with a few candles flickering. Macha and Hugo's friend Fred gamely tried to keep working on the jigsaw I brought but the wind through the slightly opened windows kept blowing the candles out. As the wind built I realized that the house we were in was a frail construction. We were protected to a degree by the big house in front of us, but we had been stupid not to go there. The owners were away and even if we had to break in, we would have been much safer. By the time we hurricane-virgins realized what we had gotten ourselves into, it was too late to venture outdoors.

The noise of the wind was so loud that it became no noise—a kind of gigantesque white noise. A loud knocking began on the roof. I don't know what it was, there were no trees close enough for limbs to be striking the tiles. It was as though the wind was so strong it was almost a solid thing, like waves of wood itself.

This little house has a hallway leading to the bathroom and the bedrooms and I got everybody to move in there. We took some blankets and pillows and cushions with us. We huddled there with the doors closed like a bunch of frightened puppies, all sort of huddling together. Glenn and I sat side by side with our knees up and the others cuddled up to us. My brave Hugo sheltered Macha and Fred by bracing himself against the door.

Funny, isn't it, that when the same unpleasant thing goes on and on and on there's a sense of no time. Just we tiny little things caught up in this great noise.

A squashed ant must feel this way just as that great sole descends upon it. So tiny in proportion to the forces around it. Despair isn't part of it. Or anguish. It's just the reality of you, the tiny thing. And it, the huge force. You just wait, to see if it's going to crush you or not. And the waiting doesn't go on and on. It just is.

The house trembled and there was a feeling that the whole thing might just fly apart. You could really feel the wood tugging at the nails. It wanted to go. Macha said, "I think we should all get into the bathroom." Maybe because it was even smaller it seemed safer. But crawl in we did, letting the water out of the tub so there was a little more room for us. Six adults in a bathroom. I suppose there are many jam-packed bathrooms tonight.

fred's hurricane

Well, the wind blew and the shit flew. Very interesting to see how people behave in what might be their last hours. I guess we're all scared, although I'm not so much really. It's not that kind of panic you get before you go onstage and you wonder if you're crazy to think anybody is going to want to watch you. Maybe I'm just too young to believe anything can really happen to me. It's all sort of happening on television.

God, that wind isn't happening on television. The curtains are standing straight out from the window. And there's kind of a rumbling on the roof like the ocean is breaking right over us.

Everybody here is sort of at their most essential. Macha gets high on the adventure, I think. She'll be lording it over her parents for the rest of their lives that she rode out the big hurricane while they were out of town.

She's not one little bit afraid. She'd probably get a big kick out of being whirled over the treetops and out to sea, even if they were her last moments. She's sort of sitting by herself, hugging her knees, listening. I think she knows this will never happen to her again and she doesn't want to miss a minute.

Hugo and his mom, they're just alike. They are the caretakers, they want to make sure that everybody else is taken care of. Bustling around, making sure the doors are locked and the windows open. Their big concern is the rest of us. Takes their minds off themselves. If your parents are your role models, he's got a good one. He was lucky his dad was out of the picture, that creep from Brazil. I hope he's out on Fisher's Island being swept out to sea right this minute. Funny how nonfaggots always want to think that an overprotective mother and a dad that's out of the picture turn you into a homosexual. My dad was certainly out of the picture but overprotective was hardly the word for Mom. All those kids, going out to clean house somewhere all the time. It was like a boardinghouse. She just felt relieved every time someone grew up and left home. I've got to send her some money; she's still got Phil and Dolores on her hands.

I think you want to go to bed with that part of you that's missing. Always was missing. Never was there. Never should have been there. That's why when boys are growing up they want to sleep with other men. Stronger muscles. Bigger cocks. What they want to have. Unless, of course, they have them already. And then nature kicks in and you feel like dominating women or you don't. If you yourself feel enough like what a woman feels, you don't have much urge to make yourself feel good at their expense.

That's certainly what's going on with Hugo and that guy Glenn. Glenn's handsomer than practically anybody, so who wouldn't want to be in touch with that? He's one of those guys who's just sitting around waiting to fuck. You wonder how they ever find the time or interest to work. You can just feel those vibrations. Fucking is what they like to do best. And what they do best.

Funny how these situations just sort of roll up into place and they don't seem hard to understand at all when you're there with them. I mean, here's this guy popping it to Hugo and his mother and it all seems sort of normal. Hugo is such a prince he wants his mother to be happy. The guy Glenn is such a fucking machine he just does what feels good and it doesn't even occur to him that this could be a pretty messy situation he's gotten himself into. I can't quite figure out why Iris doesn't get it. Her husband was gay, she was a model, she knows how the world works. But she hasn't really tipped that Hugo's making out with her boyfriend. Or is she making out with his boyfriend? I think he saw him first, by about five minutes. Yeah, Macha, I think you're right. I think we should all move into the bathroom. This place is really rocking and rolling.

Let's see, we'll let the water out of the tub. I'm going to sit down here beside the sink. Let's put that laundry hamper out in the hall. Glenn is going to sit on the toilet. . . . no, Iris is going to sit on the toilet and Glenn is snuggling down beside her with his arm around her. Ken and Macha can go in the tub, sort of like they're bobsledding. And that lovebug Hugo can squeeze the door shut and sit with his back against it. Come here, you little blond noodle, I'll put my arm around you so we can hug each other tightly out of sheer fright or something. He's really a sweet kid. We're really good friends even though we did get it on that night. He needed it. Funny how a fuck can calm you right down.

So here we are. I don't quite get the picture on this guy Ken. I don't think there's much of anything going on with Macha and him. She'd be all over him if there was. He's got that kind of gay look models have. Nothing really fidgety, but everything is calculated to attract. Men. Women like a nice ass, I know, but it's not the first thing they look for.

Gay guys really are kind of sappy. Women have it all over them. They're just like the kind of guys who read *Playboy*. Except the young blonds with big chests that they're after are other guys. They buy the package and then they're stuck with the stuff inside for the rest of their lives. Not really, of course. But you'd think they'd learn after a couple of trial runs. Women do. But gay guys never. To the end of their days they still want to latch up with a male bimbo. Well, not all. There are always those guys who like the really swishy ones. I always tell the flighty little fillies that they should butch it up a little. If a guy wants a girl there are plenty of real ones around. But that's not entirely true. A lot of those long-term relationships are with a pretty straight-acting guy and one of those butterfly boys. But some of those kids are really hung and I'd guess they're doing their Donna Reed number around the house and going upstairs and pronging the old man a good one. That's the secret of their success. Weird. Twirling around the house in an apron and then climbing aboard and screwing the daylights out of their hubby. Weird, weird, weird. You never know, you never know.

Why hasn't anybody had to go to the bathroom? That would be a real trip. Sitting here in the dark taking a big crap with five other people jammed up around you. Probably, like everything else, it's all on hold, and when this is all over there will be six large dumps to be accomplished.

This is kind of okay. Sitting here with my warm little Hugo in my arms, a banging on the roof like some kind of giant would like to come in. Everyone just sitting silently, breathing, holding. Maybe the pipes and the weight of the bathroom stuff is protecting us more. I don't know. We're sort of like sextuplets sitting in the womb, waiting to be born. The world is out there, crashing and smashing about, no wonder we don't want to go out there. But sooner or later, whether we're forcibly snatched out or whether we just walk out, one way or another we are going to be born.

macha's hurricane

This is definitely cool . . . sitting in a bathtub locked in the arms of a geek with the roof about to blow off. I love it. I love it. I love it. It's like an old Dorothy Lamour movie. If I let myself go I could be very romantic. And here I am, sitting in a bathroom with one other woman and four men and they're all queer. The men, that is.

Queerness is such a strange thing. Not at all what you thought when you were ten years old and you rode your bike down to Ocean Drive and Billy Bernstein said, "That's a faggot" at some guy who just looked short and blond, and then he yelled, "Faggot! Faggot!" And we had to ride away real fast. You thought they were boys who acted like girls, and we used to make life hell for that poor kid, Remy something or other, in the eighth grade. Well, we girls didn't, actually, but the boys did. Just because he wanted to play with us at recess and wasn't any good at sports.

I don't get it. All the really great-looking guys, the guys you could really get interested in, are gay. It's true. None of these guys are girly. Well, Myrtle can be. But a lot of the time he isn't. Hugo was on the swimming team. Ken told me he played basketball in college. Glenn Elliott was in the Marines. Maybe the whole world is queer and they just haven't told women about it. So we don't get disappointed.

Well, it makes sense, sort of. The one time I did get it on with Ken he didn't really like the smoochy part. The good part. Not a great kisser. And you kind of get the feeling that playing with your breasts and that sort of stuff is like something he read about in a manual. They just want to get it in and let nature take its course. I mean, if you don't know what good is you could really be disappointed. No wonder Peggy Lee sings, "Is that all there is?" As soon as Ken got his jollies he was out of there. He probably figures I'm too young and too much in love to know the difference anyway. When I was looking for a T-shirt and found those sex magazines in his drawer it did not come as much of a surprise. I do not think that heterosexuals are very interested in *Playgirl* or *Blue Boy*. Not to mention *Honcho, Hard,* and some of those other little beauties he had. In a way it makes him more interesting and in some ways it doesn't.

I guess I'm just old-fashioned enough to want to be a real turn-on for the man in my life. Whoever he might be.

I should probably think about the fact that I know so many gay guys. I really don't want to be known as a fag hag before I even graduate from high school. But going to someplace like the Winter Palace makes me feel free. Like I'm a little gay guy myself. No plans to get married. No ideas about how many kids I'm going to have. What kind of career my husband will have. Where I want to live. What kind of house it will be and what kind of furniture and will I work after the children come? Out the window. Just jiving around to the music and I'm not even a cute gay guy. Nobody's paying any attention to me. No problems. There's a lot to be said for it. And in my head I suppose not being able to get pregnant is all a part of it. Could get AIDS, of course, but you have to sleep with somebody first to get that. It's just the fun of it down at the Winter Palace. So much more fun than that awful place Prince has on Washington. Do I look all right? Will somebody find me attractive? Who gives a shit, right? This whole business of being good enough for somebody to love you is really boring.

And look at all the people who are gay and all the saps who don't know and don't want to believe it. The one who's such a big singer, looks a little bit like Elvis. In all his interviews he's always talking about how his heart was broken and he's taking a long time to get over it. Please. One of these days somebody besides me is going to notice he still lives with his mother.

And the one who's making all the action movies now. Started out doing a gay play in Canada. He didn't get to Hollywood because they loved the way he did *Hamlet.* Really wild when you think about it, all these girls going to bed dreaming about him at night and he couldn't care less. And he doesn't even bother to pretend he's got a girlfriend. The interviewers just skip the subject.

And what'sername. One review I read said in her last movie she played the role of a heterosexual very well. Wild. I guess little by little the public can be brought around to be interested in seeing somebody in a movie they know they haven't got any hope of sleeping with. They haven't anyway if they'd just think about it.

And there's that little Prince. In my brief life I have learned that men who like to pose nude and wear a lot of makeup are probably not interested in girls. Michael Jackson. I guess it's easier to just slip off into being a nut case than dealing with it.

So what's in store for little me? Guess I'm supposed to dream I'll meet some hunky guy someday who isn't interested in other hunky guys. I think what it really is is that they're so in love with themselves that the closest thing to themselves is what interests them. Failing that, somebody who worships them. I guess I could fall into that category. Better yet, maybe I should keep my eye out for someone really plain who thinks I'm a goddess. Those are two really poor choices.

Shit! What was that? Sounded like the windows in the bedroom just blew out.

hugo's hurricane

One thing I didn't expect in a hurricane was to fuck. But it happened. But it happened. Lately I've been wondering if I'm having too much experience for a young boy of seventeen.

Now it's over I kind of wonder if I imagined it. But when I look out the window and see the trees all topsy-turvy down the street I know that the hurricane happened, so the rest of it must have happened too. I'm being a little silly. Of course it happened.

While we are stuck in the bathroom and the storm sounds like a hundred airplanes are taking off on the roof there was a crash in the next room that sounded like the end of the house had gone. Scared the shit out of all of us. Glenn said that it sounded like the window had blown in. He said we should try to go in there and put something over the window, or up against it. Don't ask me why we hadn't already. Everything we did over at our house on Royal Palm we never did here at Ken's. I guess we were so sure that the storm was going over Miami Beach we never thought about it. Mom wasn't crazy about us going out there but Glenn said it wasn't dangerous. We were just going to go in and push the mattress up so the wind didn't do any more damage. And he and I were going to do it because we were closest to the door. So we did.

Wow. It was crazy once we opened the door. The wind banged the door open at the other end of the hall and we had to hang onto the door openings to even stand up. Glenn yelled, "Get down." So we got down and crawled across the floor to the side of the bed. We pushed the mattress off the bed but it was impossible to stand up with it. The wind kept pushing us back and we were falling all over each other. With our two bodies struggling together we kept trying and got the bed turned around so we could push the headboard up against the mattress.

I could hear Mom yell, "Are you all right?" from the hall. Glenn shouted, "We're getting it. Get back in there." We finally got the mattress up against the window and our backs against the headboard of the bed. We were stuck there, the wind whistling through our hair. The bed was caught on something on the other side of the room so it was real solid, with Glenn pinned between me and the mattress.

Glenn took my hand down and put it on the front of his jeans. He had a hard-on! Christ, I thought. He turned his head back and yelled in my ear, "Fuck me, Hugo." Pressing against his butt the way I was I had a hard-on myself. I never took cocaine, but it must be something like this. All that noise, things flying and banging outside, the wind rushing through. Glenn's pants were coming down and he was reaching to get me out of mine. And here I was pushing into him. His butt was soft and hot and he was twisting and pushing to help me get in. He put his arms around me from behind and held me as tight as he could. We could hear Mom calling, "Are you all right, are you all right?" It was pitch black in there, but you didn't even think that you couldn't see. It was as though seeing wasn't an option. Glenn shouted, "We're fine. We're fine. Stay in there, we'll be right there" while pushing his ass back and forth frantically. I felt for him and started pulling on him as I pushed further and further into him. My own cock seemed enormously long to me. As though I was pushing deep, deep into him. So soft, so hot.

He was really frantic. He grabbed himself and was jerking violently and working his ass as hard as he could at the same time.

You know how you can be really into sex and at the same time know you're sort of standing aside observing it? I couldn't see him but I knew he was wilder and hotter than I'd ever known him to be. Just as violent as the storm, I guess. We fell down on the floor between the mattress and the headboard and the mattress fell back a little, sheltering us. I really felt like fucking him hard now. I pushed up and started giving him really long strokes. The head almost coming out, then sliding way, way in again. I felt absolutely huge. He was pushing up against me as hard as he could when I went back in.

Mom called again, "What's happening? What's happening? I couldn't get my breath enough to call back but Glenn yelled back in a really calm voice, "Almost got it. We'll be right there. Stay there. We'll be right there. We're coming right now!"

And we did. Man. I never had an orgasm like that. I felt like I was pumping quarts into him. And he was groaning and pounding the floor under me. I could hear him but all those groans were lost in the screaming of the wind over our heads. I slid out of him. He reached up and pulled my head down beside his. "Went in like six and came out like ten, Hugo. That was great. Let's get out of here." We scrambled out from under the mattress and pushed the bed up against it. Bracing it with the bureau. I got my pants back up and zipped up somehow as we stumbled back to the bathroom door.

We squeezed back in and Glenn said, "That was exhausting." "You're covered in sweat," Mom said, feeling his body. And mine, too. "So is Hugo, that must have been hard."

"I didn't know if we were going to make it or not," Glenn said. "But finally we did. Hugo was great. He can be a real toughie." I thought we smelled so much of come that everybody must be able to figure out what just happened. When I woke up the wind had died down a lot.

after the hurricane

Outside, all is wreckage. Inside, all is calm. The house actually survived with little damage except for the blown-in bedroom window that Glenn and Hugo patched up with such difficulty during the storm.

The sun was shining brightly as the wind died down and we knew the house was not going to blow away. Glenn and I pulled some blankets over ourselves on the springs of the bed, and left the kids to sort out what sleeping arrangements they could in the living room. They pulled open the folding couch and just fell on it in a heap, like a bunch of puppies. Poor Hugo wasn't really awake when they dragged him in there to jampile with them. A brave kid and I know it wasn't easy for him to have Glenn here with us. He couldn't really be my brave protector and our private communication was cut off. It's part of growing up and it's just as well, but I feel sorry about it all the same.

Once we hit the bed Glenn was very much in the mood to make love and I felt very much the same. Sort of like we survived and let's propagate. Although that wouldn't be the greatest idea on earth.

He was more loving than I'd known him to be, less urgent. He is such a sexual being that once it's plain that intercourse is in the cards he is very interested in getting to the good part.

But early this morning he was very comforting and soothing, stroking me and petting me as though he really understood I needed that. He's such a strange guy, he doesn't really have any verbal thinking process, I don't think. He's not stupid. Certainly not in business. And he certainly knows how to use his charm, but his charm is really just himself. He just places himself in your path and lets you discover him.

Lovemaking is such a pleasure with him because he really likes it and understands that there are two people involved. It's not just his pleasure. Of course, that's a man who has been involved with a lot of lovemaking in his time. But when you look like he does and have his gifts for sensuality, it is inevitable. Such a great kisser. I think that tells you so much about how much a person is willing to give. Eyes can lie, but a person's mouth tells you everything. Glenn really has lips. Beautiful lips.

A really nicely shaped penis, too. Maybe the two things go together. But he has been quick to point out that the more he kisses me the more enthusiasm I have for making bamboola.

He took all of my clothes off and all of his and then proceeded to make very long and slow love. It was as though he was treating himself to a great pleasure and was in no hurry about it. He didn't seem terribly exhausted despite all the struggle covering the window. He's a very strong person physically, which you realize once you're in his arms. He could crush me if he was in the mood. Strange how with some men you can really let yourself go and let them plunge in and touch your heart. There's something about Glenn, the sort of powdery smell and the softness of his skin over his hard muscles and the way his mouth pulls on mine, that really suits me. We have virtually no small talk but I think he feels that I am dependable and that he can count on me. We don't seem to get restive in one another's company. We seem to have fallen into sharing each other without anything you could really call romance having happened. Go with the tide, I say, go with the tide.

When we woke up we were still in each other's arms. Glenn Elliott said into my neck, "This must be love when you wake up in someone's arms." I said nothing. He is not given to saying things like that. We all struggled into our clothes. There was no electricity so we couldn't cook anything but there was plenty of orange juice and I made sandwiches since we couldn't have toast or eggs or anything. Our cars were intact, although trees were sprawled everywhere. We all went out and picked up branches and did what we could to clear up Ken's lawn and his landlord's. Many men were out sawing away at the trees on the street in front of the house. Coconut Grove has many more real trees than palms, so there was a lot of work to be done. The palms seem to have swayed their way through, though many of them were tilted over at a 45-degree angle. And they stayed that way until someone came around to straighten them up.

By the end of the afternoon we decided maybe things had been cleared up enough to try to get back to Miami Beach. It was quite a trip. Wandering around fallen trees, cutting corners across people's lawns, getting out of the car to haul giant limbs out of the way.

We traveled in convoy, with Macha and Fred driving behind us. We decided to kidnap Fred and bring him back to Miami Beach with us. If we had to battle for food and water at least we would all battle together. The causeways were open and poor old Miami Beach looked battered but considerably better than Coconut Grove. Trees down and branches and torn loose shrubbery everywhere, with garbage cans and lawn furniture laced through it, but we could pass through it and find our way up Royal Palm. Those old royal palms looked good. Not one had gone down and the big one in our front yard was standing straight and tall, didn't look as though it had lost a frond. The same was true of the one in the backyard, we discovered, soon surrounded by our cats, who were delighted to be able to rush outdoors and squat under the hedges. They didn't seem to be particularly upset by their night of disorder.

They probably figure everything that goes on outside the house is the work of humans and how in the hell can any self-respecting cat understand *them?*

The house was intact. Longing to get our lives back in order we immediately set about carrying everything back downstairs that we had carried upstairs yesterday morning. We'd left Ken at home, but both Macha and Fred were staying with us, so we had lots of helping hands.

Glenn improvised a grill in the backyard and we grilled some steaks that were in their last moments. And we had some tomatoes. The ice cream was soup. Eggs we can probably fix over the grill in a frying pan. It's like camping out.

Glenn Elliott wandered off to his own flat to see how things were there. I wasn't sorry. I wanted to mull over the really satisfying maneuver of this morning. Sometimes your lover needs to be something of a fantasy to be really appreciated.

Cold showers and all of us go to bed. Macha is in the guest room and Fred dossing down with Hugo. Before Hugo went off to bed I said, "I wonder if your father survived the hurricane all right?" He said, "We can only hope he didn't." And off to bed. I asked Macha if she wanted us to go over to her parents' house to see how things were but she said, "Who cares? If anything needs to be fixed I'm not going to do it tonight. I'm hitting the sack." She is a wonderful girl. Nothing but good things are in store for a person like that. I wasn't that mature until I was years older than she is. I'm not sure I am now.

So the hurricane has come and gone. All we know is what the car radio told us. Poor Homestead got the worst of it. Pretty well obliterated I guess. Haven't heard that anyone died yet. I feel as though I've had a baby or something. As though things will never be quite the same again. We've come through something.

played out

I told Macha what was going on. I can't keep *everything* to myself. She was pretty brief. She said, "You're too calm. Get hysterical." So I did.

The hurricane was pretty well over. The electricity was back on so we could stop putting ice in the refrigerator to keep things cold. The trees were all cleared up in our part of town. Old Mrs. Rasmussen has hardly noticed the difference. She eats so little and goes to bed early so even the fact there's no electricity hardly bothers her. She hates television so that wasn't a problem either.

Of course, down in Homestead things are a real wreck. Glenn and I went down to take a look. It was like the first pioneers had just come in to clear the land. Trees topsy-turvy everywhere, all the houses looked like shacks that had just been thrown together. Hand-lettered signs nailed up everywhere telling people what street they were on or where people had gone or warning people not to mess around. Stray animals wandering about trying to find their owners. People were pretty good about that, feeding them and taking them in.

So seeing all the hysteria around me I got pretty hysterical myself. Glenn was pretty surprised. I said, "Glenn, what are you going to do? What's going to happen to you and me?"

He said, "That was a pretty good fuck you threw into me the other night. Isn't that what's going to happen between you and me."

"But what about you and my mother?"

"What's that got to do with you and me? That's between your mother and myself. Just like what's going on with you and me is just between us."

"It doesn't bother you that we're all living in the same house?"

"We're not all living in the same house, Hugo. I don't live there. I spend a lot of time at your place, but I don't live there. You and I never screw there. You must have noticed that."

"Yeah, but Mom and you do while I'm there. How do you think that makes me feel?"

"Well, how does it make you feel, Hugo?"

"You are such a shit, Glenn. A real shit. If it was somebody else I'd probably come in there and kill both of you. But I love my mom and I want her to be happy. So I just lie in my bed and feel like I'm falling all apart. And then get up in the morning and act like nothing's happening. It just makes me feel awful." And I started crying. I was all bent over in my seat crying and crying. It was really awful.

Glenn pulled off the road. We were on the Julia Tuttle Causeway so he could pull over on the grass. And he undid my safety belt and undid his own and pulled me over and put his arms around me, and I cried like I have never cried before in my life and had to get it all out. And while I was doing it at the same time I thought, Christ, what if some of the kids from school go by and see me? It'd be all over the school in five minutes. Or what if a cop car stops? But I couldn't get myself under control. I just kept saying, "I love you, Glenn. I love you." And crying some more. He held me real tight and kept rocking me back and forth and saying, "Hugo, Hugo, Hugo." Like I was his baby. But I guess that's what I needed because I calmed down and got myself sorted out. His shirt was soaked. "I got your shirt all wet," I said.

"That doesn't matter," he said. "Look, Hugo, I know you love me and I know what that's like when you're a kid. What can we do? You and I can't move in together. You couldn't do that. You wouldn't do that. You can't say, 'Look, Mom, I'm in love with Glenn and we're going to set up housekeeping together.' I can't marry you, Hugo."

"Why not?" I said. "Some men do."

"Not our kind of men, Hugo. Neither of us wants to be somebody's wife. I'm not sure I even want to be somebody's husband. We just have to hang in there and see how this works out."

We drove back to his place and he said, "I don't suppose you want to come up and fuck a little?" Actually I did but then again, I didn't. I told him I should really go home and study. So my handsome Glenn went upstairs and I rode my bike, which I'd left locked up in front of his place, slowly up Meridian and then up Royal Palm.

He made me think, Glenn. What did I expect him to do? I guess in my silly half-assed way I thought he'd come home every night and we'd fuck the daylights out of each other. That's about as far as I'd gotten.

But obviously that was on another channel altogether from my going to college and becoming a writer or whatever else I wanted to do with my life. The two things just didn't fit together. Maybe if I'd just graduated from college I could have thought about doing that. But even if I did, Glenn isn't the kind of guy who would want to take a stand and say, "Hey, okay, I'm queer and I'm going to live with this kid." He'd never box himself in that way.

And I realized something about Glenn. And people like him. Beautiful people. Sexy people. People everyone loves. Maybe I'm one of those people myself except that I don't think or act the way they do. They're sort of like things in nature. The Grand Canyon. Sunset over the ocean. A beautiful cliff where the water breaks. They just stay still and let everybody rush and crash around them. You can love them but you can't make them act. They are just there. They don't see life like I do at all. As going somewhere, becoming something. They just exist.

I guess if you've been beautiful all your life there doesn't seem to be any reason to make plans to try to interest someone in you, create something. You are the subject of so many people's fantasies you don't have to have any of your own. You *are* the dream. You don't have to have any.

So Glenn Elliott isn't ever going to do anything about me. He's just going to stand by until I kill myself, or Mom finds out and kills me or kills herself or kills him. It's all the same to him.

And Mom can't act since she hasn't really figured it out. Despite the sort of wild life she's had I think she still thinks everything works out all right. And here it is, working out all right. Being a really nice person can be a disadvantage. You're not suspicious. You think everyone is just as nice as you are. Glenn Elliott fits into that part of her life where she needs him, and the other parts of her life, like her real estate and me, are separate and she doesn't even think they might be overlapping.

Which leaves me. The person to act. So what am I going to do exactly? I'm young. I'll fall in love again. But I think there will always be like this little room inside me with someone in it crying. Crying because when you fall in love you can't just be whirled away to a desert island somewhere and live the rest of your life lying in someone's arms being happy. That's the dream, and I know I can adjust to reality, but I'll never adjust completely. I'll never stop wishing there was somewhere to go with love that was worthy of the way you feel.

And I know that Glenn Elliott Paul will always be in that little room with the crying person the way he is now. Those smooth muscles, that beautiful face, that beautiful cock. That smile and those squinted blue eyes that you think only you no-

256

ticed were so wonderful. That make you feel that he never had seen anyone as wonderful as you before. Like some god that you worshiped and that you'll never stop worshiping in that little shut away room inside yourself. Right down under your stomach somewhere.

So we had a council of war, Macha and I. What is to be done? What is to be done? I told her that Ken was an old boyfriend of Glenn's. She said that he was sort of like doing his duty in bed and that wasn't her idea of a great romance. And besides she was jealous of my great romance with Glenn. And that if she couldn't have a great romance like that she didn't want me to have one either. She's very much into being fair. She thinks I have to stop seeing him.

Which is where I had kind of gotten myself. I know he won't say anything or do anything about it. If I'm just not around he'll concentrate more on Mom. And if he has another boyfriend on the side or a girlfriend, that's his business. And her business. Even if I don't like the idea of AIDS and everything, I can't very well tell her he's a switch-hitter. And maybe if he's switch-hitting with somebody besides me she'll come out of her fog and figure it out. She did with my father.

So. So. So. Macha and I are going to see if her parents will let us live together in the little apartment they have over their garage. That used to be for servants, I suppose. We're not going to pretend we're lovers and besides there are only two single beds up there, which would be pretty hard on serious lovers anyway. We're going to explain to our parents that we want to test run what it's like to be on our own. And we're both going to get some real kind of part-time jobs that we can work full-time next summer before we go to college. I'm going to see if I can't find something over at the *Miami Herald.* Macha's mother knows someone who works over there. And Macha has decided that she wants to be a lawyer so she's trying to get some kind of part-time thing in a law office. And we're going to get serious. Except when we go out on weekends with Myrtle and go slumming. I'm going to start calling him Fred exclusively from now on.

And we're hustling Fred into doing something real. Like being a stand-up comic or something. If you can call that real. He's going to start going back to college this fall in the evening. He'll do something great once he gets started, he's *so* smart.

And I'm going to explain all this to Mom right away. It isn't as though I'm going anywhere. I'll only be five blocks away. But this way she'll have to concentrate fully on Glenn. And she knows I'm not moving out to do drugs or have a wild sex life or anything like that.

And we'll see how it goes. As Glenn said, nothing dramatic. Nothing confrontational.

What would probably be best would be cloning. A replicant that you could leave behind so you don't have to disappoint anyone. And then you could go on and see what the *true* scenario of your life will be.

And so there will be all these different possible scenarios. Mom will marry Glenn Elliott and they will live happily ever after. She might even have a little Glenn Elliott or two. Which would be very weird but okay.

I might fall in love with Macha and we will be very happy together forever and ever. Unlikely.

I might fall in love with Fred and would have some sort of meaningful relationship over a period of time. We've already done the groundwork. Unlikely, but not out of the question. Strip off those dresses and he's quite a hunk of a guy.

Or even sailor John might develop into a reality in my life.

Or Glenn might suddenly decide that he really loves me more than anyone else in the world and insists that I stay with him forever. My heart pounds even to think about it, but I don't see how Mom could ever fit into that kind of scheme so I kind of have to put that in the category: nearly impossible.

Or maybe I'll slip out of this high gear I'm in and start slipping around to meet Glenn and start fucking and getting fucked by him again and maybe my being so noble and getting things all sorted out will amount to nothing. But I wouldn't like that.

I guess I have to kind of count on Glenn's just letting me slip away like one of those waves crashing on the beautiful rock and rushing out to sea. Which I think he will do.

And now Macha and Fred and I have to get dressed up and go out to the movies and compare notes on Mel Gibson and then go the Winter Palace and fool around and get on with our lives.

I'm like the man in the yellow boat that I saw rowing in from the ocean. When I get to the shore I have to put the boat on my shoulders and walk wherever it is that I'm going.